THE EASY PART OF IMPOSSIBLE

Also by Sarah Tomp

My Best Everything

THE EASY PART OF IMPOSSIBLE

SARAH TOMP

HARPER TEEN
An Imprint of HarperCollinsPublishers

For HannaH

HarperTeen is an imprint of HarperCollins Publishers.

The Easy Part of Impossible
 For information address HarperCollins Children's Books, a division of HarperCollins Publishers, 195 Broadway, New York, NY 10007.
www.epicreads.com

ISBN 978-0-06-289828-9

Typography by David DeWitt
20 21 22 23 24 PC/LSCH 10 9 8 7 6 5 4 3 2 1
❖

First Edition

SOUTHWEST DAILY TIMES

JULY 1

Local Girl Diving into National Competition

Pierre, VA—Victoria "Ria" Williams will be traveling Tuesday with coach Benjamin Hawkins to Los Angeles, California, to compete in the USA Diving National Championships.

"Ria is easily the best diver on the East Coast," said Hawkins. "Now she will have a chance to prove she's the best in the country."

Williams started diving at age six with the Pierre Community Center recreational team. After making rapid progress, she began a more rigorous training schedule with Hawkins, a former NCAA diver for the University of Virginia. "The first time I saw Ria dive, I knew she was champion material," said Hawkins.

The Rock Dive Team practices at Memorial Pool and in Hawkins's personal gym on Bell Avenue. The private club team competes year-round. Tryouts require a private invitation.

If Williams places in the top three of this competition, her future will require even more time in the water. She will have the chance to travel throughout the world representing the United States while training for the next Olympic team trials.

SOUTHWEST DAILY TIMES

JULY 14

Scratch That

Pierre, VA—Local diver Victoria Williams reportedly scratched all events and did not compete at the USA Diving National Championships in Los Angeles, California, last week. A reason was not cited.

The Williams family and coach Benjamin Hawkins all declined to comment.

ONE

One slip and it was over.

Everything Ria had worked for, dreamed of, spent every single second of her life dedicated to, was finished. No more demanding schedule, no dictated life. She could eat whatever she wanted. Do what she wanted, when she wanted.

If only someone could tell her what that was.

"Come on, Ria," said Sean. "Hurry up and pick something. We need to get to the quarry before dark."

"You said we should bring snacks." She'd liked the idea of picking something delicious and junky, but she hadn't expected three aisles of choices in the mini-mart. "What's best? Should we go for frosted sweets? Chocolate or fruity? Or are chips better? Look at the entire line of '-ito' choices! What's the junkiest? Doritos? Cheetos? Fritos?"

"It's not a picky crowd."

She turned and faced him. "Or, maybe Funyuns are a better

time since 'fun' is right there in their name. Maybe they're the life of the party!"

Sean laughed. "What do *you* want to eat?"

"I'm not hungry." She shrugged. "You pick."

He eyed her but didn't argue as he grabbed a boring bag of ordinary potato chips.

Ever since she'd quit diving, after backing out of her biggest meet ever—the one that mattered more than all the others combined—one impossibly long month ago, Sean had stepped in, eager to fill her suddenly empty hours, happy to take her away from her parents' questions and frowns. He was an attentive tour guide to the world of being normal.

Fact was, she'd never done anything normal. For the last eleven years she'd spent each and every possible second either at the pool or in the dry gym—building strength, increasing flippable flexibility—doing whatever she could to dive better, straighter, more gracefully, and with greater power. She'd missed out on everything else. She was an alien in her own hometown.

A native alien. Which didn't make sense, but Ria was used to not making sense.

The party was at the abandoned quarry, another place she'd heard of but never been. She parked on the road behind the line of cars as Sean directed. "It's going to be great," he said. "It's like a kickoff for our senior year."

Ugh. She'd been so busy not diving, she'd forgotten to dread the start of school.

Sean led her along the sandy roadside, then stopped where the fence was bent. He held it out for her to slip through. Walking along the gravel path, she could hear the party before she could see it. She followed him around a large boulder, stepping into a wide-open space.

"Whoa," she said, taking in the view of an enormous gaping hole. The rough rock walls glowed in the late-afternoon sunshine.

"Right? I told you everyone would be here."

Ria turned her attention to the crowd gathered on the patchy grass and sandy field. She didn't know everyone, not like Sean did. She didn't know much of anyone beyond her tight circle of teammates. *Ex*-teammates. She'd only met Sean because he worked as a lifeguard at the Aquaplex, her old home. He was on the high school's swim team, part of the pack mysteriously willing to splash their way back and forth for miles of straight lines. He'd been one step out of Coach Benny's circle of forbidden relationships. Teammates were always off-limits for romance.

She watched Sean and his friends slap, smack, and crash their hellos through high-fives, head whacks, and chest bumps. She'd invited Maggie to come today too, but at the last minute, Benny called a "Board Meeting" at the pool. Code word for an in-team meet. They'd compete against each other, at the mercy of his fickle scoring, with rewards and punishments doled out on the deck. He'd probably heard about the party, and wanted to keep his team close and out of trouble. Ria, on the other hand, was now free to get in as much trouble as she wanted.

"Let's go find the keg," said Sean.

There wasn't any order to the party. This was nothing like the picture of a party she'd had in her head. Instead of beautiful people dressed in fabulous clothes having a wildly hilarious time, it was a bunch of kids standing in the dirt sipping from red plastic cups. Of course no one had set up a table for gourmet hors d'oeuvres, or even pointless potato chips. They were simply something to lug around. "Where should I put the chips?"

Sean took them from her and shoved the bag into Charlie's hand. "You look hungry."

Tony turned to her. "How did Sean finally convince you to come to a party?"

"Yeah," Charlie chimed in. "Aren't you supposed to be off at the Olympics?"

"Shut up. Go be stupid somewhere else." Sean shoved him in the chest.

"What did I do?"

"Nothing," said Ria, hating that Sean felt the need to protect her, and hating more that she needed him to. "Go get a drink," she said to Sean. "I'm going to go look at the hole."

As she turned and walked away she heard Tony say, "But the a-hole is right here."

"Shut up," protested Charlie. "I am not."

"You're not here? Am I hallucinating?"

Their voices faded as Ria walked away from the noise and

jumble of the crowd. She stood at the edge and looked down, past the sheer face of brown-and-red-streaked rocks, down to the jagged shelves of cut cliffs, and into the water. It looked deep, dark, and blue. Still. Not a ripple or wrinkle anywhere.

Behind her, bass beats played through speakers, while the melody sounded thin and tinny in the open air. Voices and laughter filled the cracks between the notes. She tilted her head and squinted, trying to imagine how the steep walls would look from below. She wondered if the sky would look like water.

She bent over, legs straight, back curved into line-up position, reaching downward. A gust of wind hit the back of her legs, and with it, quick and surprising, a flash of fear.

Ria knew Fear well. It was a necessary part of diving. Sometimes it came as a whisper sending shivers skittering across her skin. Or it could be a buzz, humming in the background. Other times it appeared with a thud and bang, demanding immediate attention. Now, it nestled in close beside her, nudging her to step away from the edge. She hadn't realized how much she'd missed it.

"I brought you a drink." Sean was back.

She stood up, face flushed, feeling caught.

He grinned, handing her a cup.

"Thanks." She forced her voice to stay even. Fear was gone now. She sniffed the foamy cup, took a sip, and immediately wondered which food group beer fit into. It tasted like pure carbs.

"How deep is the water?"

"Are you going to dive in?" Charlie asked.

"Of course not," said Sean, wrapping his arm around her waist. "That's gotta be fifty feet down."

"Oh, come on," said Tony. "Go for it. Sean's a lifeguard. What could go wrong?"

Sean clutched her tighter. "Hey dip-wad, feel free to risk your own worthless life, but leave my girl alone." To her, he said slowly, "Ignore him. You don't need to prove anything."

Fear knew what he was worried about. If someone fell from this spot, higher than a dive platform, the water's surface would feel like glass. Hard and cold. Unforgiving. And yet, from here it looked calm and inviting. Perfect. Only one bit of white skimming the surface.

"Look at the cloud in there." She pointed down.

Sean laughed. "Are you already buzzed? You always notice the weirdest things."

She looked up, searching the clear but dimming sky until she found the cloud. A small one, all alone. She never would have noticed it except for the water's reflection.

"I could dive in." She turned her attention back on Sean's friends. "But I'd go from the other side. There are too many things to get caught on here. You heard about that boy who lost his head, didn't you?"

"No," Charlie said, raising one eyebrow.

"What happened?" Tony moved in closer.

They stared at her, waiting. She tossed her hair, threw back her shoulders, and put on her performance stance, the one she used at meets. "Well, halfway down—*CRACK!*—his head hit the shelf . . . and stayed there."

"Ewww!" Someone laughed.

"No effing way!"

"The rest of him kept going, but not his head. It was on the shelf, eyes open, like he was looking around for the rest of him." Her own eyes opened wide, as if in shock.

"Gross." Sean laughed. "No way did that happen."

"Uh-uh," said Charlie.

"We all would have heard about it."

Ria peered over the edge again, searching for proof, of something. It's not like she *wanted* it to be true. She'd been haunted by Coach Benny's story. His point had been that there was nothing to fear from diving off the platform, which was free from rocky hazards. But she'd gotten lost in the idea of that particular fall. The exhilaration of the leap, stopped suddenly by the hard rock shelf. It still made her heart race to think of it.

Especially now that Charlie and Tony were wrestling too close to the edge.

"Can we go down to the water?" She pointed at the narrow trail carved into the rock, leading down to the water's surface.

"It's too late," said Sean. "It'll be dark soon."

As if to prove his point, the sun dropped behind the wall of rock. Although the sky still glowed, the rocks were disappearing into the shadows. The view was fading, turning fuzzy.

"Why did they stop quarrying?" she asked.

"Quarrying?" Charlie sputtered his drink. "You mean mining?"

"Whatever it's called. Why didn't they keep going? There's still more rock. It's all the same along the walls. They could have gotten more."

"Does it matter?"

It felt like it should.

"I heard"—she eyed Sean, ready to read his expression—"that there's all kinds of machinery under the water. When they shut it down, they left everything behind."

"Well, yeah. Look at this place. How would they get it out? Drive? They had to leave it all inside."

So that was true. The dark, smooth surface did hide dangers. "Where did the water come from? It must have been something natural, right? Is there water below the rock?"

"I guess so." Sean leaned in close. "You're obsessing again."

He nuzzled her neck, sending shivers along her skin. Now that it was darker, she couldn't clearly see the edge of the giant hole.

Suddenly impatient, she said, "Do you want to dance?"

"It's not that kind of party. That would be weird."

"Maggie wouldn't care. She'd dance anyway."

"You're probably right." He laughed, then frowned. "Aren't you having fun? This is awesome, Ria. The quarry is legendary."

"Right. Of course."

He sipped from his cup and smiled. His arm stayed around her waist, but his eyes were on his friends who had wandered into the sea of bodies. None of them had girlfriends. Ria wished again that Maggie was here. She'd be able to convince Ria this party was as fun as Sean said it was. She knew how to laugh at nothing, to take something awful and make it bearable. If Maggie had been at that meet in LA, then maybe . . . but "maybe" was regret dressed up as make-believe. Otherwise known as useless.

She slipped her hand into Sean's. She was so lucky he'd asked her out. Maggie was the one who'd spotted the cute lifeguard first. Ria wouldn't have noticed him. Lifeguards were irrelevant during their practices. Benny had his eye on his team, wound tight and ready to spring if something went wrong. She hadn't known she'd need a boyfriend when everything fell apart.

But now she was ruining his fun.

"I'm going to go home," she said.

"Why? What's wrong?"

"I don't feel well." It was the truth, but not anything sudden or new. It was the same general blah she couldn't shake. So far, none of the parties, the hanging out, the fast-food sampler marathon—where they'd ordered something off every drive-through menu in town—or even the hours in the back seat of her car had turned out like she expected. Nothing seemed quite as good as Sean promised. But it wasn't his fault. She was the one who didn't know how to be normal.

"You stay." She handed him her full cup. "I'll see you tomorrow."

"Are you sure?"

She could see him wrestling with his options. *Fun party with beer and friends vs. being a good boyfriend.*

"I'm sure."

She was relieved he believed her. It was exhausting being cheered up and doted on.

Back at the car, Ria stood on the side of the road, breathing deeply. Wind whipped around her, stinging her arms and legs. Then, suddenly, it subsided. She turned full circle, arms out. She waited, but the winds were gone. An ache of missing hit her hard, in her gut.

TWO

Home from the party, Ria took out her contacts, letting the world slip into its usual lack of clarity. Lying on her trampoline, she breathed in the rich smells of Maggie's shampoo mixed with the dust of the trampoline and the sharp clean of chlorine soaked into her friend's skin. Ria refused to ask about practice. She was used to denying cravings.

"How was the quarry?" Maggie asked.

"There's nothing there."

"No one showed up?"

"There were lots of people. It was a party. But the quarry, it's a big hole. It only exists because it's empty. Well, except for the cloud. There was a cloud in it."

"You're so random, Ria." Maggie laughed.

"Do you remember that story Benny told about the quarry? The one about the boy who jumped in?"

"And lost his head? How could I forget?"

"Sean said it wasn't true."

"Huh," said Maggie. "It must have been partly true. Or it happened somewhere. Benny doesn't lie. But sometimes the details aren't all there. He leaves things out."

Ria shifted to her side, leaving her arm under her heavy head. The light from her house illuminated Maggie's face and frizzy red hair against the dark beyond her yard.

"How was practice?" She'd waited as long as she could.

"Everyone misses you."

"Not everyone," said Ria. Then, before Maggie could contradict her, she said, "I know Chrissy doesn't."

"I think she actually does, even if she'd never admit it. The worst part is we're not allowed to talk about you. Temo said your name the other day and had to climb the ladder for twenty minutes."

Ria didn't trust her voice to answer. She couldn't talk about them, either.

Maggie rolled over, then clambered up. She stood on the springy surface, hovering over Ria. She bounced gently. Then more definitely. By the time she started circling, she was rising several inches into the night sky. Ria relaxed into the bounce of the old favorite game. She stayed limp, letting herself be lifted and lowered, following the rhythm of the jumps. Lost in the soothe of motion, then the rush of the drop, until she was elevated at least a foot off the bed of the trampoline. That's when the thrill of the fall kicked in, setting them both to breathless giggling. Maggie rolled into a flip and landed on her butt.

"I made my gainer two-and-a-half tonight."

"Maximum Mags! Why didn't you tell me right away? Did you rip it?"

"Duh. No way. But I didn't bruise anything, either."

"You're such a big-girl diver."

"I thought Benny was going to cry, he was so happy."

"Of course. Now the colleges are going to be knocking down your door. That's a real money dive."

"Should I call the coach at Uden College? Or wait until I get it on video?"

"Don't settle, Mags."

"It's not settling. Uden is a really good school."

"Why be good when you could be great?" Bennyisms had a way of slipping out of her mouth before she thought them.

Softly Maggie asked, "Why quit now? After everything . . ."

That's what diving had been for her. *Everything.*

"There's no point. Not after I blew my chance at Nationals." She had to make Benny's words her own by saying them over and over again.

"You fell. You got hurt. Stop me if I'm missing something."

"Stop." Her voice held a warning that Maggie would recognize. After she'd scratched the meet, Benny had banished her. He'd quit her. "It's over and done. And now I might as well enjoy my senior year." Maggie would help make these words mean something. She knew Ria had never cared about school. It was something to endure rather than enjoy, but she'd promised her parents—and herself—she'd at least graduate from high school. "I'm not going to college like you, Mags."

"*If* I get a scholarship," Maggie said. "I hope I have a coach long enough to sign somewhere."

"What do you mean? What's going on?"

"It's basic math, Ria. If your parents aren't paying him anymore . . ."

She didn't have to know numbers to know Maggie was right. Between paying for her extra workouts, private lessons, and miscellaneous other ways of supporting his gym, her parents had made sure Benny stayed in business. They had to—there was no better coach in town. Or the county. There was no one as good as Benny for endless miles in all directions. But now there was nothing for them to pay for. Even Benny needed money.

Ria felt Maggie's blame weighing down the trampoline. If Benny stopped coaching, her whole team would be lost. The ripples of one mistake flowed outward, expanding.

A song popped into Ria's head. *If wishes were fishes and fishes could sing* . . . Except she didn't know the rest of the words. They'd floated away, off into the blurry stars.

THREE

Ria woke at dimmest dawn. Even a month after quitting, her body was still conditioned to wake up early. Ready to be put in motion. Eager to perform. On autopilot, she got dressed to work out. She was downstairs before the sun had fully lit the sky. With nothing to do and nowhere to go, the day already felt longer than it should.

When she heard her parents moving around upstairs, she bolted for the back door. She darted across the yard, climbed the wooden fence, and escaped to the trail that ran behind her house. She sent them a text: **Went for a run**.

Then, to make it true, she bent over and stretched. Lifted her arms above her head. Twisted and turned to loosen her back, her neck. Out of habit, she did the dry-land modeling exercises Benny insisted on at the start of every water workout. She went through the motion of doing her dives, standing in place.

It was too hard being around her parents' frustration and

questions. Diving had left this big hole, bigger than the quarry, for all of them. They didn't know how to talk to each other anymore. Their lives had always revolved around it. After school and work, on weekends, all the time, all year long, everything was to make sure she could dive. Even their vacations had been planned around her meets. She'd loved Seattle because that was the first time she'd swept an entire meet, winning her age category in every event. It wasn't the Space Needle or the fish market or the ferry ride that she remembered best—it was that giddy, impatient feeling of wanting to get back to the pool.

Last year they'd skipped the vacation they'd planned in Orlando. None of them were in the mood after that meet. Benny had wanted her to do her reliable inward dive during Optionals, but Ria was sure she could nail her new gainer for more points and way more bragging rights. Which she did. It was the best one she'd ever done. But then Benny wouldn't coach her for the rest of the meet. He'd said, "You want to be on your own, be on your own." She'd completed her last two dives, but his silence was excruciating.

Her parents hadn't noticed the way he'd shunned her. They had no idea he'd been mad until he left before the medals were presented. The whole drive back her mother had ranted and called him unprofessional and immature. Dad had steamed silently. And Ria cried in the back because she knew she should have listened to her coach.

And now, ever since she'd scratched the meet in Los Angeles, he'd shut her out completely.

After she'd cycled through her list, Ria stopped diving into air and took off running. Down the trail. Along the ups and downs. Past the shrubs and boulders.

She hated running.

There was the wearing of shoes. The monotony of doing the same motion over and over. The hard pounding on the ground. Fighting the heavy pull of gravity. No adrenaline thrill to balance the effort. The awkward feeling that she was taking up too much space. Sweating. Panting.

All the ways it wasn't diving.

There was no finesse required. No precision. No power laced with grace.

But her body needed to get tired, so she ran harder. Faster. Even if she hated it, she knew how to push herself to that edge of not being able to go one more step, and then taking that next step anyway. To keep going. If it's possible, then do it. Pain is temporary. It's the body's warning, but not the defeat.

She hit a patch of gravel, slipping sideways. As a reflex she hugged her arms close, ready to roll, but she regained her balance before hitting the ground. The near-fall shook her, made her slow her pace.

It only took one slip to change everything.

If she hadn't slipped in Los Angeles, she wouldn't have fallen, wouldn't have invited all the trouble that followed. If she hadn't been running, she'd still be diving.

She left the trail, away from the slippery gravel. As she jogged down the grassy hill, momentum made her slide. Thick blades scraped against her legs. At the bottom, the land flattened out amid the weeds. This area was filled with hazards like rocks and sticks and who-knows-what living behind the bushes and trees. She should turn around before she got hurt or lost. But it was easier to keep moving in the same direction.

Her contacts felt dry and scratchy, and sweat dripped around her eyes, making it hard to see. Her breaths came rough and jagged, sounding loud and embarrassing.

As she followed the trail around a collection of boulders, she slammed into what felt like a wall.

A muddy, moving wall.

She stumbled backward, awkwardly bending her legs beneath her. "Damn!" was all she could manage around her gasps for air.

Two figures stood in front of her. One—the wall—was enormous, the other shorter and wiry, both of them covered from head to toe in mud. They each wore a yellow hard hat with a lightbulb in the middle.

"Ria?"

The enormous wall took off his helmet and wiped the mud coating his face. Now she could see it was Cotton Talley. They used to be friends back in elementary school—the kind of friendship too embarrassing to reminisce over. He was with his friend Leo, who she didn't know as well.

"Were you cleaning out sewers or something?" she asked.

"No. We were not cleaning sewers. We were spelunking."

She had no idea what that meant. "Well, you have some of it on your face. And your clothes. And pretty much all of you."

"We were in a cave. Over that way." He swung his arm outward, sending a spray of gunk through the air.

Ria wiped the mud droplets off her leg. "Is that allowed?"

The two boys looked at each other briefly. "Yes and no," said Leo.

"Technically, we should have written permission from the owner of the property," Cotton said in his usual stiff way of talking. "But as the owner is the housing developer who built our neighborhood and is based out of Alexandria, Virginia, we assume we, as residents of this neighborhood, have access rights."

He sounded so formal. Even though they were both wearing the same kind of weird olive-green full bodysuit, Leo's looked loose and baggy, while Cotton's was zipped all the way to his neck and fit him precisely, borderline tight. Maybe that was just because he was so tall. His dark brown curls, matted and twisted from the helmet, looked more rebellious.

"We know what we're doing," said Leo dismissively.

She scanned the overgrown field of shrubs and knobby trees. In the distance were hills and boulders—but also, somewhere, apparently not too far, was a cave.

"The latest rain made it muddier than usual," said Cotton.

"Looks like it," she said, even if she wasn't entirely sure how they'd gotten from one place to another. "You're completely muddened."

Cotton laughed. Loud and staccato. The same laugh she remembered from when they were little. As always, it made her laugh, too. With the way he grinned, the cave must have been worth the mess.

"Muddened," he said. "We are muddened. Completely muddened."

"Yep," said Leo, loudly, as if hitting a reset button.

She hated the way Leo looked embarrassed for his friend. She ignored him and instead focused on Cotton. "I had no idea there was a cave nearby."

She knew there were caves, in theory. They were probably composed of the same limestone that was dug out of the quarry back when mining employed most of the town. Every year in elementary school they'd been given a safety presentation warning of the dangers lurking below the ground. It had never occurred to her to look for one so close to her house. She shivered in the early sunlight, but it wasn't only the breeze hitting the sweat on her skin.

Now she was thinking about Esther, Cotton's little sister. When they were in fifth grade and Esther was in third, she'd gone out to play and never came back. She was someone Ria had seen almost every day, even if she never thought much about her. Esther was always there, until she wasn't. Their quiet town had suddenly become big news. Invaded by strangers, all wanting to help, but making everything feel wrong.

"Where's the entrance?" Ria turned to Cotton, felt him tense up. She'd forgotten he didn't like being touched without warning. She pulled away, leaving a clear space between them. She felt desperate to know more. "Will you show me?"

"I don't know."

"Please? I don't want to go in there by myself."

"No!" he said, obviously agitated. "You can't do that. Caving requires a partner. And proper gear."

"Then take me. For a peek, that's all," she begged. "So I can see where it is."

It was like she could see the struggle going on in Cotton's mind. He wanted to show her. But something was in the way. "My mother is expecting us home. She'll worry."

"Because of Esther." She knew it was true, but the shocked look on Leo's face made her wonder if she'd blown her chance by being too blunt.

"Yes. It's a matter of safety."

"Can't you call your mother?"

"I don't have my phone."

"There's no reception in the cave," explained Leo.

"Use mine."

"No, thank you." Cotton tucked his hand behind his back.

"Just show me where it is." She knew she was obsessing, but she couldn't give up, not this close to almost. The promise of a thrill hummed in her ears. "Please say yes."

“Yes,” said Cotton. Then, to Leo, “That is a compromise. Right? Isn’t this the kind of flexibility you say I need?”

“Sure, okay,” said Leo. Then, glaring at Ria: “We’ll show you the entrance, but that’s it. We’re not taking you inside.”

“And you can’t go in by yourself.”

“I won’t,” she said, not entirely sure what she was promising.

The entrance to the cave was close to invisible. A large boulder and a scraggly, forgettable pine blocked the opening, only a few steps off the trail. She could have passed this spot a hundred times and never noticed it. But once she ducked her head around the tree, she immediately saw the hole. Cool air wafted over her skin as she breathed in something like mildew, but greener. Ria moved closer, squatted, and peered in. She could only see a few feet inside of the rocky entrance before meeting a wall of dark.

“What do you do in there?” she asked, standing up.

Cotton tilted his head like he didn’t understand the question. Then said, slowly, “We explore. We walk around. We see what we find.”

“So it’s like hiking, but in the dark?”

He frowned, and for a minute she thought she’d said something wrong. But then he laughed.

“We’re also mapping it,” said Leo.

“What does it look like inside?”

“Well,” said Cotton, settling back on his heels, “it’s dark. And damp. There are tunnels and rooms. And there’s a small stream. There are several different geologic formations and types of crystals." He pulled a small notebook from one of his many coverall pockets, opened to a page filled with lines and shapes. He traced one of the darker lines with his finger and started talking faster. More animated. "You come in this way, and there are two different paths. This one"—he circled one side—"ends with a stone wall. But the other side opens up after a narrow tunnel. It's actually quite amazing." His enthusiasm poured out, filling the space between them.

"It's not something for everyone to know about. It's kind of a secret." Leo sounded borderline threatening.

"I can keep a secret." She stepped back. "You don't have to worry about me."

"Ria is not like normal girls."

Damn. She and Cotton had each spent plenty of time not fitting in, but she hadn't expected to hear the obvious truth so harshly stated.

"We can trust her."

He smiled suddenly, showing one crooked tooth on the side. Not enough to be snaggled, but more like it had its own ideas about the way it should go. Reflexively, she ran her tongue over her own teeth, feeling for the chipped spot. It was still there, even if it was too tiny for anyone else to notice.

FOUR

Ria waited for Benny in the dry gym parking lot. After running, she'd showered and gotten dressed in her dive team warm-up suit. It was the one she wore to meets. It always made her feel more confident.

She'd parked down the street and now stood behind the corner of the building so she could avoid talking to her teammates. The first week after she'd been banished, she'd driven by here every day, hoping she'd misunderstood. She'd even parked outside Benny's apartment as if she could somehow telepathically change his mind. He'd known, of course, and sent her a text threatening to call the police, or worse, her parents, so she'd been forced to face the truth, complete with withdrawal symptoms.

Right now, right here, she needed to stay focused on what she wanted to say. She knew how to fix everything. For Maggie. And the rest of her team. And for Benny, too.

She knew better than to try to talk to him during a workout. As long as everyone did their assigned reps and exercises, the team could talk about anything and everything, but he never chatted. He sat back and watched. Evaluated. Rated.

They'd probably watched film today. With their previous night's practice projected on the wall, he would have narrated each dive, stopping mid-flip, stretching flash-seconds into minutes, rewinding mistakes in slow-motion. He'd spout off his insights as to where and why a dive went wrong. He could always spot wrong. And he knew how to fix it.

That's why he was the one person in the world who understood her. Only he saw her hyper-distractibility as a good thing. She'd always been in trouble at school. The reason her parents put her in gymnastics, oh so long ago, was because she drove them nuts with her constant need to move. Tired of peeling her off the furniture and forcing her right-side up, they'd looked for a way to wear her out. Then she'd been too wild for that prissy world, too.

She'd finally found her place on the diving board. Benny knew how to channel her impulsiveness, her way of leaping first and looking later, her flaws and messes, into something that worked. Everything she'd accomplished—her dives, scores, wins, championships—were because of him.

Finally, an eternity after the last diver's car left the lot, her coach appeared. His hat blocked his face, but she knew his posture, the brisk way he walked, always with purpose.

"Hi."

He stopped, a few feet from his red SUV. Stared for a full minute before his face broke into something she was almost sure was a smile. She licked her lips, tried not to fidget.

"I went to the quarry. It looks dive-able. It must have been a freak accident when that boy lost his head."

He stared at her but didn't take it back, didn't pretend she'd heard his story wrong.

"Did you go for it? Or did you walk away?"

They both knew the answer.

"Why are you here, Ria?"

A shiver of doubt ran over her skin. But then she shook it off. "Let me come back."

"Not happening."

"Please?" Sometimes begging worked. "I'll do whatever you say. You can work me as hard as you want. We can go back to the way it was."

"I got you there, Ria. I got you ready. We were going to go all the way." His voice was steely, metallic and cold. "But you blew it. You ran away."

"I know." There was no point in apologizing. Benny hated the word "sorry."

"You could have been a champion, but now you're nothing." He shifted his bag to his other shoulder. He was getting irritated. Not quite pissed, yet. She still had time. "You were barely hurt after that fall. You *quit*!"

"I didn't mean to. I didn't understand." She scrambled to the ground. Put her hands flat on the cement, stretched herself out long, into a plank position. So many infractions she'd worked off this way. "How long should I hold it?" She tightened every muscle, readied herself for his check.

"This was the year, Ria. That was always the plan. I'm not waiting around. Seriously, what would we work for? What would be the point?"

Through clenched teeth, struggling to stay taut, she said, "We can try again next year. Or maybe even sooner, if we hit every meet."

"No team wants you now. Everyone knows you're a head case. You're too unstable."

"They can't ignore me if I keep winning."

"Go for it. I wish you all the luck."

"You don't believe in luck." Her voice was thick, filled with frustration. Her body swayed, revealing her struggle. She hadn't been working hard enough. She'd tried to stay strong, but she couldn't do it on her own. "My parents will pay whatever you want. You know they will."

"You think this is about money? No wonder you blew it. You never got what we were doing, did you?" He spat on the ground. "We're done, Ria. I'm not going to waste my time on someone I can't trust. The second you scratched that meet, we were kaput. Over. Cease and desist. The end."

She pressed harder into the cement, trying to calm the

involuntary shaking of her muscles.

"I know I screwed up, Benny. It's all my fault. But you can fix this. Tell me what to do. I promise I won't mess up again. Please, Benny. . . ."

His kick hit her right arm, too fast for reflexes to fight gravity. Her shoulder folded, giving her chin nowhere to go but down, hard, into the pavement. She should have been ready, should have ducked and rolled, should have known how this talk would end. Her ragged breathing blended with the sound of his engine, the smell of her blood with his exhaust. By the time she'd sat up, pressing her sleeve against the stinging scrape, he was gone.

FIVE

On her trampoline, between Maggie and Sean, Ria leaned back and stared up at the sky. Her glasses had a smear on the lens, but she liked the way it made the stars look like they'd been spilled behind the tree. Her chin only hurt when she touched it.

"Starting tomorrow," said Sean, "we're seniors."

"Finally!" said Maggie. "We're going to take the place over. Chrissy is already working on a class costume for Halloween."

"We've got to start thinking about the perfect senior prank, too. Charlie'll be the mastermind, I'm sure."

"And prom," added Maggie. "We'll have the most ultimate prom. But what about tomorrow? We should do something for the first day."

"We'll meet by the front window—the same spot where we'll have lunch. The Senior Roost."

"I've waited three years to sit there!"

"You made it. *We* made it. Right, Ria?"

"Okay." It wasn't the rightest answer, but it wasn't completely wrong. She hadn't given senior year a lot of thought. Or any. She was having trouble following all the plans Maggie and Sean had for this year, but plans didn't mean actually happening, either. Her plans had been to not be here. She was supposed to have won Nationals and now be diving around the world. She would have had private tutors instead of boring classes.

She and school had a tumultuous history. In elementary school, she'd always been the skinny kid with big glasses. One step behind and two levels below. She counted backward and upside down. Letters had a way of mixing up and jumping around. Playing hide-and-seek and peekaboo. Looking like one thing but being another.

Diving had saved her.

Getting her body exhausted had given her mind a chance to slow down. Plus, it gave her plenty of excuses. If she was gone at a meet all weekend, it made sense that her report was short and messy. Once teachers heard her extensive practice schedule, they were more willing to make even more adjustments and adaptations.

But now she'd failed diving, too. She hadn't escaped after all.

"We'll rule the school," said Sean.

"We'll rule the universe!"

"Ruling the whole universe sounds like a lot of responsibility," Ria said.

Sean ignored her ridiculous comment, keeping in line with

Maggie's excitement. "It's going to be awesome."

"What color is awesome?" What she really meant was, how could school be awesome? Those two ideas didn't exist together in her mind. Even for brains like Maggie and Sean, "awesome" seemed like an awfully long stretch.

"Well, Random Ria," Maggie said, tossing a seed pod at her. "'Awesome' can be whatever color you want it to be."

Cotton had made caving sound awesome and amazing and mysterious and yet he hadn't mentioned any colors besides mud-brown. He'd been muddened. That joke would be too hard to explain to Maggie and Sean. Maybe Cotton was just easily amazed.

"Let's see if we can find some awesome right here." She handed her glasses to Sean, then stood up, reaching for Maggie's hands. "I challenge you to an Awesome Add-on."

"You start."

"You be judge," Ria said to Sean, who had already moved to the edge of the trampoline. "Rate our color of awesome."

He shook his head, slipping down to the grass. "No way. I'm not starting a war. I'll film for any disputes."

They both laughed. It was true. Their competitions were fierce and unyielding.

Ria started basic, with a backflip. Maggie did her own, then reversed the direction into a front handspring. Ria took those two moves and added a front flip, the force of it launching her precariously high, setting off a chorus of shrieks. By the time they'd added a total of fourteen moves, they both staggered around the trampoline, a floppy mess of breathless, hysterical giggles.

Her chin ached now. She must have bumped it again. "Truce."

"Hell no," said Maggie. "If you quit, I win. Otherwise we keep going."

"I'm done. I quit."

Her friend eyed her mistrustfully.

"Seriously. You win, Mags." She'd let her have this one. There was no point in winning.

"Oh, thank God. My legs are Jell-O-fied." Maggie slid to the edge and off. "We worked our legs today along to the entire *Les Mis* soundtrack."

Once Maggie drove away, she and Sean stood in the driveway, near his mother's sedan. "Come closer. I miss you."

"I'm right here." She laughed, then shifted so he would be the one leaning against the car. She hated being trapped without a getaway route. Not that he'd given her any reason to need one. He knew he was her first boyfriend, and he'd been nothing but sweet. He'd put up with her weird and limited schedule. Understood when she was too tired and sore to go out.

Now, she let him pull her close. He kissed her, gently at first, but quickly warming up to where they'd left off the last time they'd been together. He locked his hips on hers, let her feel how much he liked this. She liked it too. She was curious what was on the other side of all this kissing and touching, but she also knew Sean had rules about what and when and how, only he hadn't explained them yet. And now he kept bumping her bruised chin with his.

The outside light flashed on, off, then on, above them.

"I guess I better go." His voice sounded raspy and deep.

"I guess so." She slipped out of his reach.

"Senior year is going to be better than you think." He grinned and played with her hair. "You'll look back on it and see how I was right."

"So I should look forward to how I'll look back?"

"What?"

"Forget it. I'll see you tomorrow—at the *Senior Roost*." She kissed him, then opened his door, sending him on his way.

Looking forward, looking backward, anytime looked better than right now.

SIX

The first day of school was always about seeing and being seen. Who was wearing what. Who'd lost or gained weight over the summer. New tats and piercings. The status of romances—breakups and hookups. Figuring out who's in what class and when. Where paths cross. Anticipation. Senior year was all that, on steroids.

As soon as Ria walked through the doorway to school, she knew she'd worn the wrong thing. Gym shorts or yoga pants along with dive T-shirts had always been her uniform. Here at school, she liked to be anonymous. Invisible. For today she'd let Maggie talk her into wearing a sundress, skimpy and slinky, an explosion of color. In her bedroom, with only her reflection to judge, the dress had felt right. Looked sexy. Now, in the loud and crowded space, it felt too tight and too bright. Aware of being seen, she touched her chin in reflex, even though she knew the bruise was barely noticeable under makeup, especially if she kept her head tilted.

"You look hot." Sean sidled up close, keeping one arm behind him. It was clear he had something hidden back there. He was big on surprises. Knowing one was coming was both better and worse. Then he frowned. "You always flinch when I come near you."

"No, I don't."

"I think it's because of diving."

"What?"

Ria stepped back. Her cheeks flushed. Just because he'd been at the pool, sitting in his lifeguard chair, being useless and irrelevant, didn't mean he knew everything. Or anything.

"It's okay. I understand. It's just hard for you to relax now after working so hard for so long."

"I'm fine. I'm good. Great." She grabbed his belt loop, shaking off the feeling she'd been blindsided.

"Okay, good, great. I brought you something." He swung his arm out from behind his back, presenting her with a bouquet of flowers. Before she could thank him or even get a decent hold of them, he kissed her in front of all his friends.

A chorus of "Ooooh" broke out around them. Someone coughed the word "whipped." Sean grinned. He bumped fists with his friends, making the rounds, leaving her to watch and wonder if the kiss had been for her or for them.

Maggie appeared at her side, smelling of shampoo and lotion. She greeted everyone with that comfortable way of hers.

Ria tugged her wet ponytail and said, "Did you wake up late?"

"I had practice."

"You had a morning workout? Today?" Practice on the first day of school was hard-core, even for Benny.

"It was a one-on-one. I want to get my gainer solid."

"Right," said Ria. But it wasn't. Maggie's parents never paid extra for diving. The possibility of an Uden scholarship must have influence. She hoped it was worth it. It felt like too little, too late. She sniffed the flowers in her hand. They already looked bored and wistful.

"This is for you, too." Maggie handed her a small silver thermos.

She opened it and was hit with the smell of peanut butter and banana. When she took a sip of the creamy deliciousness, the feel of cold in her throat and stomach was somehow a just-right soothing discomfort. Nerves had kept her from eating breakfast, but this was exactly what she needed.

"Did you even add a shot of . . ."

"Coffee," said Maggie, looking amused.

"Oh, Mags, I am yours. Forever. You have no idea."

"You're right. I had no idea."

"Hmm?" said Ria, still savoring the sweet perfection.

"It's from Benny. He said you'd need it today."

Brain freeze.

"You two." Maggie shook her head. "It's so messed up that neither of you can admit how much you miss the other."

Ria made her way to the counseling office to pick up her schedule. Thanks to her special-education paperwork and modified graduation requirements, she always had to be counseled before each new school year. She hadn't bothered trying to explain her schedule to Sean. He probably didn't even know her remedial support classes existed. They were the kind of thing you either needed or they were invisible.

She didn't mind discovering a crowd in Mrs. Sellers's office. It only meant she'd have longer before she had to face any actual classes. She'd spent many hours in the counseling center. This office was the first stop whenever there was a problem brewing. Diving and meds had helped her do better in school, but some things had no cure.

Ria knew Mrs. Sellers kept a stash of dark chocolate in her desk. There were puzzles and games behind the college reference brochures. She'd mastered genius level for the peg puzzle during sophomore year when she'd been accidentally put in advanced Spanish. As if maybe she'd somehow be able to read, write, and conjugate verbs in a different language. Her grade had ended up being similar to the one she had in English, so maybe it wasn't that much of a mistake. Benny understood. That's why he'd convinced her parents she'd do better to spend her time diving. She took a sip of the perfect smoothie he'd sent for her. More proof that he knew her best.

Today it wasn't the usual group of misfits and troublemakers she was used to seeing in the counseling office. Even Cotton was here. She sat in his row, two seats over. He was working in his notebook as she studied his profile, the sharp edge of his chin. Beneath his curls, his broad shoulders rolled toward his lap. His bent legs barely fit in the space between his chair and the one in front of him. His arms, busy drawing, looked like they could reach her. In reflex, she extended her own arm toward him to measure the distance. He turned and looked her. "Hi, Ria."

She got up and moved to the seat beside him, careful to keep a barrier of space between her arm and his. Now she could see the page on his lap was filled with circles, squares, and rectangles.

"I keep thinking about the cave."

"Yes," he said, like that was to be expected.

Mrs. Sellers stepped out of her office then, holding a stack of papers, so Cotton looked straight ahead and Ria settled back in her chair. She realized she'd been absentmindedly ripping petals off her flowers. Not like it mattered. They were already dead, even if they didn't know it.

As she scanned the room, trying to figure out what this group had in common, she saw what she'd missed. Cotton had mapped the room. Each shape stood for a piece of furniture. She pointed to a spot in his notebook, and whispered, "You are here." He nodded; then, a full second later, grinned.

"Good morning, Pierre High seniors," said Mrs. Sellers. "Each of you has been approved for a modified day schedule. You'll need to pick up your official paperwork and have it signed by your supervising mentor.

"If you're taking online classes, we will receive the electronic updates. Those of you enrolled in classes at the community college will need to get a signature from both your teacher and the dean of the department. If you are enrolled in a work-study program, your immediate supervisor will need to sign for you. And those of you enrolled in other endeavors"—she met Ria's eyes—"will make other arrangements."

She smiled in reply. Then felt her face flush hot and red.

Even though she'd assumed she'd be gone by now, the school had kept her minimum schedule the way Benny had arranged for last year. He'd made sure she only had to take three classes, each one designed to help her achieve basic proficiency for graduation and then she'd be free before lunch. Free to practice and work out in private lessons. Free to dive. Which she didn't do anymore. She was completely free. And completely lost.

SEVEN

After she'd finished her few classes, Ria sat in her car, letting the not-yet-cool air blow hard across her face. Her phone buzzed from the cupholder. Another text from Sean.

She replied now: **Minimum schedule. Ask Maggie.** Then, as if she was worried he'd try to stop her, or ask her too many questions, she turned off her phone. She put her car in drive and let school shrink in her rearview mirror. The sun shone bright, the music played on her radio, and she could go anywhere. Only she wasn't sure where that might be.

As she turned onto the main road, she immediately recognized the tall figure at the town bus stop. Cotton.

She stopped her car a few feet past. She eyed him in her mirror, waiting for him to react. He stood behind a dark green metal bench, slouched against the sign. He had terrible posture. He looked at her car, but she couldn't tell if he knew it was hers.

She put it in reverse and backed up along the edge of the road until she was parallel to him. He stepped back, away from the street until he was almost in the bushes.

She rolled down the window. "Do you want a ride?"

"What are you doing, Ria?" He didn't move from his spot.

"Stalking you, obviously." He didn't laugh, so she added, "I thought you might want a ride." It didn't make sense that she suddenly felt guilty. Like she had to make excuses and explanations. It must be the look on his face. It was as if he couldn't believe she would do this—whatever this was—to him. "Never mind."

As the window almost reached the top again, Cotton said, "Wait."

He opened the passenger door and looked inside. Then at her. "Are you sure?"

"It's only a ride." She now felt as unsure as he looked. She'd obviously missed some part of ride-offering etiquette.

He pulled out his phone and started tapping. "This is a blue Subaru, correct? Four doors." He was obviously sending someone her details. But then he got in.

He took up most of the front seat. His head almost touched the car ceiling. He seemed made of arms and legs in every direction. After he buckled his seat belt, Ria asked, "Is everything okay?"

"Yes," he said. Then, after a pause, "Thank you?"

"Blue Subaru enough info? Do you need my driver's license, too?"

"No, thank you. I always tell someone where I am. For safety."

"Because of Esther."

"Yes."

"Did I scare you when I stopped my car?"

"Yes."

It was hard to believe he worried about someone scooping him up from the side of the road. He was far too big for scooping. His hands were the biggest she'd ever seen. Ria fought the urge to measure hers against his, by clutching the steering wheel. "Where should I take you?"

"Home. I live at 6571 Quartz."

She pulled back onto the road. She wondered why he had a minimum schedule, but if she asked, she'd have to talk about her own reason, which didn't exist anymore.

"These need water." He'd picked up her wilted bouquet from the floor.

"I guess so," she agreed. "My boyfriend gave them to me."

"Sean."

She wasn't surprised that Cotton knew Sean. But she hadn't known he'd noticed she was dating him.

"So it doesn't really matter if they wilt," he said.

"It doesn't?"

"No. Because that won't change their function. He gave them to you to show affection. They're already dead."

Ria laughed to hear him say what she'd been thinking. Then she felt guilty, like she was making fun of her boyfriend who'd only tried to . . . show affection.

Cotton didn't live far from her. The streets required a few twists and turns, but by the time they looped back and around, she recognized the part of the trail that ran behind his house.

He opened the car door as soon as she stopped at the curb. His house was big, with pots of brightly colored flowers on the porch. He turned to her and said, "Thank you for the ride. I'm sorry I thought you wanted to kidnap me."

As he got out of the car, she did, too. She met him as he shut the door, careful to leave plenty of space between them. "I want to go caving." To clarify, she added, "Today. Now."

"Leo and I go on weekends."

"But we have time right now. Please? I don't have anywhere else to go." It was the truth. Maybe with someone else, she might have worried about sounding desperate, or pathetic, but here with Cotton, she simply felt honest.

There was an excruciating pause while he stared at something behind her. She studied the way his fingers fluttered against his thigh, wondering if he was sending her a secret message and if she could crack the code.

"Is the cave closed right now?" she asked.

"Of course not. It's not a commercial attraction. It doesn't open and close."

She waited, not wanting to push, but also knowing he wasn't easily persuaded. She couldn't make him do anything he didn't want to do. He'd been so excited talking about the cave the other day. He had to want to go again. Even if it meant bringing her.

"So if it's not commercial, does that mean it's a wild cave?"

"Wild?"

"Yeah, wild."

He finally looked at her. Tilted his head, and then, surprisingly, laughed. "Yes, it's wild. It's completely untamed."

She laughed too, sensing she'd won.

"Yes," he said. "Let's go caving even though it's not the weekend."

He led her around the house to the backyard, past a crooked play structure and an open sandbox. He walked straight to a wooden shed built against their chain-link fence, dumping his backpack on the ground. The heavy door opened with a creak and he stepped inside while she waited nearby. The contrast of the sunlight and the dark of the shed made it hard to see what he was doing, but then he reappeared with a large duffel bag.

"You can't go in a dress." It felt like he hadn't even noticed what she was wearing until that moment.

"Can I borrow something?" As soon as she said it, her words seemed ridiculous. Her head barely reached his broad shoulders.

"You're about the same size as Leo," he said, making her feel like she'd been measured. "You could wear his coveralls. They're in our gear bag."

He pulled two heavy green suits out of his bag. He handed her the smaller one, then said, "I'll see if I can find you some shoes, too. Your sandals are impractical." He started toward the house, then looked back. "Do you want to come in?"

Ria shook her head. She didn't want to see his mother. Even though—or more accurately, *because*—she felt like she knew Mrs. Talley after seeing her on television, hoping for the return of Esther, she wouldn't know what to say to her. "I'll wait here."

As soon as he disappeared inside, she kicked off her sandals and stepped into the coveralls. She pulled the thick canvas suit to her waist, then inched up her dress, slipping her arm out of it, then into the coverall sleeve. The second arm was easier, and then she pulled the dress over her head, slipping the zipper up with the same movement. She'd had plenty of experience dressing and undressing in public situations. The fit was surprisingly close to ideal. But rough to the touch. And heavy. So much fabric.

Cotton returned with a pair of old leather boots and blue socks, along with a couple of sandwiches. "Turkey or cheese?"

She shrugged, then took the cheese one.

He took a bite of the other one and half of it disappeared.

Ria turned the sandwich over in her hands. She took a tentative bite. The bread was incredible. She hadn't even known she was hungry. She ate it slowly, taking bites in between putting on the boots, which felt slightly lopsided from wear.

Casually, Cotton picked up her dress from where she'd set it aside. He turned it over in his hand, examining it from different angles. She saw the moment he realized what he was holding.

His eyes met hers, then ran over her body. She couldn't read his look. It wasn't like he thought she was being sexy or inappropriate. She felt more like something under a microscope than any kind of object of fantasy.

She took the dress from him and placed it on their back step with her sandals.

He stood and grabbed the large duffel, throwing it over his shoulder. "Let's go." He led her behind the shed, where he undid the combination lock easily with one hand and opened the gate. He was strong in an unfamiliar way. Because of his size, lifting and maneuvering seemed effortless.

He relocked the gate and headed down the trail. As she caught up, Ria glanced at him sideways. He moved easily, strolling, or even gliding, but his steps were wide. Somehow their pace matched up precisely.

"I saw you dive once. During a swim lesson." He hadn't turned to look at her, hadn't changed his pace, so she didn't answer. A few minutes later he added, "It was an impressive defiance of gravity."

She let his words hang between them for a minute. Felt the pride of being someone who could do something special. Even if she wasn't that person now.

"I don't dive anymore." She pressed the tender spot on her chin and added, "Gravity always wins."

EIGHT

The cave was only a twenty-minute walk from his house, probably thirty from hers. The borrowed coveralls felt thick and bulky. She was already sweating, and they hadn't even done anything yet. She wished she hadn't bothered with the sandwich. It was mixing with Benny's smoothie, all churned up with anticipation.

"Did you change your mind?" he asked.

"No."

Cotton pulled two helmets from his bag and handed her one. "Then put on Leo's helmet."

"Do I really need this?" She turned the surprising weight of it over in her hands.

"Yes. You really do."

The helmet made her feel top-heavy and hyperaware of every one of her movements.

"Now we test the lights." He turned the knob and the tiny

bulb in the middle of his forehead glowed.

She reached for her own light, trying to copy his motion. Her fingers fumbled, unsure of what piece did what, until he moved in to help. As he guided her hand to the knob, he didn't seem to mind being close to her, but she held her breath, keeping still.

"It's working." He raised her hand in front of her forehead. A tiny beam shone on her palm.

"We can stay in the cave for eighty-five minutes. That's when I told my mother we'd return."

He'd always been a rule-follower. Very absolute and literal. But it made sense that Mrs. Talley would worry. She must always think the worst, after what happened with Esther.

"What do I need to know?"

"I'll lead. We'll stick together."

A tremor of adrenaline thrummed through her at the simple not knowing of what to expect. It made her eager and impatient to see if the feeling would last.

Cotton ducked his head and entered the cave with Ria close behind him. The opening was narrow, but after a few steps in, they could walk upright. The air felt cooler and smelled wet and heavy.

Her helmet light seemed brighter. The tiny beam that had been inconsequential in the sunshine now shone several feet out from wherever she directed her face. She could only see one stream of light's worth at a time, making it hard to get her bearings. This place was eerie. Mysterious.

It wasn't Fear whispering to her, exactly, but his cousin, Doubt, had arrived. Once again, she'd charged into something she didn't understand. Leap first, look later. She reached out and touched the gritty, not-quite-sandy walls on either side of her.

"Are there any lions or tigers or bears in here?"

"There are no lions or tigers or bears."

It was weird how his voice sounded quiet and muffled from ahead, but also echoed behind her.

"Is there anything else living in here?"

"There is a micro-environment of cave-dwelling creatures. Most are difficult to spot." He walked faster. "But, around this corner . . ."

She almost bumped into him when he stopped.

"Look here." He pointed to an opening in the rock at his shoulder level.

"I'm too short to see in. What's there?"

"Climb up."

"Just tell me."

"I think it would be more satisfying if you saw it yourself."

He could be stubbornly rigid. He wasn't going to let this go. Even though she was feeling wary, she wondered, too. She scrambled against the rock, feeling a rough scraping at her knees. Her fingers grasped at the slippery dampness. Then, his hands were on her waist, lifting her the last few inches. She braced her weight on the damp rock and leaned forward on her elbows.

Weird little teardrop objects hung from the ceiling. One

fluttered, stretching its webby wings. She pulled back in reflex. "Are those bats?"

"Yes!" His enthusiasm sent off a wave of vibrations through his chest and into her arm. He was right, this was something she'd had to see for herself.

"There's gotta be a hundred of them." She let her light run over their small furry bodies, but they ignored her. She breathed out, making more room for the awe growing inside her.

"It would be best if we didn't wake them up."

She tried to imagine what that would look like, but she'd never seen one bat fly, much less a whole flock or herd or—

"What do you call—"

"A colony. It's a colony of bats."

She scooted down the wall, returning to the solid stone ground.

As they made their way around a sharp turn, Ria's helmet hit the wall with a hard *thunk*. "Whoa. Watch your head."

"Yes," he said. "I have been."

The path turned slippery as they headed onward. The unfamiliar shoes added to her uncertain steps. She held her hands out to both sides, using the increasingly rugged stone walls to keep from sliding downhill into him.

"Are you okay?" He sounded out of breath.

"I think so."

"Yes. Sometimes it's hard to tell."

A few minutes later he stopped.

"Leo calls this section 'baby time.' We'll have to crawl." He took off his helmet, wiped his forehead, then used its light to illuminate a low, narrow opening. "Or we could turn around and head back."

"Not if there's more to see."

"There's always more to see." On his knees, he disappeared.

Ria bent down and peeked into the tunnel. She could see the glow from his helmet, and the shadow shape of him crawling. She took a deep breath and followed.

The ground was rough, and hard on her hands and knees. Her helmet kept slipping. Walking, she'd been able to pace herself, but she had no idea how to take bigger crawl-steps to keep up. Her reach only went so far. A vague sense of worry settled in her mouth, her stomach, the back of her throat.

She heard Cotton panting, as well as occasional scrapes against the wall. Ahead, their lights crisscrossed and overlapped, bumping up and down. The result was dizzying, but maybe that was as much from the exertion and earthy smells as anything else. Her heart pounded and her jaw ached from gritting her teeth. "How much farther?"

"Depends where we're going."

This was a mistake. She shouldn't be here. This was a certifiable unnecessary risk. Danger crowded in, like the too-close walls. Fear made it hard to breathe.

"Stop! I'm done."

"Keep moving."

"No! I need to get out of here." She twisted and strained against the rock wall. "There's not enough room to turn around."

"That's why we have to go forward." His voice had moved farther away.

"I want to go back."

"Keep moving."

"Damn, Cotton. You aren't listening!"

"I hear you. You want to turn around. That's not possible until you reach the end of the tunnel."

Now she was back to thinking about Esther. Her disappearance had terrified Ria. She'd slept between Mom and Dad for months. She hadn't wanted to play outside anymore. There'd been too many orange-vested strangers everywhere, searching all over town.

Eventually, the hunt had slowed down. Ria started diving for Benny. Exhausted from the workouts, she'd moved back to her own bed. She spent the summer at the pool under his careful watch. In the fall, she went back to school and Cotton was there. He'd grown several inches in every direction. Basically, he was the same boy she'd always known. Sometimes it was hard to believe anything bad had ever happened.

Until now. Now it felt real again.

"Please, Cotton." Stupid tears.

"Count to twenty," he said, his voice maddeningly stuck in neutral.

She took a deep breath and counted, first in her head, then

out loud. "Three . . . four . . . five . . ."

Counting was good. It was simple and predictable. By the time she got to seven, her breathing felt more even. She kept her head down, not wanting to see the walls and ceiling too close. She wasn't sure how he fit in here. The idea of the walls pressing on his back and head made her squirm and feel light-headed again. The urge to stretch and move felt painful, inescapable. But, at the count of eighteen, he said, "We made it."

He stood, and she, right behind him, scrambled up, happy to get off her knees. She could feel the space of the room even without fully seeing it. The walls were far enough apart that her light strained to reach them. "Wow," she said, and the word disappeared into the shadows.

"Is this better?"

"Much. But, damn. That sucked."

"Claustrophobia is a common side effect of caving."

"Sorry I yelled."

"Fear can look like anger."

She studied his face, looking sideways so as not to shine her light in his eyes. "Don't you worry about getting stuck?"

"If I can fit in one way, I can get out. It's a matter of measurable space."

It made sense, and yet, she wasn't convinced. It was one thing to know it, another to believe it. "Are we going to have to go back that way?"

"Yes. It's the only way out."

She liked that he didn't fake it or apologize.

"Have some water. It's important not to get dehydrated. It's cool enough that you might forget you're thirsty." He handed her a metal canteen.

That was like diving. Surrounded by water, rookies always dried up at their first meets. She took the container from him. The lukewarm water tasted metallic, but she was surprised that she didn't mind.

To her right, all along the wall, were raised formations. Matching ones hung from the ceiling. "These look like teeth." She ran her hand over them. "We're in a mouth."

"That's because there's so much water. They're formed by mineral deposits." He paused, then asked, "Am I being too geeky? I do that. You can call them teeth."

"Wait! I remember this. The ones on the ground are stalagmites. They have to grow up with all their *might*. And the other ones"—she pointed to the ceiling—"they hang *tight*. So they're stalac*tites*." She was glad she couldn't see his face from here. Cotton already knew all that. Everyone knew that. "They feel solid."

"They are. They're rock."

"So the rock gets dissolved in water, but then reappears and makes new rock? It gets a do-over."

"A do-over?"

"Yeah," she said. "A second chance."

"I never thought of it that way. But yes. The minerals get a do-over." He paused. Then said it again, "Do-over. Do-over. Do. Over."

Ria laughed. It was a weird word. Especially the more times he said it. "Do you ever worry about getting lost?"

"We're careful. That's why we're mapping it."

"How do you do that?"

"We wear pedometers. And do laser calculations to help measure and triangulate." He pulled a laser pen from his pocket and shone the red light on the rocks across the dark space. "Put it all together with our notes and we get the depth and mileage—both bird's-eye and actual step-by-step. I have a computer program that converts it all. It's pretty awesome. In a geeky way."

She could tell this was something he'd been told. It was probably true, but she had to add her own opinion. "Geeky is good, Cotton. Geeky is smart."

She stared into the darkness, trying to imagine what hovered beyond the tiny beam.

"Have you gone farther in?"

"Oh yes. From here, there are two ways to go. This way, and—" He swung his light from one corner of the room to the other. "That way. We've only started mapping the lower part."

"Let's keep going."

Her hands were gritty and coated in a thin sheen of mud. Under the helmet her hair felt sweaty and mussed. But she was exhilarated, too. A buzz of the challenge hummed along her bones as she scrambled and climbed up and over rocky barricades.

"Look at this."

Ria couldn't tell what made this particular collection of

bumpy rocks different from any others, but she stopped and leaned against one. She was surprised to realize she was close to panting.

"Here's what we call the 'back door to Australia.'" He handed her a small rock and pointed to a narrow opening. "Drop it in."

She tried to peer inside it, but her light wasn't aligned with her eyes. It seemed impossibly dark in there. She dropped the rock and waited. A second later she heard a *thunk* of it hitting rock. The skittering noise continued. And kept going. Even longer, until she couldn't hear it anymore, but she was sure she'd never heard it hit bottom.

"What's down there?" She sounded—and felt—breathless, and even more determined to try to see within the rocks.

"My favorite pocketknife, Leo's compass, and a lot of rocks. There might also be another cave system, but we haven't found a way down."

"I . . ." Ria paused. "That's so deep."

"Yes." His light nodded with him.

"Thanks for bringing me here, Cotton. I didn't know what to do today, now that I'm not diving. I used to have practice every day, but . . ." She stopped. None of this mattered to him. Or, at all. It was over.

"Why did you quit diving? I thought you were going to compete around the world."

That's what she'd planned. Hoped for. Now even the wishing was over.

"Just because I asked doesn't mean you have to answer," he said. "Sometimes I ask inappropriate questions. It's because I have poor social skills."

"It's fine. You're fine, Cotton. I'm just not sure of the answer." She took the canteen from him, sipping more water.

"There was a big meet in California. I was supposed to win. That's what everyone expected." There was something about the dark that made it easier to talk. It was also Cotton's patient way of listening. It felt like he was waiting, not guessing what her words would be, with his answer ready before she finished. "If I placed in the top three, I'd earn a spot with the National Development Team. It's an elite training club. There are others, but NDT is the best. It's a *very*—with a capital *V*, *B*, and *D*—Very Big Deal."

"Got it. NDT is a VBD."

"The NDT is what we'd been working for. But then . . ." She shook her head, and her light traveled back and forth across the walls. She'd freaked out, screwed up.

"During a practice before the meet, there are always lots of coaches around. One of them yelled at me, and, well, I ran away."

"Yelling is scary."

He was right. It was that simple. But, also, more complicated. The situation had felt too charged. Benny had been on edge all week. Even more intense than usual.

"The floor was slick, and I went down, hard."

Her knees and elbows had been banged up, but her confusing

answers to their too many questions convinced them she had a serious head injury, too. She hadn't even mentioned her chipped tooth. No one could understand why she'd been running.

"The stupid thing is, that coach, the one who was yelling, wasn't mad. I'd left my shammy towel and she was giving it to me." She'd felt so scared—terrified—when that coach had yelled her name. But she'd gotten it wrong.

Then Benny got riled up because he thought the woman pushed her. He'd accused her of trying to sabotage their practice. There was too much jealousy in the air, there always had been, ever since she started winning. All the other teams resented how a small-town nobody coach had the best diver. She and Benny always had to be even more perfect because people envied him.

And then she'd screwed up in front of everyone.

When someone produced the video that showed her in the background, it was clear the other coach hadn't come near her. There was no question, the slip was Ria's own fault.

"I freaked out for no reason."

"You had a reason. Even if it wasn't a reason other people understand. I used to freak out all the time. I always had a reason."

She remembered. Everyone took turns freaking out back in Ms. Q's room in elementary school. She was their special ed teacher, but the few hours they'd spent there each week had felt more like a vacation hideaway than a real class. Freak-outs hadn't mattered as much in there.

"So, I didn't compete." Scratching the meet was the easiest way to stop the questions and the fighting. Her parents blamed a concussion. All she'd wanted was to make it all stop, right then. In the moment, it felt like her only choice. "But since I blew my biggest meet, my coach won't work with me anymore. So I'm done."

"Done," echoed Cotton.

"It's not like diving is a career. I had to quit eventually. And now it's eventually."

"Eventually never looks the way I think it will."

She laughed, setting the helmet light bobbing. "What about you, Cotton? Why do you have a minimum schedule? Is it so you can go caving?"

"No. I didn't plan to cave today. It was your idea."

That was Cotton. Straightforward and stating the obvious.

"Well, then, why?"

"I want to learn more about mapmaking. So I'm taking online classes from the University of Virginia."

"They have an awesome pool. With a brand-new platform."

"That's for the really high dives, right?"

"Yeah."

"That will never be used by me," he said.

"Not even online?" Ria paused, then said, "That's a joke."

"Yes," he said. Then, "I prefer to stay on the ground."

"And underground." She stretched her arms over her head and twisted her torso. "Are you going on campus next year?"

"No." He frowned. "I can't leave my family."

It was clear he didn't have anything else to say about that.

"How much time do we have?"

"We have three minutes before we need to head back."

"Let's go now." It would be a relief to stop straining to see beyond what her helmet revealed. This in-between place of not quite light or dark was exhausting.

When they reached the tunnel, Cotton stopped and asked, "Are you ready?"

"I think so." Her light moved more enthusiastically than she felt.

This time, instead of facing the walls on every side of her, she closed her eyes. She crawled, letting her body disappear into the motion of it. Reach by reach, only forward, no hurry, refusing to let panic settle in. She was surprised to feel a draft of cool air, and the sense of space widening. She opened her eyes again, then blinked against the reflections of the damp, sparkly wall.

"We made it through," he said. "We're almost back."

She had no way of knowing if he was right. It all looked the same to her: mud and dark.

Her knees felt raw and bruised, even under the coveralls. Whenever her helmet scraped against the rocks, it sent vibrations across her skull and put her nerves on edge. She had no choice but to trust Cotton, to hope that he was as smart as she'd always thought. She'd copied his papers all through elementary school. She could copy his steps now.

Finally, a peek of sunlight appeared ahead. As they stepped out, she blinked and squinted in the bright day. She'd known Cotton forever, but somehow she'd missed the fact that his dark brown eyes were flecked with green. His face was slightly muddy and his hair completely wild now. Seeing him filled her with a giddy lightness. But that was probably due to the sunshine and the blue sky and had nothing to do with the line of his eyebrows, his nose, and his lips. The shadow of whiskers on his face made her feel like they'd been in the cave too long.

NINE

As soon as Ria walked in the door, she heard Mom announce her arrival. "She's here."

Her mother walked out of the kitchen as her father hurried down the stairs, each of them meeting her in the foyer. They had her surrounded.

"How are you, sweetheart? Did you have a good day?" Mom stared into Ria's eyes, way too intently.

Ria looked down, tried to smooth her rumpled dress, saw that she had mud under her fingernails.

"It was fine." She skirted around her dad and headed to the bathroom sink to wash her hands. She studied her face in the mirror. She was sure she still had mud tucked into her joints. Maybe it was inside her nose. She could smell it mingled with her sweat. The exact opposite of a day spent in the pool. Her arms and legs twanged with the effort.

They were waiting for her as soon as she stepped back into the hallway.

"Are you hungry?"

"I think I'll go jump on the trampoline first." She couldn't bear the effort of eating with such an attentive audience.

"Not yet. We need to talk."

Those words never led to anything she wanted to hear. No one ever "needed to talk" about anything wonderful. Good news spilled out, fast and frantic, shared without any warning. Need was about messes and mistakes. Troubles.

They sat in the family room. Her parents on the couch, Ria in the loveseat. The same positions as when she told them Benny had refused to keep coaching her. All the time and money spent on her sport had been wasted. Dumped on the floor with her wet towel.

"It's been a while since we did a mood check-in." Dad's voice had a fake cheerful tone.

When she first started her ADHD meds, they did daily, then weekly check-ins, forcing her to examine her emotions. One of the costs of being able to focus better could be a shift in mood. But, for her, as long as she'd had her time in the pool, she could work off whatever messes filled her school day. Diving was her therapy.

"We're worried about you. You seem depressed."

"Which is completely understandable," Mom interrupted.

"But we need to know how you're feeling. What you might do."

"I'm not suicidal." Irritation burned in the back of her throat. She hated that they worried. It made her feel weak. Like she was still that wiggy little kid who'd hid in the janitor's closet so she wouldn't have to try to read her book report to the class.

After a minute, Dad broke the tense silence. "What do you know about Dayton Hill University?"

Nothing much. She had a vague idea their mascot was some kind of horned animal. She must have seen one of their recruiting scouts at a meet.

"Their coach wants to talk to you about diving." Mom joined her on the loveseat, squishing in close and grabbing Ria's hand.

"Why?" Ria pulled her hand back.

"She's interested in meeting you."

Mom couldn't contain her enthusiasm. "They're a Division One school. They're already offering money. It could mean a full scholarship!"

Ria started to get up, but Dad stopped her.

"She wants you to come for a visit. No obligation, no commitment. The pool was redone last year. All new boards. They need a new platform, but that's in development. . . ."

"But I'm not going to college." That was never the plan. They knew how much she hated school. How laughable to think this was a possibility. She hadn't even met with any college coaches because they didn't have anything for her. Benny knew that. He got it.

Once, when she'd been trying to finish her homework at the dry gym in between sets he'd said to her, "There's more than one kind of intelligence, Victorious. Don't you worry that pen-and-paper stuff isn't yours. There's not going to be tests and science reports in real life."

It had made her feel better at the time. And for a long time afterward. But now here she was at the start of senior year, with nowhere to go. The void ahead, otherwise known as her future, was too big, too exhausting, too much nothing to fill.

"She's going to call soon. You need to at least talk to her."

"I can't," Ria started, but then Mom's phone rang and they all jumped, startled. She stared at it, like it might explode. Dad shoved it in her hand.

"Hello," a woman's shrill voice greeted her over the line. "My name is Evelyn Ling from Dayton Hill University. Is this Victoria Williams?"

"You can call me Ria."

"Excellent. I won't waste your time. According to our records, you haven't yet committed to dive for any college next year. Is that correct?"

"Yes. But . . ."

"You need to consider Dayton Hill. We're NCAA Division One. Our facility is top-notch, with all the bells and whistles. Brand-new boards, with a platform coming soon. You'll look great in orange."

"If it's so great, then why do you still need divers?" It was an irrelevant question. The answer didn't matter. Not to her. But she couldn't help but wonder anyway. All the top programs had their scholarship places filled months ago. That's why Maggie was tempted to settle for a small college like Uden—she knew it was too late to get picked up at any of the top programs.

Coach Ling laughed, but it sounded like something she hadn't practiced enough.

"I like that you're a straight shooter. You'll fit right in. Truth is we're looking to expand our program, and, well, our other recruits hit a bit of bad luck and made some poor choices. You don't have a criminal record, do you?" Before Ria could respond, she went on, "I'm sure you heard about Tammy Bauer's back surgery. Hopefully she'll get another chance next year."

She remembered Tammy. Nice tight flips, a little prone to meltdowns. The better she dove at the start, the more likely she'd fail a later dive completely. But she had good scores on most dives at some point. She probably had a killer video—the kind that makes coaches hopeful they can tame the head-storms.

Ria stood up, turned away from her parents so she wouldn't have to watch them staring.

"You should look at Maggie O'Connell. She's made some serious progress lately. She's mastered a reverse two-and-a-half and is working on her inward. I'll be surprised if she doesn't have two-and-a-halves in every direction by December. Check her scores; she's super consistent. She dives for Benny . . ." Ria cut herself off before she added the "too" that used to fit.

"You sound like a scout. But we want *you*, Ria. Even if it's only for a year."

"Only a year?"

"That leaves options for all of us. By then we'll know if it's a good fit for everyone."

Ria could tell there was a whole undercurrent of conversation she was missing here. Benny would know what the coach meant and what was being said without being said. That's why all recruitment conversations were supposed to go through him. All she could go on was the seasick roiling feeling she felt at all the vagueness.

"Come for a visit. Let us convince you in person."

She shook her head no even though Coach Ling couldn't see.

"Your parents have my contact information. I hope we'll hear from you soon."

After Ria ended the call, she wrapped her arms around herself, then quickly dropped them. That was an old cue that she was upset. That she needed her parents to give her a hug. She looked at them, back and forth between their expectant, hopeful faces. Hoping they'd found what she'd been missing.

"Well?" said Dad, breaking the tense silence. "What do you think?"

"I think it could be good to dive for a woman," added Mom.

"I quit."

Why did she have to say it again? Every time was like ripping off a Band-Aid. Or part of her skin. A chunk of herself.

"How can you quit? After all this time, all this effort. I don't get it!" Mom sounded one breath away from a scream. "Tell us what you're thinking. We want to understand."

She did too.

She traced the stitching in her dress with one finger. It used to be her parents who knew what she was thinking and feeling before she did. They'd help her define the mess of emotions churning inside. They'd say, *You're frustrated. Angry. Nervous. Hurt.* They knew why she did things, even when she didn't. But there wasn't a label for this freefall feeling.

"Ria," said Dad. "I know you're disappointed about missing that last meet—"

"And Benny is being . . ." Mom cut in, then stopped. Restarted. "I still can't believe after everything we've done for him . . ."

"You paid him to coach me," said Ria. "He coached me. You don't have to pay him anymore. Think about all the money you'll save."

Mom pursed her lips, then went on. "Our point is, we need to look to the future. *Your* future."

Dad stared at her as though he thought he could read her mind. She wished he could, that they both could. But her parents didn't get it. They'd never been on the board with her. They weren't the ones who wore the bruises. Their questions only proved how little they knew. All the things they couldn't possibly understand.

Benny was the only one who knew—and said—the truth.

"There's no point diving. I blew my chance." She'd tried to fix things, but he'd turned her away. Again. He didn't need her. She would have been gone by now, if she'd competed the way she was supposed to. He must have another plan. He always had a plan.

Her parents had tried to support her diving, in the ways they knew how. They were the ones who'd found Benny. Mom had recruited him from a community college after reading how he'd coached a group of former gymnasts with no water experience to win their regional championship. They'd paid him to move.

And, every day, for weeks and months and years, they'd told her how lucky she was that they'd found him, lucky that he was willing to work with her, lucky that she was his pet. She was lucky, privileged, honored that he'd do whatever it took to make her the best. Except they thought, since they paid Benny extensive club and coaching fees, they had the right to weigh in on what she needed. But it was the opposite. As her coach, Benny's opinion was the one that mattered. Her parents only confused her, making her doubt how things should go.

Once, a few years ago, they'd thought she was overtired, so they made her take a weekend off. Then, when she returned, Benny wouldn't let her on the board. He'd forced her to sit on the side of the pool as punishment for missing practice. She'd refused, instead decided to run away. A few hours later, Benny was the one who found her walking along the highway. After that, her parents backed off and let him dictate her schedule. She'd insisted they stay away from practices. She didn't want them to even talk to him.

And now, the thought of starting over with a new coach was

impossible to imagine. If she freaked out at that meet in LA, when that coach had just called her name, there was no way she'd make it through a single workout with someone else.

"Don't you miss it?" asked Dad.

Of course she missed it. Her body literally ached to get back to work. Simply hearing Coach Ling talk about the boards and the water and the maybe of diving had made her weak in her middle.

But worse was the way she wanted to run to Benny and see what he thought. She'd belonged to him for so long, she didn't know how to be on her own.

She may have gone somewhere new in that cave with Cotton, but now she was right back where she'd started.

TEN

School already felt dim and drab and it was only the second day.

Both Sean and Maggie were so pumped up with the newness of the year and being *seniors*, it was easy not to say anything about caving. As long as Ria kept asking them questions, their focus never turned on her. That had always been how she avoided letting anyone look too closely at how she spent her school day. If Sean knew her classes were ridiculously basic it was only because Maggie had told him.

She didn't even have to lie or be vague about where she'd gone after school. There was no reason to try to describe the nitty-gritty details or the looser, more elusive feeling of caving. Now, in the ordinary world of fluorescent lights and crowds, it almost felt as if she'd dreamed about exploring underground. Except, she felt echoes of all the climbing and maneuvering around the rocks in her muscles. It had been a full-body workout, leaving her with the best kind of ache. So reassuringly familiar.

At the end of third period and all of her assigned classes, Sean latched onto her. Literally. He tucked his hand into her back pocket and said, "Walk me to class. I don't want to say goodbye yet."

On the way, he suddenly ducked around a corner, into a spot behind a display case.

He moved in for a kiss. She shifted, so she wouldn't have her back against the wall. His hands felt good against her sore muscles, but his kisses felt too frantic. Especially for school. His tongue was way too acrobatic, for anywhere. Or maybe he was doing it right. She could only compare Sean to Sean. He was the only boy she'd ever kissed.

She pulled away and pressed her fingers against his chest, searching for his heartbeat beneath the soft of his shirt. In her mind she named his muscles: pecs, abs, obliques, delts, biceps, triceps.

"Aren't you going to be late?" she asked.

"Are you trying to get rid of me?"

She was treading unsteady ground. She'd never seen him get mad before so she had no idea how to defuse him if he did. "I don't want you to get in trouble."

"I wish you would get me in trouble." He grinned mischievously and took her hands in his. "But you're never here."

"I have a minimum schedule."

"I know, I know. But it's not like you have anywhere to go." He squeezed her hands. "Stop. Don't look like that. Don't be sad."

"I'm fine."

"How can you still miss diving?" He frowned, staring too intensely, too close. "It's been two months."

Fifty-six days. But it wasn't the time. It was her. Who would she be if she didn't miss it?

"Yesterday Benny made them do yoga poses on the board. Anytime anyone fell off they had to do a dirty thirty on the deck. It was horrendous!"

She knew he was trying to make her laugh, but hearing him use Benny-lingo only made her queasy.

"But, hey, there's a football game on Friday. All the seniors sit together and go crazy. Okay?"

"Okay," said Ria. Because "okay" was a vanilla nothing kind of word. It didn't mean anything. Nothing worth caring about was ever simply *okay*.

Sean suddenly looked nervous, shifting his weight from foot to foot. "The guys are planning to go to *Grover's* after the game."

Grover didn't exist. He was a code name among Sean and his friends for when they needed a cover for partying. He was the scapegoat if anything ever went wrong.

"Which means I can stay out . . . all night? Okay?"

"Okay," she said again, unsure what either of them meant.

"You're the best!" He kissed her quickly, then said, "Crap. I'm late. Gotta go."

When she finally left school, she slowed by the bus stop, but Cotton wasn't there. She was so late leaving she'd missed him and he probably was already on the bus. Or, he was somewhere else entirely. As much as she wanted to, she couldn't show up at his house. It's not like he'd be expecting her. No way could she knock on the door and bother his mother. There was no chance of caving today. She'd even brought an extra pair of old clothes, in case. A pebble of disappointment formed in her throat.

ELEVEN

It felt like Cotton had disappeared.

For the last two days she'd run along the trail behind his house, and all the way to the cave entrance, but there was no sign that he'd been there. He had seemed certain that he only went in the cave on weekends. She didn't have to follow his guidelines. But, even though she'd brought a flashlight, she couldn't bring herself to go in the cave alone. Instead she sat by the entrance, breathing in the cool, damp air and listening for proof that he was inside. The proof hadn't surfaced, not any more than he had. All week she didn't see him anywhere, around school, or at the bus stop.

Friday afternoon she received a giddy text from Maggie that practice had ended early. She wanted to go to the football game together.

Ria went to pick her up from the dry gym. She parked around the corner of the enormous cement building, out of sight. When she'd first started diving, Benny's dry land workouts had been held on a rusty trampoline and a mildewed mat shoved in the alley behind the Aquaplex. Once Mom heard what he visualized, she'd helped him get the permits and lease. Dad wrote a business plan so Benny could get a loan for all the required equipment. Trampolines in three different sizes, weights, mats, mirrors; even a diving board that launched them into a giant foam pit. Anything and everything that would make them stronger, better, more competitive. All the divers and their parents had helped to create the fantasy wonderland.

She checked her phone again. There had to be a different time zone or magic portal surrounding the gym. Hours had flown by when she was inside it, but now, sitting in the parking lot, the minutes dragged on.

A sudden knocking on her back window made her jump, but before she could make sense of Benny's face, he'd moved beside her car, gesturing for her to open the window.

"Maggie'll be out in a minute," he said as soon as the glass slid down.

Ria kept her hands on the steering wheel, reminding herself to stay in the car.

"I've been thinking," he said, bending over and putting his elbows on her window frame. "I knew you couldn't quit."

She hadn't meant to quit altogether. She just scratched the meet. But then he'd quit *her,* even though he knew she couldn't dive for anyone else.

"You're not wired that way."

She couldn't tell if that was a compliment or a curse.

"We might be able to help each other out."

She waited. Not knowing where he was leading her made it hard to sit still.

"Nothing is for sure, but I've got some ideas. I don't want to make any promises I can't keep, but . . ." He grinned, as if she should know what he meant. "Let's just say I have a feeling your parents are going to be sorry they ever started whining about how things have turned out."

She rubbed her chin in reflex. It barely hurt anymore. For Benny, whining was one of the gravest sins.

"So, I can come back?"

"Not here. You quit this place. It would be a bad example." He frowned. "I'm working as fast as I can, but this is your time, Ria. Use it to play teenager. I hear there's a big game tonight, right? So, go and have fun with that pretty lifeguard boyfriend of yours. Go a little wild."

He must have recognized her confusion because he added, "I mean it. You deserve to have fun while you can."

Her head spun with his words that belonged to someone else. As if she didn't know he thought normal teenager stuff was a waste of time.

"But don't get soft on me."

He disappeared around the back side of the building, leaving her to puzzle what he meant. He didn't want her here, but he hadn't seemed mad, either. It was the most precarious place to be.

Finally, Maggie opened the passenger door and stuck her head in, grinning and smelling of sweat and chalk. "Hey! Do you want to come in and see everyone?"

"No!" Ria turned away, swallowing hard against the sudden ambush of ache in her throat. Clearly, Maggie had no idea Benny had stepped outside to see her. There'd always been parts of his coaching they didn't talk about. It was one of his rules—no comparison. He had to treat them each differently because they needed different things. What was said privately, coach to diver, was sacred. Secret. It was the only way to be a team.

As Maggie plopped on the passenger seat, she redid her bun, checking it in the visor mirror even though her fingers knew the drill.

"I still can't believe Benny let us out early. He was finally in a decent mood today, for the first time since . . ." Maggie looked away and got busy with her seat belt, while going on. "Anyway, when Chrissy started complaining about missing the first game of the year, I was fully expecting him to add another round of reps, but instead, all of a sudden, he said—" She paused for dramatic effect, then lowered her voice in a weak Benny-imitation, "Go *experience* a high school football game. Be teenagers."

That was like what he'd said to her. Ria forced herself to laugh along even though it knocked the air out of her that he would say those same words so casually. To the whole team. For stupid football.

"I don't know if I even want to go to the game."

"Oh come on, Ria. Don't be soggy. It's our senior year. Everyone is going to be there. Aren't you meeting Sean?"

"Yeah. He's going with Tony and Charlie."

As she started the car and pulled away from the curb, Maggie burst out, "You have no idea what it's like without you at practice. Chrissy thinks she's queen bee."

"She is. Queen bee-yotch. That's nothing new."

"But you aren't there to shut her up! And Max keeps crying. Temo is so freaking lazy. He actually hid in the hot tub last week—and Benny didn't even call him on it. Jillian is just Jillian."

"So, quit."

"Quit?" Maggie scrunched up her nose. "I can't quit. I have to get a scholarship."

"Then suck it in and dive it straight." Her Benny-quotes were so damn automatic. Their minds worked the same way.

Maggie rolled her eyes, then said, "Besides, you should have seen my backs today. They were totally kick-ass. Chrissy was so jealous."

That was diving. Bitching was part of the game. The pain and misery put the shine on the badge of honor. It had to hurt, to suck at least a little bit, to balance out the thrill. Having too much of one or the other threw everything out of whack. "I still want to see your reverse two-and-a-half."

"It's not quite there yet. That first one was a fluke. I don't know what I'm missing."

"Go more up than out."

Ria meant it as a joke. That was the catchall, the most generic of dive advice, always true, but maddeningly nonspecific.

"I bet you could fix it for me. You know I never would have gotten my inward without you."

"You already had it, Maggie. You just didn't believe it. It's all in your head."

Stupid heads. Life would be easier without them.

"Sorry," said Maggie. "Shutting up now."

"You don't have to not talk about diving." She had a million questions about what was going on with the team. And about the workouts. She didn't have the right to ask, but the wondering wouldn't quit. Now she was also wondering what Benny was working on. Maybe she wasn't done after all.

"Benny must have had a reason for letting Temo rest in the hot tub," Ria said. "You know he didn't forget he was there. Maybe Temo wasn't ready. Or he's injured, even if it's only a tweak. Then he might need the extra soak time. I can't see Benny ignoring him for no reason. Benny always has a reason." Ria caught the look on Maggie's face and stopped.

"You've never been able to convince me Benny's as perfect as you think, so let's not invite him in with us right now, okay? I'm sick of diving—it's all I ever do. Save me from my boring self. Tell me something new."

She didn't have anything to tell. Except for caving. And that was getting harder to believe it had ever happened.

"Hey, Mags, do you have any classes with Cotton Talley?"

Maggie sucked on her water bottle, noisily, for several inches' worth, then finally came up for air. "I don't think so. Why?"

Ria shrugged. It seemed like she should have run into him again after that day of caving. She'd spent way too much time making up explanations why she hadn't. Thinking that he'd been kidnapped like Esther. Or was sick and suffering all alone in his bed. He could have fallen through the crack in the cave, all the way to Australia. But, really, it was probably that he hadn't thought about her one way or another. She was obsessing for no reason. If he'd vanished, it would be in the news. Everyone would be talking about it.

Maggie laughed. "You're so random, Ria. But hey, take me to the drugstore. Jillian told me about this new hair serum. She swears it heals even the worst pool frizz."

The cool of the store's air-conditioning hit Ria in the face. "Ahhh," she said involuntarily.

"You're a cheap date." Maggie laughed.

They studied the aisle of oils, serums, conditioners. Maggie was a dedicated soldier in the battle of chlorine vs. hair. "The name is Sensational Something. Or Sensory. I think it has coconut oil. Or maybe avocado." She paused, then asked, "Are you and Sean fighting?"

"No. Why would you think that?"

"I don't know. Because he was pouting at lunch and you look miserable too. And . . . because you asked me about Cotton Talley." Maggie burst out laughing. "As if."

Ria frowned. She knew why Maggie was laughing. Cotton was nice and smart. But he was also different. Maybe even weird. He'd outgrown needing special classes but he still had that small-room way of being clueless about things that mattered to people who fit in the one-size-fits-all classroom.

She was glad she hadn't told Maggie about the cave. That was Cotton's place, somewhere he fit perfectly. He'd shared it with Ria, but it wasn't hers to pass on to anyone else. Maybe he'd take her there again. As long as he hadn't disappeared.

"Sean's planning to stay out all night tonight. With *Grover*."

"Does that mean with you?"

"I don't know. I don't think so." That was the problem with only speaking in looks and kisses and eager roaming hands. She never knew for sure if they were speaking the same language.

"Well, are you ready? What if he wants to do it?"

"That's not what he meant. We've never even talked about it."

"You don't have to talk about it, you just have to do it."

"Doesn't it seem like if you're going to be exchanging body fluids you should be able to talk about the when and where and how?"

"Ewww. Body fluids? That's a gross way to put it."

But that didn't make it untrue.

"I think he just wants to drink." She picked up a big purple bottle with silver swirls. "Have you tried this one?"

Maggie took it from her, studying the list of ingredients.

"But, sex is better for your body than drinking," said Ria.

"I guess you're right. *If* you use protection. Do you have a love glove?"

"A what?"

"A hot juice balloon. Rocket pocket. Wacker wrapper. Wood hood. Knock-me-not." Maggie sighed. "Rubbers?"

"You mean condoms?"

"Yes, Ria, condoms. Prophylactics."

"No! We haven't even . . . besides, isn't that Sean's job?"

"You have to make sure. Just in case."

A second later, Maggie dragged Ria across the store to the family planning aisle.

"How can there be so many choices?" Ria asked, utterly stunned by the expansive display. "Forget it. I'm not buying these."

"Wait, wait, wait." Maggie linked her arm in Ria's. "Do you know what a turn-on it would be for Sean if you did?"

"That's not the issue. He's turned on plenty."

"Okay."

"It's a big deal to some people, Maggie. You know, most people."

"Speaking of big deal, what size do you need?"

"There are different sizes?"

"Well, duh. So, do you think he's a medium or large? Please don't say small."

"How am I supposed to know?" She picked up one of the boxes and looked at the happy couple on the back. "I can't win with this, Maggie. No matter what size I pick—whether I'm right or wrong—it's going to make him feel bad. I hate hurting his feelings. He's so sensitive."

"Wait!" Maggie grabbed a box. "Here! The sensitive touch. Get this one!"

It was all so ridiculous. But she couldn't imagine Sean finding it quite so funny.

"I think you should do large." Maggie raised her eyebrows suggestively. "I bet there's not really a difference from medium, anyway. It's all about ego. But extra-large might look like you have certain expectations. Now, how many boxes?"

Another loaded decision. If she only got one, it might look like she was reluctant. But too many and . . .

"No way, Maggie. There are no right answers."

"Uh-uh. You mean there are no *wrong* answers. The fact that you are thinking about it and planning ahead is the right answer. So, what color?"

"There should not be different colors." Ria laughed and groaned all at once.

"Ooh. How about texture?"

It seemed unnecessarily confusing to have different sizes. Not to mention colors and textures. Did anyone actually try them on? Was there really a Goldilocks concern of too big, too small, just right? If they didn't fit, could you return them?

"Come on, Mags, pick your magic serum and get out of here."

"Are you chickening out?"

There was an edge to Maggie's voice. Ria suddenly wondered what Maggie and Sean talked about when she wasn't around.

"Why do you care so much?"

"A friend who lets you fail is a failure of a friend."

That's what Benny always said, whenever the practice turned grueling. When someone started to whine. He expected them to coax each other on, to push and cheer. Suffering was something done together. No one left behind.

"Do you think *that's* what all Benny's advice is actually about? Like, 'Halfway only gets you halfway.'"

Maggie laughed.

"Point your toes! Keep your legs straight! Your abs are your friends!"

Maggie said, in her exaggerated nerd-voice, "Could I have your body fluids?" right as an older man came around the corner.

"Come on." Ria dragged Maggie down the aisle by the hand.

"Don't be so rough. What about our maximum pleasure?"

They burst out laughing. Wild, hysterical laughter, more about them, and being together, than what they were talking about. It was the way it used to be. Maybe she didn't have to keep looking backward. There might be something worth seeing ahead.

TWELVE

Even though Friday night football games were one of those typical high school experiences Ria had never been a part of, she hadn't especially minded that she'd missed them. But the size of the crowd made it easy to believe she was the only one who hadn't cared. The bleachers were full, and more swarms of people milled around the sidewalks between the stands and the Snack Shack.

Sean had stopped texting her every minute, now that he was sure she was coming, but she knew he was sitting in the senior section. Up high and near the end zone.

"Didn't you say Tony will be here?" asked Maggie.

"Yeah. Why?"

"He's friends with Sean. So maybe we could double-date. He's kind of cute, and I don't want to waste my senior year."

Ria shouldn't have been surprised. Maggie had always been better about balancing life with dive practice. They were so different.

In looks, too. Her own dark blond hair was straight and thin while Maggie's thick red hair went everywhere. There was so much more of her—more height, more curves, everything more, more, more. On the diving board, it had always seemed like more was harder to reign in. Ria had never envied any of the extra inches. Now, seeing the confident way Maggie moved through the crowd, she wasn't as sure she'd mind.

She followed Maggie up the bleacher steps. They were taller than average stairs, an awkward distance apart, making her aware of each and every level she climbed. She was headed straight for the people she'd been avoiding.

"Prunes!" cheered Maggie, greeting the huddle of swimmers, water polo players, and divers—the ones who lived at the Aquaplex. Their proud nickname was from the way their skin wrinkled from being waterlogged. The result was a very certain look. The fried hair, the tanned skin, honed physique beneath their clothes.

It was the first time she'd been around her team since she quit. Half of the team went to Chappelle, the other high school in the area, and with her minimum schedule she hadn't even seen Devin or Jillian. She stood in the aisle next to Maggie and scanned her old teammates.

She almost didn't recognize them anymore. It was always weird to see each other in real clothes. Everyone wore workout gear in the gym and next to nothing at the pool, so any other attire seemed foreign. The tiny Speedos that the boys wore didn't leave any doubts regarding anatomy, and yet it was seeing them in jeans and tight T-shirts that made them look definitely male. It was the reverse of normal people suddenly seeing each other in swimsuits. "Hey there, Ria." Temo stood up and gave Ria an awkward hug, then looked her over. She was suddenly glad to be disguised in all black.

"Let me in," said Maggie, settling beside Devin. She must have already forgotten Tony.

"Hey, Ria, I'm surprised you're not down on the field," Chrissy said, pointing. "I figured that's why you quit. To be a cheerleader."

Ria forced herself to laugh, over the simmer bubbling up. It was a nothing kind of Chrissy comment laced with something sharper. Benny scorned and belittled cheerleaders. Ridiculed their waste of tumbling and flipping abilities.

"Oops, Chrissy," said Ria. "Your bitch is showing."

"Better be! I wear it proudly." Then Chrissy winked. "I miss you too."

Tears sucked. Damn Chrissy. They'd always been at war. She had the skills to be Ria's strongest competition, but she wasn't willing to dedicate the time. It figured she'd be the one to ambush her in public now. Ria moved on down the row and squeezed into the spot next to Sean. She leaned into him, desperate to think about anything but the fact that her team wasn't hers anymore.

"You're finally here." She could tell he'd been drinking by the size of his smile. Whenever he caught a buzz, his teeth seemed to grow and multiply. He slipped his hand around her waist and nuzzled her neck. Then leaned back, eyeing her. "Why are you dressed like Batgirl?" He held out his cup. "Have some."

"I can't. I'm driving."

"Damn right. You're driving me crazy." He was kind of adorable, all messy and grinning. Loopy and goofy was way better than serious and romantic.

By the middle of the third quarter, the Rockhounds were winning and Ria was tired of sitting. Somehow, right beside her, Sean had gone from affectionately buzzed to sloppy wasted. His eyes were little more than slits, but his grin was wide.

"Let's get out of here." She ran her finger along his arm.

"The game's not over. Is it?" He stared out at the scoreboard.

"Does that matter?"

Around her, the divers exploded with groans. "Can you believe him?" yelled Maggie, laughing. "What do you think a Drumstick Chorus looks like?"

"It sure as hell doesn't mean fried chicken," answered Temo. "And I guarantee the Biscuit Beaters will leave us flat."

"We're so gonna be hurting!" Maggie whined.

It was obvious that Benny had sent one of his infamous group texts, letting them know the plan for practice. So typical for him to have tricked them into thinking they had the night off, then hitting them with a warning for what the next day would be like. To keep them focused. Remembering they still belonged to him.

When she checked her own phone, it was blank. Her cheeks flushed hot and red and her eyes stung. Out on the field, a football player ran, all alone, with a trail of other players straggling behind him, slowing and giving up before he crossed the end zone. Around her, everyone stood to cheer.

"Some of us are going to get food," said Maggie, grabbing her arm.

"Fried chicken?"

"Maybe. I was thinking I'd do a carb-o-load of fries and biscuits."

"Tough workout tomorrow?"

"Always. You know how it is."

She thought she'd known, but it felt too long ago to be certain.

"You could come with us."

Ria looked at Sean, glassy-eyed and swaying on the bleacher seat. It wasn't his fault she didn't belong with the team anymore, but she gestured toward him and said, "I can't."

It was painfully true, for plenty of reasons. Mostly because there was no doubt Benny would find out if she went, and she wasn't sure she was allowed to be a part of their team bonding. Someone would say something, a picture would be taken—there wasn't any question as to *if*; only the specifics of *how* were uncertain. Besides, she barely knew her old team anymore.

As she watched Maggie swish down the steps, she pressed her legs firmly against the bleachers to keep herself from running off to follow. She focused her breathing, imagined her body growing roots, planting herself into this spot. She let herself blend in with the strangers around her, talking, laughing, staring, eating, being. She was only one small part of a bigger picture, a smudge of black within the swirl of colors.

THIRTEEN

Sean was the drunkest Ria had ever seen. Not only the drunkest Sean, but the drunkest anyone. Talking to him made her feel like she was dealing with someone with multiple personalities. Or all the personalities were Sean, but at different ages. It was like reasoning with a three-year-old Sean who had ten-year-old Sean's sense of humor while seventeen-year-old Sean groped her butt and old-man Sean wobbled and teetered, completely off balance.

"Stay with me, Ria. You wouldn't leave me, would you?"

His question annoyed her, seeing as she was obviously here, holding him up. Charlie and Tony were the ones who'd left him behind. She was alone trying to get him to her car.

Drunk Sean was heavy, with no sense of direction. When he started weaving and wandering, crashing into people as they left the stadium, Ria threw her arm around his waist and braced her leg against his. Instead of keeping him moving in a straight line, the reinforcement made him crumple. He leaned on her as if his skeleton had turned soft and rubbery. At this particular moment, it was hard to believe he was any kind of athlete. Or someone who could speak without spitting.

"You know I love you. Right? Don't you? Do you know that I love you?"

That was such a weird way to say it. Like it was all on her somehow to get right or wrong. Heading along the sidewalk and seeing the security guards ahead, she said, "Walk."

Behind her, she heard a familiar clipped voice. Almost monotone, but with its own distinctive rhythm. She looked over her shoulder and finally, with a huge surge of relief, like she'd just this second raised her head above water, she spotted Cotton.

"Ria! I'm so glad to see you!"

She waited for him to explain why. To follow it up with a reason. A question. Something he needed to tell her. But his greeting seemed to be the end of his point. She was glad to see him, too. Except she had plenty of reasons. Maybe it was the way his eyes opened wide to meet hers. And the smile that followed, as if had been trailing behind. Or it could have been the way his crazy whirl of curls went every which way. Mostly it was that he hadn't simply up and disappeared.

"Do you need help?"

"I'm good," she said, even though "good" had been left somewhere in the stands before the start of halftime.

"She's good, Cotton Talley," said Sean, too loud. The effort of his protest made him lose his balance again. He staggered and fell to his knees. "Shit, Ria. You dropped me."

"What's wrong with him?" Cotton asked. "Is he having a medical emergency? I know first aid."

"I don't think so," she said.

"He smells drunk."

"Yeah."

"Shhhh!" Sean spit and sputtered. "Come on, Cotton Talley, be cool."

"Cool," said Cotton.

Ria looked down on her noodled boyfriend, then up at Cotton, who actually looked like the definition of cool—as in calm and collected. Not impressed or disgusted. Neutral. "Can you help me get him up again? My car is still a ways down the row."

"Yes." But then, instead of holding out a hand, Cotton circled Sean, looking at him from every angle, all the while his hand flapped against his thigh. She wasn't sure if he was studying him or performing some kind of ritual. Either way, Sean was still on the ground, now with his head hanging between his legs. She had to try again.

"Come on, Sean, get up." She held out her hand. He grabbed it, then pulled, almost dragging her down until she braced her legs. Finally he was on his feet again, but swaying. She slid under his arm, so as to hold him up, but then Cotton stepped in front of them. "We need to walk that way," she said. "Maybe you could be on his other side."

Cotton reached for Sean with both arms—for an extremely weird second Ria thought he was going to hug him—but then all of a sudden, Sean was lifted in the air and slung over Cotton's shoulder. It was the same way he'd carried his duffel. Sean was either groaning or laughing, but at least he was in motion.

And Cotton still managed to bounce when he walked.

At her car, Cotton dumped Sean into the back seat. He promptly lay down, groaned, and closed his eyes. Ria reached around him and buckled the seat belt. She didn't bother moving the strap off his face, but she grabbed his phone out of his pocket.

"Thanks, Cotton."

She scanned Sean's phone for messages with his mom. She obviously thought he was staying at Grover's and didn't expect him home until tomorrow. The last text she'd sent said **Make good choices!!!!!** Maybe she thought the extra exclamation marks would hold him up.

Ria turned to Cotton. The contrast of the field lights left this part of the parking lot in the shadows, with everything coated in a soft and fuzzy glow. "I don't know what I would have done if you hadn't shown up."

"I'm glad to help. It was clear he was in the midst of a gravity storm."

She laughed.

"Shhhh. Make that noise stop." Sean groaned in the back seat.

They were both quiet while all around them cars drove out of the parking lot. In the distance, cars honked to each other, loud and insistent, announcing the win.

"How are you getting home, Cotton?"

"Leo. He and my sister Flutie are over there."

Ria saw him a few rows down, standing near a green minivan with a tall, thin girl.

"How about if I give you a ride? That way you can help me with Sean. I won't be able to move him without you."

She waited, knowing he needed time to adjust the plan in his mind. She could tell he was evaluating, making sure the variables were acceptable. Finally, he said, "Yes. If Leo agrees."

Judging by the way Leo was nuzzled next to Flutie, she was sure they wouldn't mind if she borrowed Cotton.

Once he'd talked with them, Cotton climbed into the passenger seat. His knees barely fit without hitting the dashboard.

After she parked in her driveway, Cotton carried Sean from the back seat, following Ria around her house to the backyard.

"Put it there. I mean *him*. Put him there." She pointed at the lounge chair on the patio.

He dumped Sean on the chair.

"I love you," said Sean.

"I love you too," said Cotton. "But as a fellow human. Not in a romantic way." He looked at Ria. "What? Do you think he was talking to you? I'm the one carrying him."

She giggled, trying to keep her voice down. But it must not

have been enough, because there was Dad standing in the patio doorway.

"Hi, Dad. This is Cotton. And"—she pointed in the direction of her passed-out boyfriend—"you know Sean."

"Hello, sir." Cotton held out his hand. "My name is Connor Talley. But everyone calls me Cotton. I live over on Quartz. Sorry to disturb you. I know it's late. I can leave."

He was so earnest. Extremely stiff and slightly awkward. Probably nervous. Somehow it added up to cute.

"You don't have to leave," said Ria. "Right, Dad? Can Cotton stay for a while? And Sean, too?"

"Are you sure he's okay?" Dad peered over Sean.

"He's tired. I think he had a super-intense practice."

Sean sat up suddenly. "I'll have her home by midnight," he said, then fell back again.

"Well," said Dad. "He kept his word. You are home. . . ."

"Exactly."

"Okay. You two have fun. But keep the noise down."

"Your father is very accepting of intoxication," Cotton said as Dad slid the door shut.

"Or completely clueless." Ria added, "You don't have to stay. I can take you home if you want."

"I don't want. Is that a trampoline?" He pointed across the yard.

Ria laughed at the marvel in his voice.

On the trampoline, she resisted the reflex to jump, waiting as

Cotton sat on the edge and swung his legs around with a grunt. He rested for a second, as if getting his bearings, then rolled sideways onto the springy part.

"This is huge. Isn't it? Isn't it bigger than a normal trampoline?"

"It's better for working on tumble sequences and hurdles." She did an aerial into a front flip to show him. "My parents got tired of me bouncing on the furniture when I was little. Plus, it's a good way to release stress."

Awkwardly, as if he wasn't sure where his legs ended, Cotton moved into a crawl position, then finally lifted himself to his feet. He stood with his legs slightly bent and his back curved forward. He slid his feet across the surface, slowly, his body stiff and holding his hands straight out. Then, suddenly, he threw his hands up over his head and said, "Ta-da!"

"Very nice." She laughed, moving along the edge.

"It's been a while since I've been on one of these." He tilted and turned his head, as if he was looking at it sideways. "I thought I used to be able to flip. But now I can't see how that could be true."

"That might have to do with your center of gravity. It changes when you grow. How long has it been?"

"I don't know. It was part of my sensory therapy. I wasn't very good at being a little kid. I had to learn how to finger paint, chew bubblegum, and roll around on a trampoline."

"And to cave?"

He looked confused.

"It seems like caving might bother you too. All that gooky mud. And the dark. Caving is kind of annoying . . . I mean in an amazing kind of way."

"Yes. The amazing makes it worth the mess. Now I know what to expect. I can learn to like things that are at first unpleasant, if there's a reason I should."

"You could also learn to flip again. I could teach you." She moved to the center of the trampoline.

"I think that center-of-gravity issue might be at odds with your plans."

"Only if you let it be. Gravity is overrated."

"I'm too scared."

"You can't be scared. Not if caving doesn't scare you."

"Caving? I told you, the mess doesn't bother me. Why would caving scare me?"

"Because you go crawling through the dark. With hundreds of bats. You squeeze yourself into tight little crevices. You go marching off into a place where you might get lost. Or you could fall in a hole that goes to Australia."

"I take reasonable precautions." He tilted his head. "Why doesn't diving scare you?"

"It does. When I think about it too much. But fear is part of getting better, too." She stretched her arms over her head. "If my coach says I'm ready to do a dive, I know he's right. My body might still have to figure out the details, but it's going to happen. And if I smack, well the pain is only temporary."

"Right. Your coach sets reasonable precautions. Like caving."

She wasn't sure she totally agreed, but she didn't disagree, either. That sounded so cut-and-dried. Not like the swirly mix of colors and energy that she'd been trying to describe.

"Show me something, Ria. Make me doubt gravity. I've heard it's overrated."

She bounce-walked to the center as he crawled to the foam-trimmed edge, out of the way. She jumped. High and straight. Up, up to the treetops. She flipped backward, which was easy but impressive. Handsprings in both directions. The layouts—flips with a straight body—were the thing that made him say, "Whoa."

She'd almost forgotten she had the power to impress. She knew her own sense of average was skewed, but she didn't know how far.

She collapsed to her back on the springy bed of the trampoline, letting her breaths return to a steady state. She stared up at the stars beyond the tree branches. Looked at them with only her left eye. Then her right. Thanks to her contacts, the stars seemed closer with the left one.

"I looked for you this week, Cotton. I wanted to go caving again."

"That was a good day," he said. "I liked caving with you."

It was a simple thing to say. Something she agreed with. Somehow it made her feel lighter. Like she could float.

"Where were you all week? Were you caving?"

"No."

"Were you sick? You look good now," she said, suddenly thankful for the shadows.

"We had to travel out of town to meet with the police. As part of the ongoing investigation."

"For Esther?" She sat up.

"Yes. You've said her name to me. You remember her."

"Well, yeah." She tucked herself into a ball, facing him.

"No one ever says her name. My little brother and sister don't even remember her. Flutie won't say what she remembers. No one talks about her. Except for reporters, once a year, on the anniversary of when we couldn't find her."

"I think people don't want to make you sad."

He tilted his head, into his thinking pose. "I'm always sad about Esther."

Ria hugged her knees even tighter against her chest.

"The first time I found the cave, I thought she'd be there. I was sure she wandered in and got lost. Or hurt."

She held her breath, dreading his words, but needing to hear them, too.

"My dad and I searched and searched. The police came too. But we never found any sign of her. And now we've gone too far in. There's no way she would have made it all that way. Not in the dark, not by herself."

"Is that good or bad?" It was a stupid question, but she felt desperate for the answer.

"Both. Or, neither."

She stared at the stars still peeking through the trees.

"I'm going to find her. She's going to come home."

The lump in her throat made her eyes sting. There was no way to answer. Even if she'd had the right words, they couldn't possibly squeeze through the tightness in her chest.

"No one else believes that. Not anymore. My parents want closure. . . ." His voice faded into the darkness. Then it came back, stronger, almost harsh with its stiffness. "On Tuesday a man found a child's bones buried near Lake Manning. But it wasn't Esther."

"Do they know who?" Ria wanted to bite back her words as soon as she'd said them.

"Her name was Rebecca Salisbury. She died ten years before Esther was born. But every time there's a chance we're going to get an answer, everything stops."

She nodded, unsure if he could see the motion. Even more unsure if it mattered.

"That's why I wasn't at school."

"That must . . ." Ria couldn't find the right word but she felt it.

"Yes," he said.

He gently slapped his hand against the bed of the trampoline, sending vibrations across the fabric.

She tapped in reply.

"I'm going to release stress." He stood, suddenly, awkwardly, looking unsure but determined.

He got into jumping position, legs straddled, hands out. She kept her distance, so as not to throw off his balance. Finally, she had to laugh. "Jumping usually means actually going up. And then down. Off the surface."

"Right! Like I'm doing."

"Give me your hands." She bounced lightly toward him.

"I can't. I'm busy jumping right now."

She bent her legs, pushed a little harder, rose a little higher, lifting him with her bounce. His hands reached toward hers, stopping an inch before they touched. Up and down.

When she took his hands in hers, he didn't pull away. Under her thumb she could feel a rough, rounded spot along his. He had a hangnail by his pinky finger. They jumped together, slowly, barely enough to even be called jumping.

She bent her legs, pushed a little harder, rose a little higher.

They were a funny match. His weight brought him much lower, but he was less willing to release on the way up. She had to compensate for the space between the up and down. It added an unexpected thrill to the nothing kind of jumping.

They weren't quite laughing as they bounced up and down, but the longer they jumped, the closer she felt to giddy. Silly. Buzzing. The dark of the night and the bright of the moon and the cool of the air, along with the funny little wrinkle between Cotton's eyebrows added up to something she couldn't name.

But then she pushed a little too much, went a little too high, and their rhythm was off. She came down a split fraction of a second later than he did. It wasn't a big enough double-bounce to worry about, but there was a moment of off-centered movement in multiple directions.

Cotton collapsed on his butt, with his legs splayed out. She flipped over him so as not to land on top of him. She burst out laughing, and a second later, he joined her.

As their eyes met, something new—hot and surprising—hit Ria in her middle. She held the gaze, all the while feeling awfully close to breathless until he dropped his eyes.

"I'd better go home now." He crawled toward the edge.

Ria balanced her weight on the narrow frame, then leapt, landing in the damp grass. The ground felt excessively solid and unforgiving after so much time on the springy trampoline. Gravity reminding her there was no escape.

"Leo and I are going caving tomorrow. You can come with us." Cotton sat on the frame of the trampoline with his legs dangling over the edge.

"I'd like that." She held out her hand to help him down. A painful shock traveled between them.

"Ow!"

"Static electricity," said Ria. "Sorry! It builds up."

Cotton kept his hands tucked behind him, like he didn't quite trust her. He was taking reasonable precautions.

"I can give you a ride home."

"No, thank you. I'll call my dad. It's late. And you have . . ."

They both looked over at Sean. "I think he's going to feel ill tomorrow."

"Probably," she agreed. "But Sean doesn't seem to mind hang-overs. I can't stand it when my body won't do what I want it to."

"He has no idea where he is. I could never let myself be that out of it. Not if I have a choice."

He was thinking about Esther again. Still. Always. Esther had made the choice to go out to play, but something had happened to keep her away. She'd gone somewhere, expecting something, but then . . . At what point was her choice not her choice any-more?

After Cotton left, Ria threw a blanket over Sean. She stood near, watching him sleep. He mumbled something. Cotton was right. Sean had no idea where he was.

She brought her pillow and sleeping bag out to the trampo-line, the way she and Maggie used to do. She looked up at the stars through one eye, then the other. Bringing them close and letting them go again.

FOURTEEN

Ria woke to the sound of the back door opening. She felt warm in her sleeping bag, but the outside of it was damp, and the air felt cool on her face. Fall was creeping in, bringing a new hint of chill to the air. She'd left her contacts in all night and now her eyes ached. She blinked to clear them, then lifted her head and saw Mom peering out on the patio where Sean still slept. Ria waved and slipped off the springy trampoline, into the wet grass.

Mom raised her eyebrows in question and mimed talking on the phone. Ria nodded to confirm that Sean's parents wouldn't be worried about him.

They'd had plenty of practice communicating through sign language. She'd learned from Benny, who could coach an entire dive list without saying a word. He'd simply gesture and point to the body parts he wanted her to focus on. She and Mom had created their own communication system during meets when

Ria was stuck on the pool deck. Those conversations had been predictable. *Good job. I'm hungry. I need a new towel.* Having her passed-out boyfriend there in the morning was more complicated. There'd be a follow-up debriefing. But those had happened after meets as well.

Mom motioned that she should wake Sean and then went back inside.

Ria stood over him. His blond hair covered one eye. His lips looked chapped, but full. He was cute again now that he wasn't wasted.

"Good morning." When he didn't stir, she sat on the lounge chair beside him and traced the line of his jaw with one finger.

"Mmm?" He opened his eyes a crack. "I gotta get outta here." He swung his legs around to the ground. "Before your parents . . ."

"They know you're here."

His eyes grew wide and panicked. "They *know*?"

"Obviously. It's fine."

"What happened? Did we . . . anything?"

"You passed out before we even got here. I thought you'd turned boneless."

"That's harsh." He frowned. "Did Cotton Talley carry me in here?"

"Mm-hmm." She wondered what else he remembered. What he'd heard from the trampoline.

"That's so weird. I was so trashed." But apparently that's

all he thought. Because he turned to his phone, getting all his updates and missed messages. "Maggie's taking me to work."

"Maggie?"

"Yeah. Benny wants me to help set up some pads or bars or something for their workout today. Maggie said he's going to pay me extra to get there early."

"You talked to Maggie?" A sudden heat filled her cheeks. She scooted away from him.

"Only texting. When I woke up in the middle of the night, I freaked. I wasn't sure why I was here. You were sleeping."

"So you asked *Maggie*?" Irritation prickled her.

"I think your phone was dead."

Ria stared at him, trying to comprehend. He'd woken up wondering where he was—actually, no, he knew where he was *and* where she was, only fifty feet or so away—but he'd had other questions. So when he couldn't reach her by *phone*, he texted Maggie. Who apparently was also texting Benny. Busy night for Maggie.

"Seriously?"

Now that his eyes were open, she saw the red veins and bloodshot look of them. His breath didn't have the liquor-y smell of last night, but something related, and sour.

She went to get her phone from the trampoline. It had been almost out of its charge by the time she and Cotton stopped texting last night. He'd let her know he made it home and then she'd had some questions about caving that somehow led to them trading funny memories of Ms. Q's room, and, well, now it wouldn't turn on. So Sean was right about her phone. But apparently, he couldn't make it across the yard to ask her what had happened. And now he and Maggie were going to go to the pool.

"I'm sorry about last night, Ria. Please don't be pissed." He sounded truly remorseful. Pitiful. He looked like he was honestly suffering, even if that was his own fault.

"I'm not mad." It was the easiest way to end the conversation. And besides, since he'd been such a mess, Cotton had to help. And that meant she was going caving today.

After Sean left with Maggie, Ria headed inside. She could hear her parents in the kitchen, their voices blending in and out of their oldies songs playing in the background. The smell of breakfast made her mouth water as she paused outside the kitchen, getting ready to face them. They were going to have questions, but she wasn't sure where the focus would be.

"Is Sean gone?" asked Dad.

"Yeah," she said as she took the plate of eggs and fruit from him, settling in the sunniest spot of the kitchen table.

"That sounds like the start of a new hit song. *Sean is gone. Gone, gone, gone.* It works on multiple levels. As in gone drunk. Gone, gone. Gone so long."

"All right, Dad. Don't quit your day job."

"Did you have fun last night?" Mom leaned back in her chair.

Ria thought a minute. There had been moments. Sean had been funny before he turned completely useless. The football team had won. Jumping on the trampoline with Cotton had been the best part. "It was okay."

"Okay?" Mom said with a definite edge to her voice. "Your boyfriend was passed out on our lawn furniture. Don't tell me he wasn't drinking."

"I won't."

"I hope you weren't drinking too."

"Of course not."

"I know it can be tempting when everyone else is doing something," said Dad. "Especially when you're feeling unhappy. . . ."

"I was driving. I'm not completely stupid."

Dad handed her the bottle of meds. It was as if she'd reminded him to, simply by saying the word. Even after all the promises that her ADHD didn't mean she was stupid, somehow the two ideas always ended up together.

While Ria swallowed her pill, Mom went on, "Do you know how many calories are in a beer? Wine coolers and mixed drinks are even worse."

Mom wasn't counting calories. It was the days of no diving and what they'd all lost. If Ria had been drinking, maybe Mom could admit she was mad.

"You miss Benny keeping me in line, don't you?"

"We miss you doing what you love," said Dad.

She got up and took her plate to the sink, dumped the food down the garbage disposal, let the grinding roar drown out her parents' worries.

She was used to their concern wrapped up in irritation. But, as usual, they had their focus on the wrong thing. They saw what she told them to see, and yet she was still amazed at all the things they ignored. But then again, bruises from smacking the water look the same as bruises from getting smacked from a hand. Or pushed into a wall. Being held face-up in a shower of cold water didn't leave any mark at all. They still didn't know she'd chipped her tooth.

Sometimes she'd picked fights with them, thinking they'd see how she was hurting, but all the while afraid of what would happen if they did. They'd be so disappointed, so disillusioned if they knew everything she'd been through. She couldn't do that to them. So, she'd learned to swallow her frustration, to ignore their blatant obliviousness. She couldn't blame them. She knew how easy it was to miss what was right there.

When she turned around, Mom was beside her, waiting. Looking weird, her cheeks all red and blotchy. "Did Benny do . . . something . . . inappropriate? Did he try something sexual?"

"You can tell us," said Dad. "No matter what happened."

"God. No. You know he's not like that." Ria needed to do something, anything, with her arms and legs. She paced back and forth in front of them, her mind a swirl of confusion. "He would never."

And he wouldn't. He was the one who insisted everyone wear clothes over their suits whenever they went anywhere at meets. He'd broken a reporter's camera when he took a picture of Ria on the deck. Photos of her in motion, at work, were acceptable. Photos of her posing in her suit were not. Benny was obsessively, passionately, desperately all about the diving. He was far closer to a rubberband-man than seducer. She'd never even thought to worry about anything like that.

She headed out of the kitchen.

"Where are you going? We're not done talking to you."

"I'm going to go for a run. To look for fun. In the sun. Won't come back until I'm done. Look, Dad, I can write a song too."

"Don't go. You didn't even eat your breakfast."

"I had enough calories."

"Well, all right," said Dad. "Running will be good for you. You know that exercise produces endorphins. You've been missing that."

Except she had been exercising. Running, jumping on the trampoline, but even more, caving. That was a full-body workout.

Her parents didn't know all the things they didn't know.

FIFTEEN

Ria met Cotton and Leo at the entrance of the cave, as planned. She got there first and was worried for a minute that they'd gone in without her. Then, with a bluster of voices and laughter, they appeared on the trail, already wearing their coveralls and helmets.

Her old sweats didn't have the official look of the coveralls, but they fit her better, felt like a second skin. She didn't own rugged boots so her running shoes would have to do. Cotton had promised he'd find her a helmet, which turned out to be an old bike helmet with a headlamp duct-taped to the brim.

"I know it's ugly, but I think it'll work."

"I don't care how it looks," said Ria, knowing her grin was big and goofy. "It's what I can look at with it."

"That's right! Not how it looks, what you look at. Looks-at, not it-looks. Looks-at, not it-looks."

"Let's go," Leo said, clapping him on the shoulder.

"Yes. Oh, and Ria, my parents want to meet you."

A whiff of dread fluttered by. She would have no idea how to act around them.

"They were surprised I was at your house last night," Cotton continued. "Apparently I didn't tell them we went caving together. They assumed I was with Leo that day."

"Yeah," said Leo. "We were all surprised."

Cotton's bounce of a walk implied he didn't feel any more guilty than she did.

At the cave's entrance, Ria suddenly felt hungry. Or full. Or maybe her stomach was feeling the dread that had snuck up on her remembering that panicky feeling of the tight tunnel.

She eyed Cotton. So much bigger than she was, in every way. She reminded herself: If he fit, so would she. Except logic didn't always work for her.

"Let's go." She knew better than to prolong nerves. She needed to get in that tunnel and deal with it.

They headed in, with Ria in the middle following Leo, and Cotton bringing up the rear. Her makeshift helmet shone brighter, but at a different angle. Higher, and straighter, so the shadows of her peripheral vision felt darker.

She was aware of the rock walls, and the smell of damp, the sound of their breaths and footsteps, but her mind was set on reaching that tunnel. It probably wasn't even that narrow. She'd freaked herself out with it.

Except, when they got there, it seemed even smaller than she remembered. It occurred to her they were *inside* the hill, heading downward, deeper underground. She could practically feel the weight of the ground above them.

"Is this the same tunnel?"

"Yes. There's only been one way to go. The cave doesn't split until we get in deeper."

"Deeper" was such a creepy word.

"Do you want to lead?" asked Cotton.

"I don't know where to go."

"Forward. There's only one way in the tunnel. If you're in front, you won't be closed in."

"But if you go first, I'll know you fit."

"I fit." He made it seem so reasonable. So matter-of-fact.

"What if I panic and can't move?"

"I'll drag you out."

She laughed, mostly because she knew he was completely serious. "I can do it."

It was awful. Again.

But, finally, counting her crawl-steps and breaths, she made it through. The boys didn't pause to readjust or acknowledge the tunnel in any way. They hustled onward.

Her shoes didn't have the right traction. She could barely keep up with Leo. She sensed Cotton behind her, close on her heels.

As she hurried around a rocky corner, she skidded, completely freefalling along the trail. Her tumbling training kicked in and she hugged herself so as not to break a wrist or arm when she hit the ground. Which she did, with a clatter and crash. Her helmet ricocheted off the walls on either side of her. Cotton tripped over her and landed in a heap at her feet.

Adrenaline and relief battled inside her. She burst out laughing. A few seconds later, Cotton did too, short and hiccuppy.

"What happened? What are you doing down there?"

"We fell. And we're fine," said Cotton. "You are fine, right, Ria? Leo meant to be concerned."

"Yes." She stood up. "I'm fine. But damn."

"Then let's keep moving."

She readjusted her helmet and brushed off her gritty hands. She already felt a bruise forming along her left hip.

"What's the hurry?"

"We have a limited amount of time," said Leo.

"My parents' rules," added Cotton.

"If we use it all traveling, we don't go as far. We're hoping to explore new territory. There's no point seeing the same part of the cave over and over."

"It's all so amazing. Every bit of it." She ran her fingers along the wall.

"We've already mapped this part," said Cotton.

Now that she knew their expectation, she wasn't going to be the thing that slowed them down. She knew how to push. To ignore the scenery in favor of reaching the goal. She didn't even sit when they stopped for a water break.

"Left today, right?" said Cotton.

Ria laughed.

"I don't know," said Leo. "Maybe it's not a good idea to go into uncharted territory."

"That's why we're here," Cotton protested.

She wondered if he was still searching for Esther. "Don't change your plans because I'm here. It's all uncharted to me. I have no idea where we are or where we've been. It makes no difference."

The trail led them downward, steep enough that she braced her forward movement with both hands pressed against the walls.

"Are you measuring this shift in elevation?" Cotton called to Leo. "Let me go in front of you, Ria."

"I'll go faster."

"I don't want to flatten you. I've got a lot more mass than you."

She pressed herself against the wall and let Cotton pass. He stumbled down the hill, a clatter of movement, his light bumping and jostling against the walls. Alone, she allowed herself a moment to stand still. To listen to the rustles and echoes. To breathe in the smell of damp rock. With all the exertion she'd forgotten that the air was cool.

"I'm going to slide," she called to them. She squatted, then pushed herself off the walls. Being low gave her a better center of balance as she slid downward. She felt more in control than when she'd been trying to step carefully.

The boys jumped out of her way as she arrived on the flat space where they'd stopped. Their lights flashed and danced as they each turned their heads in every direction, trying to get a sense of their surroundings.

"Let's get accurate diameters. We'll have to chart the crannies."

While Cotton and Leo chattered their cave-talk and made measurements, Ria scanned the wall. A white line within the darker brown looked like a trail. She traced the line with her finger, up above her head. It kept going, up and up, way past Cotton's head. Even higher, she could see deeper shadows. "It looks like there's an opening up there. I can climb it."

"That's probably ten to twelve feet," said Cotton.

The wall had plenty of knobs and indentations. It wasn't hard to find toeholds and places to grab the rock. Her shoes were flimsy and flexible, but too slick. "I'm going barefoot."

Once her feet were free, she easily scrambled up. She'd go faster without the annoying helmet throwing her off balance, but she'd hit her head enough times to know she had to wear it. Plus, it was her only light. Funny how she kept forgetting that.

"There's a ledge," she said at the top, straining to see ahead. "I want to follow it."

"Don't go anywhere on your own," called Cotton. "That's the rule."

"I can't see where it goes."

"I'm coming up," he said.

Once he'd joined her, the passageway felt tighter.

"You have fifteen minutes to explore," yelled Leo.

With Ria leading, they crawled onward. She had to duck, which made the helmet slip and slide, sometimes covering her eyes.

"I think I hear something."

Her next movement only met air. There was no spot to put her hand. She'd almost gone over the edge. Her heart raced suddenly at the near-miss. A rush of fear washed over her.

"There's a drop-off." Her voice gave away the lurch she felt in her gut.

Cotton leaned over her, his cheek brushing against hers as he peered down. His weight pressed against her back.

"Trade spots with me," she begged.

He moved back, and awkwardly, she managed to climb around his broad shoulders and over his everywhere-legs until she was behind him.

"We're going to have to come back with ropes and climbing gear."

She was pretty sure this was a good thing, but it was hard to know from the tone of his voice.

"Three minutes!" Leo yelled from the dark behind them.

"We're being summoned," said Cotton.

Back at the bottom of the wall, she retrieved her shoes. Her feet were cold, but being able to feel the ground, to use her toes for grip, felt better, more secure. It would be easier to get up that slick hill without them. She tied the laces together and hung them around her neck.

"Ria has made an excellent find. There is a major chamber, not too far away. I think it keeps going. It had a different kind of echo."

Leo let out a whoop. "Nice! We've been hoping to find something like that."

Suddenly Cotton hugged her, with one arm. Her helmet clunked against his chest. The surprise of it, along with the narrow space, knocked her off balance.

She felt proud but wasn't sure she'd earned it. If she'd fallen off that cliff they wouldn't be so thrilled. At least she hoped not. They probably would have found this place on their own. But they were acting like she was the one who'd made something special happen.

When they reached the narrow tunnel to return, she waited as Leo disappeared.

"Hey, Cotton. Can we turn our lights off for a minute? I want to see how dark it is."

"Well, you won't *see* much. Only dark. But yes. You go first."

The knob on her helmet felt damp and slippery from the condensation in the air. Even her skin was slick with it.

"Here comes nothing," he said, turning his light off.

Her eyes met black.

They searched for something to see, and ached with trying

to focus. She turned from side to side thinking maybe she saw a shape or shadow. Cotton was right. There was nothing. Absolutely the darkest dark of darks.

She moved toward the warmth of him. She found his elbow and grabbed on. "That's enough."

"Yes." His voice was deep and close to her ear.

She felt him fiddle with her helmet and then there was a flash of light. Her pupils contracted in response. It made her dizzy. He must have felt it too because they stood in place for another minute, hanging on to each other. Then he pulled his hand back and stepped away.

Now, she saw the cave. Really saw it. It wasn't only the different dimensions and shapes—there were colors too. All along the many formations, she spotted pretty ribbons of various browns and grays, almost silver. It was closer to beautiful than she'd realized.

If only it didn't all look so foreign. She had no idea which way to go.

SIXTEEN

By Monday morning, Sean had apologized way too many times about getting drunk and she'd forgiven him every time, which was easy since she wasn't sure why she should care.

During her last class she received a pass to go to the counseling department.

She swallowed a groan of disappointment. They must have found out she didn't have a reason for leaving school early. They were probably going to fill her schedule with more pointless classes, forcing her to stay all day. Or maybe it was something else. Back in freshman year, Mrs. Sellers had called her in to ask about her bruises. A teacher had noticed and wondered if her parents, or a boyfriend, had hurt her. She'd told the truth—those particular bruises were from falling short on a new back dive. Bruises from diving were forgivable. Expected. Admired.

"I'm glad we caught you," chirped Mrs. Sellers as soon as Ria walked in. "I wouldn't want to waste your time driving to the pool when your coach is waiting for you here!" She laughed.

Benny.

Here. At school. In Mrs. Sellers's private office. Dressed for a meet in his red button-down shirt with the team logo on his chest. Standing up from a chair positioned next to the counselor. "Hello, Ria."

Still sitting at her desk, Mrs. Sellers said, "Mr. Hawkins—"

"Call me Benny."

"*Benny* was showing me videos of your dives, Ria. You're fearless!"

"Ria's better than fearless. She knows what she's doing is downright dangerous. It'd be reckless for most anyone else. But she's a pro. She tames fear and then kicks its—well, you know what I mean. Wouldn't want to cuss and end up in detention."

Mrs. Sellers giggled. She was under the spell of Benny's grin and swagger.

"It's just falling with style," Ria played along, using the old Buzz Lightyear joke. She knew how to act bold, like Benny expected.

"Well, I could never do any of that. Ria, you're an inspiration. Feel free to use the counseling space for your business."

"Let's talk." Benny led her out of Mrs. Sellers's office, then gestured toward one of the round tables near the farthest wall. He pulled out a chair for her. "Sit, Miss Victorious Marie *Where-There's-a-Will*-iams."

She sat like he'd told her to, but she didn't let herself smile at the old nickname. If she let herself relax, he might knock her over somehow.

"I thought I was doing you a favor, getting you out of school early. But looks like we got that covered already." He smirked. "That won't matter for long."

"Why are you here?"

He didn't make her wait. "The NDT wants you."

A flutter of something that felt an awful lot like winning and hope and hell-yes, started in her middle. "The NDT?" she asked, the letters clumsy on her tongue. "The actual NDT?"

He laughed, and she knew she'd gotten it right. The NDT—the National Development Team—wanted . . .

"When? How?" Her head swirled with the news. "What does that mean?"

"When you stopped by the gym that day, insisting we keep trying, well, it got me thinking. I decided to make some calls. Everyone knows you were supposed to win that meet." He leaned back in his chair, looking pleased.

This was it. The thing she'd been wishing for. An invite. A chance. And Benny was happy, too.

"We'll show them we belong."

"We?" The one short syllable stuck in her throat.

"That's right. We. You and me. I'll be your personal trainer. They know we're a package deal. They were a little worried about your head space considering what happened in LA."

Shame made her face flush hot.

"I've assured them I can keep you on track. They know you need me."

"What about the team? Your gym?"

"This is too good an opportunity to turn down. For both of us. We're the best. We're not like everyone else. You and me, that's the team that matters. Here are all the details. You sign the last page. Use your whole name." He pulled a large manila envelope from his satchel.

Her hands shook as she obediently scrawled her name across the line, *Victoria Marie Williams*. As she handed him the papers, a weight of worry settled in her gut, right below her rib cage. She whispered softly, "What if I'm not ready?"

"Then get ready."

"When do I have to decide?"

"There's nothing to decide. You just signed your letter of commitment! This is the NDT, Ria. The real deal. This has all the details. I'll leave it to you to unveil the great surprise to your parents." He handed her a second envelope. "We leave whenever you and your parents work out the details. The sooner the better."

His voice was sharp. Edged with impatience. But he wouldn't do anything here at school, not with Mrs. Sellers swishing by every few minutes.

"This is our best shot to get you ready for the Olympics. You blew one chance already. Don't blow this, too."

Abruptly, he pushed himself back from the table. Stood,

towering over her, but only for a second. Then, with a wave to Mrs. Sellers, he was gone.

She sat at the counseling table playing with the manila envelope.

The NDT wanted her.

Even after screwing up Nationals, they wanted her to train with them. To try for the Olympics. This was where she'd been aiming. She'd still have to prove herself, but Benny had found her another chance. He'd brought her here to this place she longed for, wished for, ached for. So why did she feel so confused?

She wasn't ready to tell her parents. Not until she figured out how she felt.

She couldn't tell anyone. Sean wouldn't understand. He might be sad that she was leaving. They'd have to break up. Even if the NDT's facility wasn't on the other side of the country, she wouldn't have anything to give him once she was there.

Maggie would be happy for her, but there'd be jealousy, too. They had an uneasy understanding of how competitions turned out—Ria always in first—and next year they'd be headed in different directions. But the NDT making an offer, even after she quit, was completely unexpected. And Benny leaving would put Maggie's scholarship at risk. This changed everything.

Or nothing, if she didn't go.

When the bell rang, she grabbed the envelope and headed for the exit. As she reached the door, a voice from behind said, "Hello, Ria."

She turned around. "Cotton! Are you leaving? Do you want a ride?"

"Yes and yes."

She matched her step to his bounce. It wasn't until she reached her car that she realized she hadn't said goodbye to Sean.

She stuffed the manila envelope under the driver's seat, started the engine, and headed out of the parking lot. Damn, Cotton smelled good when he wasn't covered in mud. She opened the window a few inches so she didn't feel quite as aware of him being within touching distance.

"Do you remember Mr. Guillot? In second grade?" she asked.

"Yes."

"Did you hate having to help me?" The steering wheel felt slippery in her sweaty hands. She loosened her grip, but kept her eyes on the road.

"No," said Cotton. Then, "Did I?"

"Did you hate it? I don't know. That's what I'm asking."

"I mean, did I help you?"

"Cotton, I copied the answers off your papers every day, all year long! Once when I missed school, you did my work for me, like I was there. Mr. Guillot knew. Maybe Ms. Q suggested it. I think that's why he kept me next to you."

"I did not have a lot of friends in elementary school. I had trouble acclimating to and interpreting social nuances. But I remember you were always acceptable."

Acceptable. There was something about the way Cotton said

it that let her know that was something special. Different. She smiled, keeping her eyes on the road, letting the good buzzy feeling fill the space between them.

"Do you want to go caving?" she asked.

"I don't know."

"You don't know if you can? Or you don't know if you want to?"

"I can. And I want to. But Leo prefers we don't go without him."

She didn't have the right to be disappointed. Caving was their thing. But the thrill of finding that new chamber made her want more. She didn't know enough to imagine all the possibilities of what else they might find. She had to be there with them. It wouldn't be enough to hear about it.

"Would you like to work on climbing skills?" Cotton asked. "I could use some tips."

A place immediately popped into her mind.

The spot wasn't far from Benny's dry gym. He'd led them there, past the ugly streets of warehouses and on out to where the town fizzled away. None of them had been used to running such a long distance. It wasn't long before Maggie and Temo started walking. Max was bitching about a blister. Chrissy was mad because she didn't have any gear or gadget to measure the impact of their workout. But Ria had loved the surprise of it. Changing up workouts was always a good way to erase bad habits and start over, fresh.

She didn't think anyone else would be there today. There were plenty of prettier spots to go. She worried she wouldn't be able to find the way, but as soon as they started along the trail, her body remembered. The smell of the trees and the moss and the air were the same. Except, instead of following Benny and being with her team, she was leading Cotton to the clearing.

Enormous boulders sat in the middle of shrubs, and beyond them, a grove of tall, willowy trees circled the area. She watched Cotton study the place as if he was mapping it in his mind.

"What is this place? Does it have a name?" He looked troubled and unsure.

"I don't know. Not officially."

Benny had called it Stone Revenge. Like Stonehenge, but with a vengeance for physical exertion. He'd assigned them each a boulder and they spent the next thirty minutes doing push-ups against it, first right-side up, then upside down in handstands. It was hard, but it had felt like a challenge, not a punishment. It had been a good day, after an awful one. The weekend before, the rest of the team had a bad showing at a local meet. So the first day back he'd raged at them all. He let them get wet, then made them sit on the deck, shivering while he yelled. Only she had been allowed to stay warm and dry, her reward for first place. Her team's resentment had been a different kind of punishment. But then he'd planned the trip to this magical spot. That's how it went. Whenever he felt bad for losing his temper, he made up for it with something better.

"I thought we looked everywhere when we were trying to find Esther. But I don't remember this place."

"There were a lot of people looking. I'm sure someone was here." Her voice felt close to cracking. "Do you want to leave? We could go somewhere else."

"No. It's a highly satisfactory place."

She swallowed. Took a deep breath. She needed to switch his attention to something other than Esther. "How did the rocks get here, Cotton? Where did they come from?"

"They're most likely from a prehistoric eruption. Or a flood."

Ria pictured the wonder of a world where enormous boulders moved locations. Despite their size and weight, they'd been picked up and transported here. They'd had no choice. Like Esther.

"Each boulder has a slightly different surface," she said, avoiding those thoughts. "Try to plan your route. It'll be easier if you already know where you're headed."

They started at one of the smaller rocks. Even so, its top was a couple of feet over Cotton's head. She tapped the spot around her knees' height. "You could probably make this work for a first step up."

He did as she suggested but couldn't secure the foothold. He pushed off, fell back to the ground with a thud.

She needed to make the climb before she could try to break it down for him. She forced herself to analyze what she was doing, step by step, inch by inch. From the top, she looked down at

Cotton, the top of his head a few inches below her view. "You need to use the rock more. Lean into it. Let it hold you. Each angle and curve can be part of your lift. Use your legs for the force and let your hands help your balance."

"You make climbing look simple." As he made his way up, slowly, awkwardly, she realized she was leaning too, as if she could will him upward. Maybe she did, because he made it to the top.

Going down was more of a free fall, but he looked exhilarated.

"Let's climb that one." He pointed to a rock made of obvious handholds.

By the third or fourth boulder, Ria understood the rocks in a whole new way. Rather than seeing them as enormous blocks of rough stone, she saw each one in terms of nooks and crannies, fissures and slivery places to tuck her raw and tender fingers.

As Cotton joined her on top of a flat boulder, she made no move to climb down. They sat in the sun, feeling the heat stored in the stone beneath them. She wished she'd brought water. She'd hate to leave simply because they were thirsty.

Sitting still, all the thoughts she'd been not-thinking poked her brain again.

The NDT wanted her. Getting a chance to train for the Olympics was what she'd worked for. But she'd given up that hope. She'd resigned herself to living with a dive-shaped hole in her heart. Recently the hole had started to shrink. She wasn't sure how to fit it back in.

"This has been very helpful, working on potential climbing experiences," said Cotton.

"But we don't know what we'll find in the cave. Not for sure."

"That's why we need to go. So we find out."

"It's all so uncertain and unknown. Don't you worry?"

He frowned, tilted his head. Made her wait.

"The cave requires being careful and aware, but the possibilities for trouble are limited. There's limited uncertainty."

Limited uncertainty. That sounded manageable. Contained.

"I want to tell you something, Cotton. Okay?"

"You don't need permission to tell me something. That's how conversations work."

"I just haven't told anyone else yet." She laughed.

"I'm listening."

"I've received an official invitation to join the NDT."

"The NDT that's a VBD?"

"Yes, exactly. It means a whole year of special training before the Olympic trials."

"Congratulations."

"Thank you." For a minute she let herself be happy. "It's in Colorado."

"That's approximately one thousand five hundred miles away."

"Oh. I know it's far." It wasn't the distance that nagged at her.

"I don't know if I'm good enough. Or if I'll fit in. Benny will come too, as my personal trainer. I didn't know he'd be invited. But there will be new coaches, too." She paused. "That means new rules."

Just the thought of trying to adjust to new rules, regimens, and expectations started Fear's murmurings. What if she freaked out again?

"With Benny, I know the rules. I know when he's happy with my dives."

And she knew what his angry looked like. Even when it was awful, at least she knew what was coming.

"Can't you learn the new rules?" he asked. "Since you're the one who has to do the dives."

Some rules were never said. They had to be learned by breaking them.

"I have to trust my coach. I have to know I'm safe. But I have to push myself to do things that scare me, too. It sounds easy, but really, it's impossible."

"Everyone has their own impossible."

He somehow managed to understand things he didn't know anything about.

"I just had an idea, Cotton. Since we won't be able to see as well in the cave, we should try climbing blindfolded."

"Yes."

A lightness bubbled up in her chest. "Really? You want to?"

"I don't want to," he said. "But I can see that it could assist with caving. And there is no point arguing. You have surprising and effective ideas. You are relentless and determined."

His words hung in the air between them a minute. He meant that she was prone to obsessing, but he made it sound like a good thing. Fighting the sudden wave of shy washing over her, she said, "You could use your shirt as a blindfold."

Cotton looked uncertain. Or was it embarrassed? It suddenly occurred to Ria that she was curious as to what he'd look like without a shirt. His body was so different from all the divers and swimmers she knew. Like Sean. Where they were lean and trim—and bare, due to both chlorine burns and shaving—Cotton wasn't. She'd gotten used to his size, felt comfortable with the way he towered over her. Now, with the possibility of seeing his chest and back, her own skin felt warm and flushed.

She turned away, scolding her body into behaving. Not everything had to be about touching and kissing and . . . damn. Cotton never even acted interested in any of that. And, she had a boyfriend. That's who she needed to be thinking about. But liking everything about Cotton didn't mean she didn't like Sean anymore.

"Maybe we'll come back with an actual blindfold." She bit back the word "tomorrow." Somehow, it felt like making plans, setting up a time to get together, would be crossing a line. When they bumped into each other the way they did today, simply as a coincidence—that wasn't anything to feel guilty about. Even if her body was reacting, making everything more confusing, it's not like she'd done anything wrong. But making a date to get together, knowing full well she had no plans to tell Sean, or even Maggie, about it, well, that was a whole new thing.

Except she was leaving. Going to the NDT meant she'd say goodbye to everyone. There was no use planning anything. "We should go," she said. "I need to meet Sean after school."

"Yes." He was already moving on.

The afternoon sun had disappeared behind the trees. The shadows around the boulders looked like puddles. It was easy to imagine the prehistoric flood that had moved them. Maybe that forced movement had been exactly what they'd wanted. After all, it had brought them here, to this safe and quiet place in the woods.

The place she had to leave.

SEVENTEEN

On Saturday, Ria woke to her phone beeping and buzzing.

"What are you doing?" Sean's voice sounded scratchy with morning.

"Sleeping." She checked the window, wondering if she'd slept late for the first time ever. But no. It was early. Way too early for Sean. "What are *you* doing?"

"Wondering why I never see you."

Her insides flipped. Had he heard something about Cotton? She should have told him where she'd been. There wasn't any reason for their time caving and hiking to be secret. She just didn't want to risk him thinking he should come along too. Cotton and Leo would never take her caving again.

Before she figured out an answer, she heard a voice in the background. "Are you with Maggie?"

"Yeah. We're at the outdoor pool. I'm working on closing it for the season."

Then Maggie must have grabbed his phone. "Ria. Get over

here before I lose my nerve. It's now or never if you want to see my gainer."

She was eager to see Maggie dive. It sounded like she'd made real progress. Diving was like that. One step in a hurdle, a hold, a miniscule shift—mere inches could make all the difference.

Fifteen minutes later, Ria stood in the empty parking lot. No echoes of shouts and whistles welcomed her. There was no *thunk* of the diving board in the distance. And yet, as soon as she spotted deep blue rippling through the bars of the fence, she was hit with a wave of recognition. Home.

Maggie appeared near the side gate.

"Why aren't you at the gym? What about practice?" asked Ria.

"Benny had other plans."

Inside the fence, Sean waved to them from across the pool. Barefoot and wearing his official red trunks with a snug white T-shirt labeled in all caps, *LIFEGUARD*, while holding the long skimming net in one hand, Ria recognized the boy she'd fallen for. She'd forgotten that giddy feeling of knowing Sean was watching her. She'd been shocked when Benny hadn't minded. He'd teased her about his prettiness, but he'd let them talk after practice. She hadn't had to hide him.

"Come on, get changed." Maggie headed for the boards.

"I'm here to watch. I'm not diving."

"As if."

"I might not remember how." But she was already digging through Maggie's bag, looking for a spare suit. The song of water lapping against the concrete sides, the glitter of early morning sun reflecting below the white boards, the smell of chlorine, all of it called to her.

She didn't bother with the locker room. She held a towel around her sides. Modesty in diving was a hassle, and pointless besides. There are few secrets beneath wet Lycra.

Except Maggie's suit wasn't as tight as she liked. Ria scooched the fabric around, trying to rearrange it.

"You still look ripped."

Ria looked down, eyed her body. She held out her arms, comparing them to Maggie's freckled ones, right before she took off her glasses. She'd only been trying to stay busy and tired. Running and caving were keeping her strong. A perfect example of why Benny was such a stickler for cross-training.

She still hadn't told Maggie about the NDT's offer. She hadn't told anyone besides Cotton. Instead, she'd rolled the idea around in her head, trying to imagine all the different ways it could go. It was like she'd hurdled off the diving board, launched higher than she'd ever been—and then discovered the water wasn't there. The worst part was she still hadn't landed yet. The longer she went without telling anyone the less real it felt. Besides, if she didn't go, it was an empty brag. Hollow, and easily popped.

From the very first free fall off the board, letting gravity have its way, the cool whoosh as she broke the surface; Ria felt like she'd slipped back into her own life. Her lift wasn't as high as it should be, her turns moved a little slower, but her body remembered the motions.

As she climbed the ladder to the three-meter board, Sean

came out with the team's tripod and video camera.

"Good idea!" she said. "We need to make sure we get Maggie's money dive taped."

"Only if I make it."

"The video is running. I'll be in the office." Sean waved and disappeared around the center building.

A few dives later, she said, "It's time, Maximum Mags."

"Soon."

"You've already prepped it. You're going over, which means you'll make it."

"I know, I know. But I did a really sweet one yesterday. I don't want to mess up that feeling." Maggie set herself on the end of the board. Dried herself with the shammy. Stretched. Reached. Turned. All the little quirks that were absolutely her. They all had their own superstitious rituals. "Ugh. Here I go."

As Maggie rounded her second flip, Ria could hear Benny in her head. *Hollow. Hold. Don't get loose.* When she entered the water, only slightly bent, Ria cheered.

Maggie surfaced, grinning. Then immediately started the self-coaching comments. "I didn't keep my head up long enough. As soon as I lifted, I started the tuck."

"That was damn awesome!"

"I don't know."

Ria eyed her. She couldn't convince Maggie of something she didn't believe. She needed to get her praise from someone who didn't care about her feelings. Someone brutally honest. In other words, Benny.

"I'll be back in a minute. Keep going." Maggie pulled herself out of the water and headed toward the locker room.

Ria didn't need persuading. She went through her list, checking to see if she still had her dives. Repeated the ones that felt off.

She wasn't sure how long she'd been diving when she stopped to take a break. The cool air on her wet skin made her shiver, in a good way. She lay on her back, let herself bobble and float. Most of her body hid beneath the surface of the water, but bits of her—her face, breasts, tops of her thighs took turns peeking out of the wet. She stared up at the sky, let herself feel empty and still.

"You're holding back."

She flipped upright and met Benny's stare. He stood at the edge of the pool, looking down. The way they'd talked a million times before.

Now it felt like she'd forgotten how to tread water. The clenching—in her jaw, her gut, deep within the very core of her—made her feel heavy and slow, in danger of sinking. She wanted to hear what he had to say while simultaneously wanting to run away.

"You're not supposed to be here," Ria said. "The pool is closed."

It was a stupid thing to say. He had his own key. How many times had he brought the team here without the pool being technically open? She'd never complained when he had them sneak in, not even the nights of diving in the dark with the lights off. Right now, it was obvious. He was here to see *her*. Maggie and Sean were conveniently not on the deck. She'd been set up.

For an instant, she blamed Maggie. Then Sean. But seeing Benny's smirk, she knew it had been all his idea. He always got what he wanted. This place that had seemed so inviting when she arrived now looked dingy, cold, and gray. Chlorine burned in the back of her throat.

"You still have the grace you always had. But you're too slow in the flip. If you aren't going to do the work, you gotta use the board."

"I know," she said around gritted teeth.

"The NDT is waiting to hear from you."

She scrambled out of the pool, onto the firm cement. Then instantly wished she was back in the water. Back where she wouldn't feel his automatic evaluation. He always watched, judged, measured. Found the nicks and wobbles. The soft and wavering spots. She hugged her own shoulders, trying to fold her body into itself.

"What did your parents say?" He wore his winning face, cocky and bold.

"I'm not ready."

"You've had your break. Enough screwing around. It's time to get back to work." His expression shifted, turned to steel.

She blinked hard. Concentrated on standing in one place, centering her weight, every inch of her pressed down and still. No sudden movements, not in front of Benny.

"You're running out of time. The longer you wait, the more

they'll doubt you have what it takes. Everyone knows you freaked out. They're worried about your head space."

She tasted blood, realized she'd bit the inside of her lip. "I can't. . . ."

"Dammit, Ria! You already signed with them."

"I signed because you told me to."

"You signed that letter of commitment because it was the smart thing to do. And now you need to get yourself together and get ready to join them. *Now*, before they lose interest or find someone else. Goddammit, you're so stubborn."

He used to think that was a good thing.

Benny stepped toward her, fists clenched. She braced herself, concentrating on standing firm. Ready. Once again she'd pushed him to this point. It was her own fault. Again.

She hadn't even realized Sean had joined them from inside. "Hey," he said. "You guys hungry? We have to clean everything out. We have a ton of peanut butter pretzels."

Even Sean knew Benny's favorite snack. But he was not supposed to interrupt practices. She wondered what he'd heard. He was breaking the rules. Except this wasn't practice. *She* was the one who didn't know the rules anymore.

Ria snapped, "Don't you have some laps to swim?"

Benny laughed. Then, as she bolted, he called to her, "I got you everything you wanted!"

But everything had changed.

EIGHTEEN

Even if it had been Benny's idea, Ria wasn't ready to talk to Maggie or Sean. Not with the way her heart pounded and her eyes stung. They'd set her up, with no warning. Sean didn't even belong to Benny. They knew she was pissed. Either one of them—or both—might show up at her house trying to apologize. Besides, all the telltale wet spots in weird places—over her breasts and hips, her butt—clearly from a swimsuit under her clothes would lead to questions from her parents.

So, instead of going home, she drove to Cotton's house. She parked on the street and sent him a text before she could decide if that was a good idea. He didn't answer, but she knew he didn't always keep his phone with him. Or even on. But then he came around the corner from his backyard and looked up and down the street until he found her car. She got out and leaned against it. She ran her fingers through her hair. It had finally gotten to where it looked healthy and now she'd gone and let the chlorine back in.

"Hi, Ria." Cotton scanned the street as if there might be someone or something following her. Or maybe that was the way she felt. He met her eyes with his brown ones, then looked upward and to the left, the way he tended to do.

He also looked pretty damn delighted that she was there. He didn't smile all the time, but when he did, it was worth the wait.

"You're wet."

She knew she looked like a wild mess. Disheveled and damp. Hair mussed and sticking out in all directions. She pulled her shirt away from her damp body, tried to will it dry.

"Do you want to come inside?"

"I'm fine here." She wouldn't know what to say or how to act around his family.

"You look cold."

She couldn't deny it. Not with the way she was shivering now that her fury was fizzing out. "Are you sure I can come in?"

"Yes."

Standing outside the front door, Ria heard voices inside. She took a deep breath, steeled herself; ready to meet this family who had been through every kind of awful.

Cotton opened the back door and the smell of something baking made her breathe deeply in reflex. Laughter from upstairs rang out and there was a thud of footsteps running overhead. A girl's voice shrieked from down the hall.

"I hope you weren't looking for quiet. Because that's not here."

"You have a big family." She knew too many facts and details from all the television coverage to ask questions.

"Yes. There are five children."

He was counting Esther.

Mrs. Talley came down the hallway then, carrying a wilted but large potted plant, yelling over her shoulder, "Jelly, clean up your soccer stuff. And Bo, turn that TV off and get your homework done." She paused, then smiled at Ria. "Oh. Hello." She was taller than Ria, but not as tall as Cotton. Her hair was fair, but Ria couldn't tell if it was more blond or gray.

"Mom, this is Ria Williams."

"Nice to meet you, sweetheart." She adjusted the plant to one arm. "You're the diver, right? I read about you in the newspaper."

She was hit with a hot panic, not knowing how to reply. She'd seen *their* name in the paper too many times to count. She'd seen them sobbing and pleading on television. There had been articles in magazines. But this house was so warm, so happy. If Esther made her way home now, she might never leave again.

"I understand Cotton took you caving." Mrs. Talley raised her eyebrows in question. "I didn't realize you two were friends."

"Yes. We've known each other a long time."

"We went to pull-out with Ms. Q together," added Cotton.

"Oh, that's nice." His mother smiled as if it actually was nice. "Well, Cotton, get your guest a towel."

"Yes, ma'am." He motioned for Ria to follow him. He led her down a hallway lined with shoes, sports bags, and backpacks, and on into the garage.

There wasn't room to park a car. One side was full of tools and boxes and clutter. A treadmill stood against the back wall with rags draped over the handlebars. Toys were strewn across the shelves and overflowed out of a large plastic box. In the far corner, there was a couch beside a wooden desk covered with papers and a laptop computer.

Cotton grabbed a yellow towel from the laundry basket on the floor and handed it to her. It was soft and warm, and smelled like it was fresh from the dryer. Ria eyed the pile of clean laundry. "Can I borrow a sweatshirt, too?"

The bottom hem came to her knees, as if it was a dress. She pushed up the sleeves to find her hands again.

Even though he hadn't asked, she tried to explain. "I was at the pool with Maggie. Then Benny showed up. He'd planned it with her. Sean let him in."

Cotton waited silently, giving her time to figure out what she wanted to say.

"I'm so mad at Sean. I can't believe he set me up. I'm literally shaking." Maggie had to do whatever Benny said, but Sean had no excuse. He'd even offered him a stupid snack.

She pressed her hands against her eyes so hard she saw flashes of light. When she let go, a swirl of dizzy hit her. She breathed in, waited for the feeling to pass.

"Do you want to sit down?" Cotton pointed to the chair by his desk.

She shook her head. Sitting was never a way to calm down.

She needed to move. To do something. It felt as if her body was about to explode.

"Did Benny hurt you?"

"No. Why? What did you hear? Who said he did?" The surprise of his question hit her in the chest.

"You said diving doesn't scare you, so I thought maybe Benny did something."

"He didn't touch me. Not this time. He's just impatient for me to make plans with the NDT."

People outside never understood. Benny was the only person who cared about her diving as much as she did. Between his intensity and her maddening way of screwing up, it was inevitable they'd have their conflicts. It wasn't anyone else's business what they needed to do to make her the best. He'd told her she was the only one tough enough to take it. She was the one he cared about the most.

She ran her tongue over her teeth, found the chipped spot.

The thing everyone forgot, a smack on the water hurt as much as anything. Pain was part of the process. It was all part of getting stronger, better. She was so out of shape now. She wasn't sure she could get back to where the NDT expected her to be.

She moved away from Cotton, avoiding the flecks of green within his brown eyes. And the little dimple at the top of his lip. That crooked tooth that was her favorite part of his smile. Instead she focused on the enormous sheet of paper hung from one wall, next to a pegboard of tools. She studied the lines and swirls, the tiny numbers written at various spots, all within long and twisting tube shapes.

"Is this one of your maps? You made this?"

"That's the cave." He stood beside her, studying what he'd created. "It's a topographical map. It shows the different elevations and land formations. It can be difficult to translate if you're not familiar with the codes."

He was right. Ria didn't know how to read the lines and amoeba shapes. She traced one dark line that snaked along the middle. "What's this part?"

"That's the hill you slid down. When the lines are close together, that's a steep incline. But over here, there aren't as many lines because it's almost flat."

Ria tilted her head, studied the shapes around it.

"And the numbers and the shading—that's to mark the volume. It indicates the ceiling so we know how much room we have to navigate."

Slowly, almost more of a feeling than a thought—like that moment of knowing when to open up out of a flip midair—she could see what he meant. The cave she'd seen, heard, smelled, merged with the lines in front of her. She ran her fingers over the paper as if she could find a way inside. "Is this the place you called the 'back door to Australia'?"

"Yes. That's it. You get it."

"This is amazing. Except none of this shows how beautiful it is." She turned to face him.

"There's never only one way to see something. You have to

get all the different sides and versions."

She nodded. Swallowed. Had to look away.

On his desk, she saw a white card with gold writing across the front: *Congratulations! You have received an award.* She picked it up and read the inside: *You are invited. A night of celebration.*

"Ooh. An award. What for?"

Cotton shrugged. "I'm not sure. I have to go to the ceremony to find out."

"You have no idea? Does that make you nervous?"

"No. My mom thinks it's for school or my online classes. Or maybe for the map work I did over the summer. Whatever it is, it's something I already did. I don't need to worry about it now."

"Impressive. That's a lot of options."

"Was that inappropriate bragging?"

"No. You aren't bragging. I'm curious. The only awards I've ever gotten were for diving." Since he still looked uncomfortable, she added, "Tell me how you made this map."

"Do you want to see it on the computer?" He plopped down in the chair. "Here's the program I use."

She moved closer, stood beside him.

He stared at the computer screen. He tilted his head, rubbing his chin and working his mouth so she knew he was thinking. He clicked on one of the icons, then another.

"This is our map."

It looked so precise and official. Hard to believe it was based on the numbers Cotton plugged in. He could make the world look any way he wanted. More hill? *No problem.* A tunnel to hide in? *Let's put one right here.* Except he wouldn't invent or adjust. He liked facts and measurements. Besides, she'd been there. She could recognize the places he'd reported.

"If there's another opening to the same cave, where would it be?"

"We won't know until we find it."

With Cotton sitting, she was a little bit taller than him. She glanced down at the mess of waves in his hair. It wasn't one color. There were different shades of brown tangled around reddish highlights. The swirl of it was a little bit like the lines on his maps. She played with her own wet hair so she wouldn't run her fingers through his. He turned suddenly and met her eyes. His stare was intense and unwavering.

If he moved to kiss her right here, right now, she wouldn't stop him.

Her heart thumped faster, rushing her blood hot and fast throughout her, making her feel too warm, but shivery, too. Except he didn't try. He didn't move at all.

"Do you have a map of the quarry?" Her voice came out shaky and too thick. "Of what's under the water?"

He turned back to the computer. After a few clicks, he pointed at the screen, helping her to read the shadows and symbols. It included the old equipment and different rock shelves. She moved closer, trying to align the image with her memory of the place.

"They searched the quarry looking for Esther. They hired divers and used underwater cameras. It allowed for updated accuracy."

Damn.

"I'm sorry." She immediately wished she could take the words back. She felt more than sorry. More than wishing. More. So much more.

"I think Sean had good intentions."

Confused, Ria glanced at the chart on the screen, then back at him, trying to figure out where Sean fit in.

"I'm sure he didn't know you'd be angry. Benny was your coach, right? Did he know you'd be upset to talk to him?"

"You're on Sean's side?" she asked.

"Why are there sides? It's something that happened. You got upset and you came here." He paused. Then said, "Why are you here, Ria?"

Maybe it was as simple as the fact Cotton didn't know Benny. He didn't have anything to do with diving. He was completely separate from that part of who she used to be. "Because we're friends. Aren't we?"

"I don't know," said Cotton.

He turned in his chair suddenly, away from her. It was clear he was done with their conversation. It was like she'd disappeared. He wouldn't meet her eyes, not even when she said, "Do you want me to leave?"

Cotton just kept typing frantically, as if he'd make the right answer suddenly appear.

Except there wasn't one.

NINETEEN

Later that afternoon, Maggie tiptoed into Ria's room, looking wary and carrying a plate of peanut butter fudge and brownies. "Do you want to have a horror marathon?" Except they both knew she said it as *whore-er* in honor of all the poor slutty girls who'd fallen to their deaths immediately after having sex.

Ria raised her eyebrows. "Can we fantasize that Chrissy is the first to go?"

"Of course. Are you okay?"

She shrugged away the concern she heard. Maggie knew Benny, almost as well as Ria, but *almost* wasn't an exact match. With all the not-talking they'd done, she'd lost track of what Maggie knew to worry about. "You brought me sweets and promises of bloodshed. What else could I need?" She'd always loved a good solid night of terror. It was a way to flirt with fear.

As Maggie sat beside her, she reached out and pressed her finger against Ria's arm.

"Ouch! What are you doing?"

"What are *you* doing? That's one helluva bruise."

Ria turned her arm so she could see it better. Maggie was right. The large yellowish spot traveled from her elbow halfway to her wrist. She didn't remember hitting her arm specifically, but all the many bumps and knobs inside the cave were hard to see. There was a fair amount of crashing into things. "From this angle it looks like a penguin. See the feet?"

"Maybe. How'd you get it?" Maggie twisted her head around, obliging.

"I must have bumped it on a rock," Ria said.

This might be the time to tell Maggie about caving. Except how could she explain it, and whatever she felt about Cotton, when she didn't understand it herself?

"Are you diving with someone else? Did your parents get you a new coach?"

She stared at Maggie, not following this ricochet of thoughts.

"You have that bruise. And others, too. I saw them when we were at the pool. You're still as strong as ever. Is that why you were upset to see Benny?"

She'd certainly had bruises from diving before. Bruises meant she was pushing past easy, making progress, moving on to something tougher. But to have Maggie question her now made her suddenly aware of the giant chasm between them. On the one side they had all this history, all this shared experience. But on the other side were the places they didn't go together anymore.

Futures that had nothing to do with each other. She had to be careful where she stepped.

"That was the first time I've been on a board since LA." Not meeting Maggie's stare, she tried to shift the focus back to the comfortable topic of horror. "So, what movie should we watch? Remind me, which one made you cry?"

"They're all sad. Everyone always dies."

"That's the point!" Ria laughed, until she looked up. "Are you already crying?"

"Are you breaking up with Sean because of Benny?"

"What does that even mean?"

"Sean told me you aren't answering his texts or calls. I know you're pissed that Benny showed up at the pool. But that wasn't Sean's fault. That was me."

"That was *Benny*. I know he put you up to it."

"We should have warned you." Maggie looked miserable.

True. But if she'd been warned, she wouldn't have gone. She wouldn't have been on the board, wouldn't have surprised herself how easily it all came back, wouldn't be phantom-diving in her head.

"I had to do it. He insisted. I didn't know you'd get so upset. You were always his pet."

"I was his diver." Ria peeled back the foil and sniffed the sweets more closely. Maggie baked whenever she was nervous. "If we watch *Prom Night* we'll learn what to expect." Maybe that would help her figure out if she'd miss not going to her own.

"What did he want?"

"Who? Your prom night lover? He wants you, of course. I bet it's Principal Roglio."

"You know I meant Benny. I thought he was going to beg you to come back. That's why I did it. But, ewww, Ria, Mr. Roglio must be a hundred years old. And he has nose boogers."

"So he must be a very experienced lover. You can bring tissues. Bad news is, if I get slashed, it'll be all your fault. Good news is, if we're still virgins, we might survive." She was actually kind of freaking herself out.

"He's changed lately. He seems almost human. Definitely more relaxed." They both knew Maggie didn't mean their principal. "But he's still different with you."

Ria could hear the old familiar resentment in her friend's voice. The cost of being special.

"I think Benny's starting to worry about money. He sold the extra trampoline."

Maggie blamed her, but she had the details wrong. Benny hadn't told the team about the NDT. He hadn't been part of the original plan, the one before Ria lost her mind and ran away from nothing at her most important meet. The team didn't know he might be leaving. She should have told Maggie as soon as she got the invite. Keeping the news in the dark had made it grow. It was too enormous to simply say. Not when Maggie looked so desperate. Besides, telling Maggie the truth now would make it one step closer to true.

If she went to the NDT, she'd be gone. Really gone. She'd say goodbye to Maggie and Sean . . . and Cotton. She'd skip the rest of her senior year. She'd miss prom night, whether or not it was the bloodbath shown in the old movie. And Maggie would lose her chance to keep diving. Because Ria would take Benny away too. She'd be with him a million—or, according to Cotton, 1,500—miles away, with no one else around.

She'd signed that letter of commitment, but they couldn't *make* her go. Her parents didn't even know about the invitation yet. She couldn't go if they didn't pay.

"Don't worry about Benny, Mags."

"But I need to get that scholarship. If he shuts down . . ."

"He can still help you get a scholarship even if he isn't here. Make him talk to coaches for you."

"I can't make him do anything."

It was true, but only because Maggie wasn't willing to push. She was too afraid of hearing no.

"Help me eat these brownies," said Ria.

Now she was thinking of all those girls who didn't get asked to the prom. They must have stayed at home, crying into their pillows. They had no idea they were the lucky ones.

TWENTY

Early the next morning, Dad interrupted Ria's *croga*—cross-yoga—stretching, with random-weighted objects designed to increase the challenge.

"Are you cooking or cleaning?" he asked from the doorway.

"Am I being too loud? I dropped the potatoes."

"Get ready. Mom's waiting for us. We're going out."

He was up to something. She recognized that mischievous way he was trying not to give something away. He had a terrible poker face.

In the back seat of the car, she didn't bother wondering where they were headed. It had been ages since they'd done anything together, so the possibilities were wide open.

She'd finally texted Sean last night, after dinner. He'd come over and stayed late to make up. Cotton was right. Sean hadn't meant to make her upset when he'd let Benny surprise her. She'd had no right to charge in on Cotton's life, dumping her misplaced mad on him. No wonder he'd ignored her in his garage. He didn't need to get dragged into her messes.

She and Sean had carefully avoided mentioning the pool or Benny or her storming away or pretty much anything except the video she'd sent him of stunt-fails. Someone else's pain was always good for a laugh. They'd moved on to other safe topics. Or, more accurately, kissing was an excellent way to not talk about anything.

She couldn't stay mad at Sean when she'd been such a disloyal girlfriend. She'd trade being mad at him about letting Benny into the pool for not having to tell him the way she'd thought about Cotton in his garage. She wasn't sure it was completely even, but close. Anger had never been easy for her, anyway. She'd dodged other people's so often; she didn't know how to hold on to it herself.

As soon as her parents pulled into the parking lot of Donna's Diner, Ria's stomach clenched. Damn. Something was up.

They only went to Donna's for celebrations or punishments. When she did her first back-double, they came here straight from practice. The time she was suspended for coating the girl's bathroom ceiling with wet-paper-towel bombs in order to avoid a math test, this was where they had a recovery-strategy meeting. After winning Junior Nationals, it was their first stop as soon as they were back in town. The morning after the night in eighth grade when she and Maggie snuck out and walked to the all-night doughnut store at two in the morning, they made her eat at the plastic counter while watching the cooks and breathing in all the grease and sweetness. Pancakes had always had a bittersweet flavor.

Once they were tucked into the booth, and her parents' coffee and her freshly squeezed, extra-pulp orange juice was set in front of them, Mom asked, "Is there something you want to tell us?"

Ria wasn't sure what they'd discovered. Less sure what they'd think about her caving trips. They'd probably see it as another one of her impulsive irresponsible actions. Or maybe they'd found out she was behind in her classes, as usual. She wasn't going to guess or offer anything up. She could wait. They hated silence. It wouldn't be long before they rushed in to fill the quiet.

They used to know everything she did, but never because she was the one to tell. Her teachers used to call or send home daily progress reports filled with stickers. When she first started diving, Mom or Dad always watched her practices. They knew everything because they were there. Then she'd sent them away, unable to have them interfere with Benny's demands. Once she'd started driving herself to practice and had doubled up on the number of private workouts, she'd insisted they stay away from him completely. All communication had to go through her. It kept things simpler, cleaner. She couldn't afford to have their doubts in her head when she was on the board. But right now they knew something.

"Congratulations, Ria."

"The NDT wants you!"

Then, without a second for her to catch her breath, there was the shift.

"Why didn't you tell us? Why are we hearing this from Benny? He said you're feeling uncertain."

"Are you worried about the expense? It's no more than college. The better you do, the more sponsorships kick in."

"I know it's far, but we'll come visit. I might even be able to work remotely. At least until you're settled."

"We can figure this out. We're so happy for you."

Ria set her forehead on the edge of the table, face down, breathing. They were moving so fast. In circles. Spirals. She'd barely wrapped her head around the fact Benny had told them. She was supposed to be the in-between. They weren't supposed to talk to him.

"Ria? What are you doing?"

"Sit up," said Dad. "Talk to us."

She lifted her head. She knew she was reverting, back to acting like a wiggy little kid. Like someone who needed everyone else to decide what was best.

"You talked to Benny?"

Dad said, in the most annoyingly slow and even voice, the one he used to break down the most obvious of problems, "This is what you've been working for, Ria. You did it. You get to be part of the NDT."

"This is an incredible opportunity. You are so lucky that they are still interested in working with you." Mom's voice carried a whiff of shrill.

"Do you know how few divers are chosen?"

"Do you know *anything*?" Ria couldn't keep the scorn from her voice.

She knew she was being ungrateful. After everything they'd given her, all the money they'd spent, all the time they'd dedicated to making sure she could reach this point, she was awful to feel unsure. Maybe she could find a way to tell them the truth. To let them know the parts of diving she'd kept hidden from them. Maybe if she confessed her secret shame, that she wasn't as perfect as they thought, maybe then they'd understand.

"Benny said . . ." Dad started.

There it was. If Benny said it, they believed him.

They trusted him. They knew she needed him. She could never dive without him. On her own, she always got everything wrong.

TWENTY-ONE

Ria was late getting to school on Monday morning. She'd gone for a run, heading in the direction opposite from Cotton's house. Not that she was likely to see him in the early dawn, but it was time to change up her route. Except she'd misjudged the distance and stayed out too long. Now, in the quiet parking lot, her mind raced, fast and loud. She couldn't remember if she'd taken her medicine today. Or yesterday. Or when the last time had been. There was no point sitting in class if she couldn't focus. Besides, she'd already missed too much of first period to bother, and with only a couple more classes, she might as well skip them.

So, she headed home. Now that she'd ruined things with Cotton, she didn't have anywhere else to be. She hadn't heard from him since she left him tapping away on his computer.

Her room didn't fit her mood. It was too yellow, too crowded, too weighed down with clutter. All the pictures on her bulletin board and mirror and in the frames placed in line of every view were old. Outdated. She gathered them into a stack and stashed the collection into the bottom of her desk drawer. She grabbed a pillowcase and filled it with her medals. Each one stood for a long-gone victory.

It was too heavy to lift, so she dragged it to her closet and pushed it to the back, behind her shoes and dirty clothes. Then, because all the remaining holes seemed too big and glaring, she swept away everything else, too, until finally her room looked clean and bare. Anonymous.

Ready for her to leave.

Or, to once and for all, forget diving.

She wanted to move her bed to the opposite side of the room, closer to the window, but she wasn't sure it would fit. She'd have to move her dresser and desk, too. She got out a piece of paper and drew her room, a view from above, mapping each piece of furniture in relationship to the other. Once she was sure the scale was close, she cut out each shape and moved them around her room, trying out new arrangements. It was like playing with a flat, boring dollhouse, figuring out where everything could move.

She moved the smaller furniture first, getting it out of the way, then finally she pushed and shoved, using her hips to move her bed near the window. After she'd rearranged the rest of her furniture, she lay down, checking out her new view of the tree-tops.

She had no idea what a room with the NDT would look like.

She needed to have a window. If there was no window, she'd have to leave. But what if she hated the view out the window? What if Colorado looked ugly and wrong? She knew it wasn't ugly in general as a place, but the view out her unknown window might be.

Ever since she'd gone back in the pool, every time she closed her eyes, she found herself falling off the edge of the quarry. She'd slip, then fall. Over and over, but she never hit the blue below. Lying here, she felt so damn tired. The fatigue started behind her eyes, but then it spread through her veins and arteries. Like oxygen, but thicker. It wasn't a physical, overexertion kind of spent. It wasn't that she wanted to sleep, either. Gravity had shifted. Realigned. It tugged at her. Made her body impossibly heavy. Maybe it was the weight of memories. Or the imaginary view she couldn't picture.

It was exhausting being in this place of *used to be* and *no idea what the hell to do next*.

The first time she met Benny was at the community college where he worked in northern Virginia. Mom had been emailing and calling him for months, he later told her. She'd begged him to meet with them. Ria was a skinny hyper kid excited to miss school for a road trip. There had been two boards at the pool. One was springier, better for getting height, but the fulcrum was tight, and she was little, so she'd had to use both hands while sitting on the ground to turn it.

After her first dive—a one-and-a-half pike she'd fallen in

love with, the one that made her feel like she was part bird—Benny had given her a correction. "Go more up than out."

It was the simplest advice. Something she'd heard a million times since then. But that day, it was new. She'd gone again, doing what he'd said. She went up, up, up. It was glorious. The feeling of spring without care for the board, the attention on that flash of a moment in the air before ever hitting the water—that was all that mattered.

She knew she'd done something beautiful. She could feel it in her bones and muscles and cells that she'd done it right—even before she heard the cheers and applause when she resurfaced.

After that, Benny had taken her through a beginner novice list. She'd done each dive twice. Once to show him, then again with whatever advice he gave her. It was a simple formula. When she did what he said, she dove better.

Her coachability was the reason he agreed to move to Pierre and start a new club. She was his one and only diver. But then Mom talked to parents at the rec center, spreading the word. Before long, other divers filled in the space around her, making it a real business for him. That same coachability was one of the things Benny put on his recommendation of her for the elite teams. She was willing to do whatever it took.

She never questioned his techniques. If he got mad, she accepted her punishment, knowing it was all part of the process. Being the best demanded strength and endurance. No backing down. No complaints or protests.

And for a long time, for years and years, it worked. They worked. Ria and Benny. Working hard, working together. Getting better all the time. She started winning, everything, no matter how far they traveled. But, eventually, because that's the way it always went with adults, she started making Benny mad. She got lazy. Overconfident. She played too much when she should have been working.

She couldn't let her parents know how often she got in trouble at practice. They were so sure diving was the one thing she was good at. There had been times when they thought Benny was too intense. But that's how he had to be. She was, too. Mostly, they were so proud that she was exceptional. Instead of being the parents called into the principal's office for another one of her impulsive mistakes, they were now the parents of the girl who always won. Suddenly other parents asked them for advice on nutrition and training time, even bedtimes. They were stars too. All of them, as close to perfect as possible.

One day, a long time ago, when Dad noticed her icing her ribs and didn't like the look of the bruises on her arm—the ones that looked like fingers—she'd almost told him the truth. She was so close to admitting how she'd temporarily lost trust in her coach. She'd refused to do a new inward dive. Fear had shown up, she'd thrown a fit, and Benny had to set her straight. But she didn't want Dad to be disappointed in her again. Benny had promised her he'd never make her do anything that was impossible, but she'd forgotten. It was all her own fault.

So, instead, she'd lied. She made up a ridiculous, over-the-top story about slipping off the board and wrestling with Chrissy and later she'd accidentally run over a deck chair, somersaulting onto the concrete—it was a story wild and bizarre enough to be believed because she was the star. She was always doing something reckless and goofy. Dad laughed and told Mom and she laughed too and everyone was happy. It was way easier to make up stories than to try to explain the truth: she was still a screwup.

Benny had been the one to suggest she keep her parents away from practice. He'd shared with her in secret that the reason Chrissy would never make it big was because her parents weren't on board. They were the weak link in Chrissy's pyramid: coach, diver, parents. Ria hadn't understood the geometry, but she'd understood the result. Her own success was because she and Benny worked together, without interference.

It wasn't fair that now he'd told her parents about the NDT. They couldn't make that be the right thing simply by wanting it. Not when they didn't understand what it all meant.

The NDT was a second chance, the kind that doesn't always come along. It was a flashy burst of good luck—but she'd been trained that luck didn't exist. It couldn't be trusted. She might freak out again, the way she had in LA. She'd been so absolutely, positively certain that she was in danger when she took off running. Even when no one else would admit that she'd been chased, she'd felt certain they'd missed it. But then when they'd all watched that video—it was obvious that she'd bolted for no good reason. If she couldn't understand how her head and her body had gotten so mixed up, she couldn't be sure she wouldn't do something like it again. No wonder the NDT wanted Benny to come with her. She couldn't be trusted on her own.

Her phone beeped, surprising her with a text. It lay in the spot where she'd dropped it on the floor. It was almost too far away to bother getting.

She hung over the edge of the mattress, dangling and stretching, finally grasping the phone with the tips of her fingers. It was Cotton. She'd been avoiding him, but when she saw his name pop up, she couldn't remember why.

TWENTY-TWO

The text from Cotton was short.

No words, only numbers.

With anyone else she might have thought it was a butt-text, random typing. But coming from Cotton, the digits had to be a code.

She left her bed, headed out to the trampoline to think. Halfway across the yard, she imagined a grid lining up the patio and the fence and suddenly she knew the numbers were map coordinates. Longitude and latitude. She recognized the pattern from his mapping program.

Inside her car—wearing sweats and running shoes, ready for wherever Cotton might lead her—she plugged the coordinates into the map on her phone. Driving, she followed the robotic directions spoken through her phone, making her way across town. A wave of uncertainty hit when she turned onto a small quiet road, but the bus stop on the corner reassured her. Cotton could be here.

Once she parked in a clearing just off the pavement, she studied her phone again. She zoomed in closer and saw that she hadn't quite reached the marked location. She was going to have to walk the rest of the way.

This spot was unremarkable in all the ways a place could be overlooked. There were the same greens and browns that lined a hundred roads. Anonymous gravel beneath her feet led her to the insignificant patchy grass she crossed to reach the nothing special line of trees. It didn't match the buzz of anticipation making her walk faster.

The shade of the trees felt cool and damp against her skin. She reached out and caressed the bark of a slender young tree yearning for the sunshine peeking through the thick branches above her head. A minute later she stepped out of the shade and into a long and narrow field.

All around her, woven within the grass and shrubs were hundreds, thousands—maybe more—of tiny blue flowers. She squinted and the whole world turned a fuzzy bluish-green.

"Hi, Ria," Cotton said from the spot where he sat on the ground, out in the middle of the field, as if he'd been planted there.

"I found you."

"I sent directions."

As if that was all she needed. Numbers. Coordinates. A spot on a map. Apparently, he was right.

Ria walked through the field with her arms outstretched,

wishing she could scoop up this place and hold it close. She found her way to Cotton. She stood, towering over him.

"I thought you would like it here."

"I do, Cotton. I like it a lot."

She sat next to him, keeping her arms pressed against her sides, hands in her lap. She studied his face, let her eyes travel down his broad shoulders, long arms, to his giant hands tapping the denim stretched across his knee.

"Cotton?" Her voice was small enough to blend into the flowers and stems.

"I'm listening." His was deeper, sleepier, like it was nestled into the soil.

"Are these flowers a sign of your affection?"

"Yes. You asked if we were friends. I would like to be friends."

"Oh, good. Me too. I thought you were upset with me."

"I was upset thinking that your coach hurts you." And here she was assuming it had something to do with Sean and her disloyal feelings. But no, it was back to Benny.

"I told you, he didn't."

"You said 'not this time.' So, not that day. But sometimes."

He was right. He was the only person to say it, not ask. Questions from her teammates: *What did he do? Was he mad? Are you okay?* made it impossible to admit exactly what Benny did. They knew she'd messed up again, but she wouldn't give them the satisfaction of knowing exactly what that meant. Pain always faded, but shame festered. It grew worse on the replay in her head.

Right now she didn't have to deny it, but she might be able to explain.

"It's not all the time. If you add up all the days, hours, dives I've spent with Benny, that would be an enormous number, like . . . pi."

"The number pi? That's not actually a large number. It has endless digits, but it's not a huge quantity. It's not even really a number, I don't think. It stands for the relationship between a circle's circumference and its diameter."

"A number that's not really a number?" Even though she had no idea what that meant mathematically, that might work for what she was trying to say. "Well, then, think of my diving like a giant pie. One that you eat. A pie-pie."

"Pie."

"Pie." She echoed his echo. "So with that pie, the number of times he's hurt me, it's only a slice. If one slice gets dropped on the floor, there's still way more good pie on the plate."

"So diving is like pie?"

"No." Ria laid back in the flowers.

"Okay. I like pie."

She really liked this field of flowers.

The uneven ground felt bumpy beneath her head, her shoulder blades, the edges of her hips, on down to her calves and heels. The leaves and blossoms tickled against the places where her skin peeked out from beneath her clothes. The sun felt warm and the breeze blew cool. Her body was aware of his beside her.

Solid. Close, but not touching. Not crossing any lines or breaking any rules. He was her *friend*.

The deliberate concentration of not touching, not reaching out and taking his hand, not measuring the length of her legs against his, not not not, made her feel inexplicably trembly and quivery. Within all the not, she felt the unsettled heat of wanting to. She might spontaneously combust. Or turn into molten lava. If she melted into the flowers, she'd make a long puddle. But eventually she'd cool and turn to stone.

Here and now, she breathed in the heat and the buzz and hum of them, together.

TWENTY-THREE

Saturday morning, Mom met her at the foot of the stairs, blocking the way.

"I spoke with the NDT coach yesterday."

"Why didn't you tell me?" Ria sat on the stair, hoping Mom would sit beside her. When she didn't, Ria scooted up a stair so their eyes would be even.

"I'm telling you now. Benny suggested I call, and it's a good thing I did. They have a training trip in Florida next month. Not everyone is invited to travel, but to be considered you need to join their team. Officially."

"Officially."

"Right. You signed the commitment letter, but we need to move forward with plans."

"Officially." It was such a serious word, but it sounded so silly, too. Oh-fish-ally, oh-fish-silly, ohohoh. Officially seriously silly.

"Why are you hesitating, Ria?"

"Officially?"

"I know it must be scary to think of working with new coaches. Especially after that run-in with the terrible coach in LA."

"She didn't do anything wrong."

"She never should have yelled at you." Mom grabbed Ria's hand and squeezed. "You have to remember that Benny will be there. He'll make sure everything goes right."

"Officially."

"Why do you keep saying that?" Mom was getting annoyed. "I wish you'd talk to me. You always make me guess what's wrong. I can't help if I don't know what's bothering you."

"You," said Ria. "Officially, it's you bothering me. Right now, right here."

"Ria!"

Apparently, but probably unofficially, that was the end of Mom's point. At least she moved out of the way when Ria stood, so she could finally make it downstairs.

Needing to escape, she ran all the way to Cotton's house. She was so intent on getting there she forgot to hate running on the way. She arrived, sweaty and mussed.

"Come in," he greeted her. "Leo's here. You're here. We can go now."

"And you, Cotton."

He turned his head and looked at her from the side.

"You're here, too."

"Of course I'm here." He broke into his brilliant grin.

Leo didn't look nearly as giddy and happy as Cotton. He wasn't clearly rude to Ria. Not mean, but not nice, either. She wasn't sure his obvious annoyance was personally directed at her, or if that was simply his mood.

Flutie followed them out to the shed, stood with her socks in the damp grass. Her hair was as thick and unruly as Cotton's, but lighter and longer. "Can I go too?"

"No! That would not be satisfactory. You might get hurt."

"Oh, come on. I want to see the cave."

"I think it would be good," said Leo. "We can take care of her."

"No. Absolutely no. We can't take care of people. We're going into an unknown area."

"But you're letting Ria go," whined Flutie.

"Ria is tough," Cotton said, like it was a fact. "She's strong and brave. You are not. You can't come."

After Flutie headed toward the back door, Cotton beamed, like he had no idea he'd caused the scowl on his sister's face.

"I am very much looking forward to our exploration of the new chamber today."

"Maybe next time we could bring Flutie," said Leo.

"No. We're wasting time talking about it."

"I'm ready when you are," said Ria, hoping to clear the awkward air.

The boys each wore a rope wrapped crosswise over his chest. Leo wore a beanie under his helmet.

Inside the cave, the three of them stayed close to silent. All their energy went into moving forward. No pausing for breaks or taking time to marvel. They wanted to hurry back to the newly found chamber.

The slippery hill was drier this time, or maybe she was ready for it. Even now that she was starting to know this place, to recognize certain points of the dark trails, she was still in awe of the cave. Its size, both big and small. The way the damp rocks glistened in the light. The occasional crystal mixed in with the more common sandy browns and grays. Even the most ordinary pieces were part of this huge mystery.

"Let Ria lead. She's the best climber," Cotton said when they finally reached the spot that would lead them to the new section.

She kept her shoes on in case she wanted them when they traveled beyond the drop-off.

"I can do it," said Leo.

"This was her find. Let her take you up there."

"Go ahead, Leo. But watch the drop-off. I know you know, but it's a gnarly one." She laughed nervously. "There are more handholds along the left side."

Leo gestured for her to take the lead.

"I'll wait here," said Cotton. "Until you two get to the chamber. It's too crowded for all of us."

Ria knew Cotton was right, but wished it was him behind her as she crawled along, slowly, feeling for the drop-off. She was so relieved to find the spot she forgot to warn Leo she was stopping. She swung her feet over the rock shelf and sat on the edge. With a tremendous thud, Leo's helmet slammed into her back, scooting her forward.

"Damn!"

"What happened? Are you safe?" Cotton sounded worried, calling from below.

Ria laughed, half from nerves and half from sheer gratefulness to still be sitting on solid rock. If she'd been in crawling position, Leo would have hit a mouthful of ass and she might have slid face-first into the dark.

"You should have told me you stopped," Leo snapped.

"Do I need to go for help? Tell me you're safe." Cotton sounded frantic.

"We're safe," Ria yelled. She heard him moving along the trail. Then, quietly, she said to Leo, "Why don't you want me here?"

"It's fine."

"I'd be happy for Flutie to come. It's not my fault she's not here."

"That's not it." He sighed. "You're confusing Cotton. He doesn't know how to play games."

"What games? Monopoly? Twister? Twenty Questions?"

"You know what I mean. You have a boyfriend."

"We're friends, Leo. Cotton and me. I'm not going to confuse him." Only herself. And confusion was her standard mode of being.

A flash of light announced Cotton's arrival seconds before he crashed in, filling the tunnel with his excitement. "Isn't this incredible? Isn't this the best?"

"Yeah. It's awesome." Leo's voice had shifted to a surprisingly gentle tone.

"I heard a crash. But you're safe. Right?"

"Yep. I'm here, not there." She pointed over the edge.

Cotton grabbed her arm. "Don't. Lean."

"Look," said Ria. They were on a rock balcony. Even with the dark corners and tucked-away shadows, it was clear the space below was as big as the Aquaplex. There was plenty of room for an Olympic-size pool here. Except it looked more like a field. Rolling hills of rock spread out and around. The way her light hit the swirls of white crystals nestled in the darker rock made her think of sprinkles of snow. Breathing in the damp cool air, listening to the silence of Cotton and Leo being equally impressed hit the back of her throat. This dark and hidden place was so damn beautiful.

"Let's get the ropes set up."

As he attached an anchor ring to the wall, Cotton sounded like he was apologizing. "We hate to mess with the cave, but it's too risky to climb down without being secured."

Once the rope was through the ring and firmly knotted—they

each tested it—they fixed a metal bracket to help control the rope's release as they descended. It was a matter of moving the rope out, then in, then out. Simple, yet the kind of thing that could be tricky in unexpected ways.

Cotton went first. His long legs and reach would be an advantage when dropping. He attached the rope to a harness. It wrapped around his middle, then down and around each of his thighs. If there had been fabric instead of straps, Ria would have called it a diaper.

After getting himself adjusted and attached, he went, backward, to stand at the edge of the dark chasm. Ria joined him at the edge.

"Get back! You aren't latched in."

"Don't you want light?" She lay on her stomach and pointed her face—with the lamp of her helmet obediently shining where she directed it, a few feet to the side. That way he could see the shape of the rock wall but not have the bright in his eyes. "I can't fall from this position."

"Thank you. The light helps."

Keeping his feet braced against the rock, he inched down the wall while Ria and Leo waited at the top. His grunts and heavy breaths braided with the click and shudder sounds of the rope letting him down, deep, and then even deeper into the dark.

Once he hit the bottom of the shaft, he looked up, his face a wild pattern of shadows and lines in the weird light. "This is an enormous space."

Ria paced back and forth a foot from the edge, waiting for Cotton to send the rope and lever back up.

"You go next," said Leo. "So you don't get left at the top."

"Thanks." She meant it, passionately.

She had to adjust the harness to fit, trying to make sense of how the parts worked together. She was so much smaller than Cotton that she ended up with a long expanse of strap trailing down by her feet.

"Tuck the extra length around you," said Leo. "You don't want to get tangled in it."

The lever was harder to manipulate than she'd expected. It was an awkward motion and she felt her own weight working against her, making it hard to lift and release. Worse, it was a frustratingly slow way to drop. It wasn't the height. She was used to falling, but not in tiny increments. Not in a way that required so much thought and patience. As she reached what she estimated was about halfway, she figured out how to lock the release open—and down she went in a rush of speed and drop. She hit the ground hard, but instinctively bent her legs, saving her knees from the impact. Her hands burned with the hot sting of the rope, but she laughed with the heady feeling of success.

Then quickly, she undid herself from the harness, so Leo could have his turn. Finally, once Leo stood beside them, Ria turned to see where she was.

The dips and swells of the rock were more gradual than

they'd seemed from above. The smell of the place was heavier. Thick with something she recognized, but couldn't name.

"It's slippery."

Moving slowly, she slid her shoes across the slick rock, little by little.

One wall, to her right, was a mostly smooth surface. To her left, there was a collection of rocks. Not quite big enough to qualify as boulders, but close. She'd started to climb one when something flickered on the other side.

It was the reflection of her helmet lamp. There, nestled amid the rocks, was water. That's what she'd smelled. "There's a pool!"

They joined her at the edge, leaning over the rocks until three lights shone into the still, dark water.

"There must be a stream coming from that way." Leo pointed into the nothingness to the right. "Which means there's more cave."

"We might be able to use the stream as a guide," said Cotton. "Wherever there's water, the rock will be worn away. But this is definitely more pond than stream."

"Let's see how deep it is." Leo held up a rock the size of his fist. He dropped it. The rock immediately disappeared.

"Did that tell you anything?" She laughed.

"It's deep," said Cotton.

"How very scientific." Ria ran her fingers through the water. "It's also cold."

"That's to be expected."

She shone her light in, but it didn't go far before it turned too fuzzy to be more than a soft glow. "I'm going in. To check the depth. So you can make the map more accurate."

"You'll be cold if you're wet. We're a long way from sunshine."

Leo was right. She was plenty warm from all the effort of climbing, but the air was cool and the water was downright frigid. But, she couldn't be beside a pool and not go in. Even if they determined the depth of it, numbers wouldn't mean much to her. She had to feel it.

"I'll keep my clothes dry."

It made sense to strip. She didn't want the extra weight of her clothes in the water, or to be wet afterward, climbing back up the rope.

She removed her shoes and sat on the rock to peel off her socks. Beneath her feet, it felt cool and slick. As she started to pull down her leggings, Cotton shoved Leo. "Turn around."

They both did. Her sports bra and spandex underthings wouldn't be as revealing as a bikini, but Cotton and Leo didn't live at the pool. Their lights shone against the shiny walls and they became two mismatched silhouettes to her. Ria left her clothes in a pile. The cool cave air felt good against her skin. She felt instantly more vulnerable as she took her helmet off and carefully set it on the edge. It would still light up the space, even as she went down below. Fear, quick and surprising, skittered across her skin.

"I don't know," Cotton said, his back to her. "Are you sure this is a good idea?"

She couldn't be sure, but it felt important to try. She slid over the curve of rock and let herself drop into darkness.

Cotton and Leo met her at the edge as she surfaced. She gasped, bobbing up and down, holding the side while she tried to catch her breath.

"Damn. So. Cold."

"Let me help you out."

"Not yet. I want to see how deep it goes." She was already feeling better. Not quite so shocked and pained. Or maybe she was numb enough not to care. She pressed her toes against the rock. "I'm going down."

"Go slow. The ground might be closer than you think."

It was strange to sink into darkness. Her skin felt cold and tingling. The weight of the water pressed against her, held her tight. She drifted down, her legs loose and ready to hit the bottom. Until she didn't. She buoyed up again, rising above the water's surface to breathe. "It feels really deep," she said, her voice full of air and shivers. "Shine your lights into the water."

Using the wall for leverage, she sank deep enough to feel it in her ears, but her feet dangled free and loose, hitting nothing. Looking up, she could see two circles of light shining down on her, the water holding the beams in tight orbs. She reached out, swam her way back to the surface.

Again and again she tried, all along the wall, to reach the

bottom. She even climbed out, then jumped in to gain more momentum. Each time, she sank into nothingness. There was no bottom.

When she finally climbed out, ready to call it quits, a great wild shivering hit her, hard. Her shoulders shook, her teeth chattered. Her hands felt stiff and close to useless as she tried to pull her T-shirt over her head and down over her wet body. She missed her shammy desperately.

From a couple of feet away, Leo said, "I see where the stream enters. I think it must be behind this rock face. We need to keep going."

"N-n-n-not today," Ria said, her teeth colliding between each word.

"No. We need more time. And more supplies. Food. Matches. A scale." Cotton's robotic list was laced with enthusiasm.

Her clothes clung to her wet skin, deep, racking shivers making it hard to think.

"You're too cold," said Cotton, sitting across from her.

"My feet are the worst."

She sat to put her shoes on, but her hands shook wildly, like her nerve endings had become disconnected.

"Skin-to-skin contact works best for warming up," said Leo.

She had no idea what he meant, but then, without a word, Cotton took her feet in his hands. Rubbed them thoroughly. A sound, way too close to a moan, slipped out between her lips. It was clear it had started somewhere in her middle. She couldn't tell if she was still shivering or not. Her body was doing its own thing.

At first, the heat from his hands was more thought than feeling. It was as if she was watching someone else's feet being massaged. Then she felt the rhythm of his fingers in time with his breathing. The inner vibration of him. It almost tickled. All of a sudden, the numb broke and she felt pain, like needles, but quickly they melted into a warmth that felt like something to crawl into. Except this was Cotton. It made no sense that he didn't like being touched, not when he had the power to melt her feet this way.

"Do you think you can move yet?" asked Leo. "We've been here a long time."

"I'm good. Let's go." She sat up, pulled her feet back and stuffed them into her socks and shoes.

At the rope, they all looked up the wall. It was much steeper-looking from below.

"Go ahead, Cotton," said Leo. "We'll catch you if you fall. But try not to."

"I'm counting on the rope to catch me."

Ria knew Cotton was nervous. Maybe even self-conscious to have them watch him adjust himself into the harness. But once he got started, he was fine.

"Why couldn't I climb the rope in gym class?" he asked once he reached the top. "I must have gotten stronger. Our practices have paid off, Ria."

"It's also the rock. You do realize the rock makes it easier than a dangling rope?" She felt like she must have missed something.

Cotton was quiet a minute, then burst out laughing. "I was so excited for a second."

"It's still impressive."

Damp and cold, she felt anxious waiting for her turn. Agitated and impatient. She counted the seconds it took for Cotton to send the rope and harness down for her, the ridiculous slow of her fingers fumbling until Leo finally helped her get it right. She was eating up more of their time. No wonder Leo didn't want her tagging along.

Her rush to climb made her clumsy. It didn't help to have numb fingers and clompy feet. At one point she slipped off the rock and fell backward, sliding at least three feet down before the rope snapped tight, stopping her from falling, but banging her knee against the rock. Damn, that hurt.

Somehow, in a fog of motion, they were back to the main tunnel. The tight fit didn't bother her this time. She was too busy concentrating on making her hands and knees move forward. Every inch of her felt too heavy. So slow. She was such a wuss.

As they stepped into the late-afternoon sunshine, she was hit with a wave of dizzy. Something about the angle of the sun through the branches and the smell of the woods and the way she'd been tense and tight for the last couple of hours made her waver. The world was out of focus. She blinked, realized she must've lost her contacts when she'd been opening her eyes in the cave pool. Her legs turned limp and rubbery, like her vision. Instinctively, she squatted. She put her head lower than her knees and concentrated on breathing.

"Could you be hungry? That was a lot of work swimming."

Cotton was right. She felt dumb not to think of it. But the way her head ached, she wasn't thinking much of anything. All she felt was relief that he was here. Of course he'd never leave her behind. She murmured, "If wishes were fishes and fishes could sing . . ."

"Then we'd all be musicians with a line and a string."

"You finished it, Cotton. I couldn't remember it, but you did."

"We sang it in Ms. Q's room."

"Give her a ride," said Leo.

It took a minute, but then Cotton said, "Yes. Climb on my back." He squatted in the dirt.

"Like a piggyback?"

"Piggyback." He laughed. "Piggy. Back. Piggyback."

"Oink, oink," she said.

Even Leo laughed. "Oh boy. We need to get home."

TWENTY-FOUR

At Cotton's house, she slipped off his back, murmuring, "You have such a different view of the world."

Her stomach and chest, the part of her she'd had pressed against him, felt suddenly cool. His shirt had a damp imprint of her. He turned around and stood beside her, watching. Positioned like he was ready to catch her.

"Sorry about that." Standing in his backyard, with the sun low in the sky, she felt better. Not enough to be embarrassed she'd let him carry her, but at least her head felt reconnected to the rest of her. She took a step and felt a rush of woozy behind her blurry eyes.

"Get her food. I'll clean the gear."

They left Leo with the hose while Cotton led her through the garage, stopping to wash their hands and faces in the large metal sink. The swirls of mud circled around the drain, little bits and pieces of dirt swimming and floating and sinking toward the grate. The smallest bits looked bright and shiny, close to brilliant against the silvery basin.

"Here's a towel." Cotton broke her gaze.

Stepping into his house set off every one of her senses. First there was the smell—sweet and yeasty, like baking bread, mixed in with something clean and lemony. She heard voices from somewhere, maybe upstairs, and the light from the corner made the room cozy. It was so much warmer inside. It felt like the air was pressing on her, hugging her from all around.

Cotton yelled down the hallway, "I'm home!" then turned to her and said, "Sit."

She settled on a stool at the counter overlooking the kitchen. She wasn't sure of the time, but couldn't bring herself to care, either. Feeling slow and dozy, she traced the lines of minerals within the granite countertop. It reminded her of the cave, but this surface was smooth and even beneath her fingertips. The television, from down the hall in the family room, sent out bursts of laughter—both canned and live. A talk show blared from a radio on the counter, but Cotton clicked it off. "My house is always loud."

"Will your parents mind that I'm here?"

"No." He cracked eggs into a bowl. "Do you need to call yours?"

"No."

She knew the idea of her parents not knowing where she was would be incomprehensible to him. But they were so used to her being gone for diving workouts, they still didn't think to ask where she spent her time. They worried more when she was home.

Something was sizzling in Cotton's pan by the time Leo came in with clean clothes and wet hair. Flutie followed, asking about the trip.

Ria looked down and realized she was still in her cave clothes. Her damp underthings felt clammy against her skin. Coveralls made for a more streamlined cleanup. Cotton looked rumpled in the T-shirt and shorts he'd had on underneath, but at least they weren't smeared with mud.

Standing at the counter beside her, Leo pulled out a notebook. Flutie joined Cotton in the kitchen, monitoring the ins and outs of the toaster. All the cooking food smells were dizzyingly scrumptious.

"I gotta say, that was incredible. We're going to need a lot more time to keep going. We could spend hours in that room alone." He turned and looked at her. "I have some ideas as to how we can measure the water's depth. If you're willing to go back in."

"Absolutely," Ria said as Flutie chimed in with, "I'd try it."

"No," said Cotton.

The omelet tasted even better than it smelled. "What's in here?" Her mouth was too full to be polite. "It's incredible."

"A little cheese and garlic and mushrooms." Cotton handed her a steaming mug of hot chocolate. "When was the last time you ate?"

She was too busy chewing to answer, but she wasn't sure, either. It wasn't that she'd been deliberately not eating, but without structure to her day, without a schedule and necessity, it was one of those things that she sometimes forgot to do. She'd been trained to disregard physical discomfort. Hunger was barely noticeable. Especially since her meds dulled that feeling anyway. Benny had put her on a strict timeline for eating. He'd paced her calories and proteins and carbs throughout the day.

She'd finished her second piece of toast by the time Cotton and Leo started eating their own plates of delicious goodness. Flutie was sipping hot cocoa too. Eating didn't slow the conversation.

"It might be a new discovery," said Leo.

Cotton shook his head and swallowed. "I can't believe that. It's such a huge chamber. And the pond. Think about the pond. How could no one have found the pond before?"

"Pond," said Ria. But didn't have a point. She just liked the way the word sounded. As different from "pool" as the two things were.

"Well, then, they're keeping it secret. Unless it connects with one of the others, no one has been here before. There's no word of it on the forums."

"We need to keep going and see if it connects," she said.

They both looked at her, their stares intense and unwavering. She wasn't sure if it was because they'd forgotten she was there or if they truly couldn't understand her point. It seemed so obvious. If there was a chance it went on and met up with another cave, they should know it. "When can we go back?"

"We'll need more than a few hours. We lose all our time getting to where we've already been."

"If we bring more supplies, we can stay longer."

"Why haven't you done that before?"

The two boys looked at each other, clearly not wanting to answer.

"Fatigue," Leo said finally.

"And the bathroom!" yelled Flutie. "That's the real reason."

"Ooooh," said Ria. "What does that look like?"

"A box," said Cotton.

There was an awkward silence seeing as there wasn't a lot more to say about that.

"Well, if we have to put up with a box, we should go ahead and stay overnight," said Ria. "It would give us more time to explore."

"What do you think, Leo?"

"That's what the extreme cavers do." Leo pushed his empty plate away.

Ria felt a rush of pride, then asked, "Will your parents let you, Cotton?"

"I don't know. We'd need to figure out the details. I'm not going to ask until I know what I'm asking."

"Do you have to tell them?" Sometimes these smart, geeky boys missed the obvious. "Wouldn't it be enough to tell them you're camping, and when we'll be back? Do they need to know the exact details? We could leave the specifics with someone. Like Flutie."

"I'm coming too," said Flutie.

Cotton glared at her, but Leo said, "Cotton, remember, flexibility." He went on, without missing a beat, "This could be sketchy. We need a backup plan if something goes wrong."

"There are three of us," Ria said. Looking at Flutie, she changed it to "Or four. We can't all get into trouble at the same time. As long as one of us can go get help, we're good."

"That's a scary point of view," said Leo. "We need to make a more foolproof plan."

Ria turned back to her sweet, warm drink. She knew those kinds of plans didn't exist.

TWENTY-FIVE

After Leo left, Ria stood in the front doorway. She rocked back and forth, from left to right. Inside, outside. Here, there. She didn't have a reason to stay, exactly, but she didn't have a reason to leave, either.

Mrs. Talley poked her head around the corner. "Cotton, remember you need to get a haircut today. Your father will take you when you're ready. Not to rush you out, Ria."

There was her reason. "I should go," she said.

Cotton wouldn't meet her eyes. His forehead creased and wrinkled. His fingers rhythmically tapped his thigh. He looked worried and bothered. So unlike Caving Cotton.

"Is something wrong? You don't want to get a haircut? Do you like it better long?"

"I want it to be shorter. But I don't like getting it cut."

Knowing how particular he was about things, she wasn't especially surprised, even if she wouldn't have guessed it was a problem. "What don't you like about it?"

"It always grows back. It seems like a waste of money. Plus, they play annoying music."

She bit back a laugh just as Bo came running down the hallway, making a great sliding entrance in socks. He stopped in front of Ria, staring, until she stuck out her tongue. He laughed and held out his tablet. "Is this you? Flutie says it is."

She immediately recognized the intro to the video clip. Bo—or, apparently, Flutie—had found the link to her old recruiting film. "You tell me."

"I think it is. Want to see, Cotton?"

"Yes."

Heads together, Cotton and Bo stared at the device. A million dives completed, months and years of practice boiled down to seven minutes.

She crossed her arms and squinted as she watched Cotton watch her dive. Eyebrows raised, then pinched together. Mouth open. Surprised. Puzzled. Awe. His face was a roller coaster. And beside him, Bo hooted and hollered. At the end, they each looked at her with eyes wide. "That was awesome!" Bo took off running, calling out to Jelly to watch too.

"Hey, Cotton. What if I cut your hair? I won't charge anything and I won't play music."

"How are your skills?"

"Somewhere between professional salon and paper doll cutting." Then, in answer to the worried look on his face, she added,

"I'm good. I have very reliable skills."

"You have actual experience cutting hair?"

"Yes."

He stared at her, waiting.

"You want names and references? I've been cutting Maggie's hair for years. It gets fried in the pool, so she'd be spending a fortune if she went in every time she needed her split ends tamed. And, there was this one time when the boys on my team lost a competition against us girls, and we shaved their heads as the prize." She grinned. "I won't shave your head unless you want me to."

He shook his head with tiny staccato jerks.

"Got it. No baldness. I promise." She smiled and said softly, "You can trust me. I wouldn't offer if I didn't think I could do a good job."

He didn't answer at first, but then he said, "Yes. You can cut my hair."

She clapped her hands together. "I got the job! Oh, but should you ask your mother?"

"No. It's my hair. Like I said, it always grows back."

After he'd retrieved the things she'd requested: scissors, a razor—with promises for restraint, no baldness—and a towel, they went into the garage, which seemed to be Cotton's personal haven. Ria pulled out the chair from the desk. She moved purposefully. She didn't want him to think she wasn't completely sure.

He sat in the chair and she stood behind him, looking at the mess of curls headed in every direction. "How short do you want it?" she asked. "Do you have a photo you like?"

He shook his head. He had a bored look on his face, unless it was closer to resigned.

"Let me see your phone." She took it from him, scanned through his photos, but they were all of places and objects, not people. No selfies. She checked Leo's social media, scrolling through his pictures, looking for ones of the two of them.

"He has many pictures of Flutie," said Cotton.

"You know they like each other, right?"

"Obviously they like . . ." He paused. "Oh. They do?"

She let him file this information into his brain. She held out a photo with Cotton in the background behind a grinning Flutie. He was slightly out of focus, but his hair was shorter. "How about like that? Do you want your hair that length?"

When he agreed, she smiled. "I think we should have a boundary word. Like we used to have with . . ."

"Ms. Q."

"Exactly. If I do something you don't like, or you need me to hit pause, you can say the word and we'll stop. That way you won't get annoyed. And I won't worry you're mad."

"'Squid.'"

"Squid?"

"It has to be something we can remember, and something we wouldn't accidentally say." He shrugged. "I'm not interested in talking about squid."

"Me neither. All right. 'Squid' it is." She made a face. "That's a word that sounds like what it is. Now you should cover your shirt. To keep things clean."

He wrapped a towel around his shoulders.

"Nice cape. What's your superhero name?"

He grinned. She saw a flash of the Cotton who used to let her copy his papers. "I always liked Green Lantern. But he doesn't wear a cape. Most superheroes don't."

"Really? I thought that was a requirement. But I guess a cape could get in the way." She held a lock of hair between her fingers on one hand and cut with the other. The sound of the scissors was metallic and harsh. She paused, waiting to see if Cotton seemed bothered.

"A cape is mostly aesthetic," he said. "But it's also useful at times. For hiding or providing warmth. It can be a kind of tool."

She let him talk about the various superhero characters, classifying them by costume, then by origin of power, strengths, weaknesses, geography, and sidekicks. She murmured agreement, soothing little sounds of listening, while she concentrated on her job. His hair felt smooth and silky between her fingers. Now that it was damp, the smell of his shampoo was stronger. It mixed with the smell of his skin, along with the warm and musty smell of the garage, and the clash of mud-smell from her own clothes. She stepped away, took off the offending sweatshirt, then moved back, wearing only a T-shirt. She wasn't cold anymore.

The trick to cutting his hair was to focus on each individual section, not his entire head. There was too much hair, too many different directions the curls wanted to go. She had to tame each lock before moving on to the next one. Clip by clip, snip by snip, one bit by one bit.

Once she'd made her way around his head, she stood in front of him, studying her work. He looked younger without all the extra hair. Or maybe it was older, now that she noticed the strong line of his chin, dusky with stubble.

"It looks good." She meant it. "But I need to clean up the edges. Can I use the razor?"

"Yes."

She used her fingers to lather soap along the nape of his neck. She pressed the blade firmly against his skin, so as not to tickle, but gentle enough not to nick, either.

"Squid," said Cotton.

She froze, with the razor in her hand. She'd only made two runs along his neck.

"Did you ever shave Sean?"

"No."

"You can keep going now."

But the sound of her boyfriend's name in Cotton's mouth made her falter. "Squid," she whispered.

She stepped away from him, needing to clear her head. She wiped a few suds against the hem of her shirt. Then she took a deep breath. There was still another side of Cotton's neck in need of her attention.

"I guess we should have a 'go-for-it' word too. So we know we can start again."

"'Humdiddle,'" said Cotton.

She laughed, feeling a warm relaxation seep into her middle. "That's from the fishes wishes song! All right then, 'humdiddle.'"

She ran the razor down his neck again.

"I'm sorry," he said. "About Sean."

"You don't have to apologize. You can ask me anything, Cotton. If I don't want to answer, I'll call squid."

"I meant for him. I'm sorry for Sean. This is very pleasant."

She ducked behind his head where he couldn't see her ridiculous smile. He had such a way of surprising her, in the best, most wonderfully odd kind of ways.

"Don't be sorry. I'm not."

"I take it back."

"Good. You can have it."

"Thank you," said Cotton.

"You're welcome."

And then she laughed because they spoke the same language, even if it didn't make any sense.

Humdiddle.

TWENTY-SIX

Ria lay on the trampoline, reacclimating to having her contacts in again. She stared up at the sky, watching the clouds and waiting for Sean. They had a dinner date—he was taking her somewhere "special"—but she was still full from Cotton's delicious omelet. Maybe if she concentrated, she could will her stomach into digesting faster.

That underground pond was so mysterious. The cold dark of it. With no bottom, no way to know where it ended. That had been risky, going in. But worth it. Definitely. Fear had been right to make an appearance, but she was glad not to have let it hold her back. And cutting Cotton's hair had been so . . .

Sean.

She needed to think about Sean.

She held herself as still as she could, keeping her muscles taut and tense. Trying not to move the trampoline one tremor's worth. She tempered her breathing to slow, working toward totally immobile. Every bit of movement, no matter how small, sent a shiver across the tight bed. It was a silly game the team used to play at the dry gym. Someone always started laughing, setting off all kinds of vibrations that always led to more. Now she remembered, the trick wasn't holding herself tense, it was the not-holding. Complete and utter relaxation was key.

She let loose, trying to be noodled. The cave set her mind racing too much to be still. She needed to focus on something solid and steady. Like Cotton. Only he didn't calm her either. She laughed to herself thinking of his superhero talk and squid.

"What are you doing?" Sean's voice broke into her daydream.

She sat up, blinking and reacquainting herself with here and now. She could feel her hair, loaded with static electricity, sticking straight out.

Sean wore pressed khaki slacks, the crease down the middle of his leg looked sharp and straight. It was obvious his crisp white shirt was brand-new. It fit him snug in the shoulders, and the short sleeves wrapped around his biceps, showing off his swimmer's tan.

"Do I need to change?" She slipped off the trampoline and landed next to him, trying to convince her hair to lie flat.

"I thought you might wear a dress. But you don't have to." Something in his voice sounded off.

Ria thought a minute. Not so much about the dress, but the way he looked stiff and nervous. She smiled and tucked her arm in his. "You can be the pretty one tonight."

At his mother's car, Sean opened the door. He reached in and grabbed a bouquet of pink roses. "These are for you, my lady."

She hesitated, then played along. "Thank you, sir."

Inside the car, the smell of his cologne, musky and deep, filled the air. She buried her nose in the roses, but the smell of his after-shave was stronger. He had a tiny spot of blood on his cheek, from shaving. If she told him, he'd be embarrassed. Maybe if she ignored it, it would fade away.

The restaurant, La Roche, was a small white house perched beside the dam, overlooking the river. The sound of rushing water was almost deafening, and yet had no specific sound. It was like an overwhelming wall of white noise.

"Let's go look."

"After dinner. We're going to be late for our reservation."

He put his arm around her as they walked up the cobbled stone path to the front porch. A green sign on the lawn said *Gastronomie* in fancy curlicue letters. "What does that mean? It sounds like a stomach bug. Or a snail. Isn't that a kind of snail?"

"It's French, Ria. Shh."

"Shh?"

Sean was too busy opening the door with a flourish and bow to explain. She had the distinct feeling he had practiced this move at home. Probably in front of a mirror. Several times.

Inside, an overwhelming smell of lavender and garlic hit Ria in the face.

"Whoa. Looks like they're expecting a fairy-princess invasion."

The entire restaurant was decked out in fluff and lace. Little white lights that hung from the ceiling blinked gently amid pink and white ribbons. The hostess led them through the main room and around the corner into an alcove. Here there were four small tables, two taken by couples, each one covered in a white linen tablecloth with a doily topping that made her think of homemade valentines. China bowls filled with white roses sat in the center.

She'd never liked the unforgiving color white.

"Let me help you," Sean said, standing between her and the chair.

"Help me what?"

"Sit."

"I'm trying."

Finally, in her seat, Ria breathed deeply, trying to reset her attitude. To see this place the way Sean meant it.

"Are you okay?" he asked. "What's wrong?"

"Nothing." She smiled at the waitress watching them from across the room. She leaned closer to his ear and whispered, "It's so white. And breakable."

"We'll be careful."

Ria studied the ornate menu. She couldn't decipher the flowery cursive. "Do you think they have a kids' menu?" she whispered.

"We're getting the special."

She closed the menu. Immediately the waitress was there to take their order, with lots of nods and murmurs of approval.

As she left them alone again, Ria folded her hands in her

lap. She didn't trust them not to suddenly throw something. It was the old impulse to immediately do whatever she wasn't supposed to do. The one that had always led to her being seated at the front of the classroom.

"Isn't this romantic?" asked Sean.

It was a very nice restaurant. She knew that, and yet she wanted nothing more than to run outside and scream at the top of her lungs. Even at dive meets, while waiting for her turn, the needing to be quiet would get to her, make her twitchy and restless. That's when Benny would give her jobs to do. He'd have her bring snacks to refs, make her coach one of the younger kids, or she'd take pictures and videos. Any kind of job to keep her body busy.

She needed a job right now.

"I wanted to bring you somewhere special to celebrate."

Her mind raced. It wasn't her birthday. Or his, she was almost sure. Maybe it was their anniversary of something. She hoped he wouldn't quiz her.

"Congratulations on getting picked for the NDT!" His smile was way too full of straight teeth, white and bright. "I mean, of course I'll miss you, but this is perfect! Like your dives!"

Perfect was clearly a matter of perspective, and they had different views.

"Thanks," she said carefully.

"You should have told me. Benny said you don't like to brag."

"Benny?"

"Yeah. He suggested this place." He ducked his head, grinning sheepishly. "He's even helping to pay for our meal."

"Maggie," she said, but Sean knew it was a question. He nodded. So Maggie knew about the NDT now, and Ria hadn't told her. "What—" But her unclear, roaming question was cut off by the arrival of their food.

She was relieved to see the small portion on her plate. The sauce was delicious. At first. But then, suddenly, mid-bite, it tasted too rich and creamy. Suffocating.

"I need to use the restroom." As she got up, she bumped the table. Water spilled on the tablecloth. "Oops." She pulled her plate over the damp spot.

She ducked behind a partition painted with tiny pink flowers. The bathroom was barely big enough to turn around in. She could sit on the toilet and wash her hands at the same time if she wanted. She wet a paper towel and held it to the back of her neck. She had to power through, like any other workout. Only this time it was the inside of her stomach that was being forced to perform.

She returned to Sean, wearing her most convincing smile. But when she saw the food on her plate again, she couldn't pretend.

"What's wrong with you? Why aren't you eating?"

"Can we go? Please?"

He stared into her eyes, his expression hard to read. She wasn't sure what she was trying to say either, except that she needed to escape.

She was so relieved to leave the crowded fluff of a place that they were already in the car and down the road before she remembered that she hadn't looked over the dam. Disappointment made her eyes sting, but the look on Sean's face kept her from complaining. She would not obsess about the damn dam. Her stomach ached, but it had nothing to do with the food.

"I'm sorry you didn't like the restaurant."

She stared at her reflection in the glass window. She looked muted and fuzzy. She leaned in, pressed her forehead against the cool, smooth surface and counted to ten.

"It's not your fault."

He hadn't picked the place. He'd been following Benny's orders.

He smiled, grabbed her hand, and squeezed. Ria leaned back against the seat. She closed her eyes, enjoying the heat of him, the way he rubbed his thumb against her wrist.

When he stopped the car, she sat up and tried to see out the dark windows. He'd brought her to a playground. The swings and slides looked like giant insects in the shadows.

"Ria."

He gazed into her eyes and smiled. He licked his lips. Those lips she'd kissed so many times before. She could, so easily, move to him. Forget talking. She could press herself against him. Let his hands roam over her. And hers would wander too. She could lose herself in that.

If only her head wasn't attached.

He reached behind her seat, opened a cooler, and pulled out a bottle of wine.

"I know your news calls for champagne, but I couldn't get anyone to buy it. This is my mother's favorite white wine. It's sweet and we can pretend it has bubbles."

"Did you ask Benny?"

"Ask him what?" Sean pulled out a corkscrew, sharp and twisting.

She played with the bouquet, regretted not putting the poor roses in a vase at home.

"Did you ask him to get champagne? Was that part of his plan for tonight?"

"Of course not." He stopped messing with the bottle. "He'd probably kill me. Is this a bad idea?"

"Now you're asking me?"

"What the hell is going on, Ria? You apparently got really good news, but you didn't tell me. Or even Maggie. So, whatever. But at least I thought you'd finally be happy."

"You should have told me that you knew about the NDT."

"You're the one who didn't tell me."

"It was *my* news."

"And I'm your boyfriend. I should know your news. It sounds like the NDT is a fantastic opportunity. You should be telling everyone."

But everyone had it wrong.

"You should have asked me what I wanted to do tonight.

Wine? Why would I want wine?"

"I wanted this to be special."

"I want to go home."

Instead of answering, he started the car. Drove silently away from the playground. She studied him, blond and gorgeous, a perfect gentleman. The tendons in his jaw pulsed and his knuckles looked white against the wheel, but still he did what she asked.

She cradled the bouquet in her arms, breathing the flowers in, knowing their smell wouldn't last.

Once he'd parked in her driveway, she turned to him and asked, "Why me? Why'd you ask me out?"

He didn't say anything. The quiet lasted long enough for her to wonder if he knew the answer.

"You're special." He reached out and played with a lock of her hair. "You never hesitate, never back down, no matter what Benny says or does. You make it look easy. That's why you're going to be famous someday." He was smiling now, caught up in being sweet.

"You wanted to date someone famous?"

"What? No. At first I was going to ask Maggie out. She would actually talk to me."

"So then what?"

"Well, Benny knew. I guess it was obvious when I kept following the two of you after practice every night. But he thought I liked you. He threatened me a little bit, about treating you right and all that kind of stuff, but then he said I should go for it. That you needed something besides diving to think about." Sean wrinkled his nose and went on, "Don't be mad. I'm glad how things worked out. I just never would have thought I could have a chance with you. So when Benny gave me permission, it felt right."

"He gave you permission."

"Well, yeah. And that was a good thing. I never would have stood a chance if he didn't want you dating."

He was right, of course. But so wrong, too.

"I hate cut flowers."

Even after the entire mess of a night, he looked stunned.

"They're dead," she continued. "But they don't even know it."

"What?"

"I don't drink wine. I hated that fluffy restaurant. You didn't let me look over the dam."

It had all been a mistake.

Benny's mistake. Months ago, he'd set Sean on the wrong road, and then he'd gotten it wrong again tonight.

"Don't take romance advice from a single man who only loves one thing." She opened her door, stepped out onto her driveway. "I want to break up."

"I know," said Sean. "I've always known."

TWENTY-SEVEN

Ria peeked in her parents' bedroom. Dad lifted his head from the pillow.

"I didn't mean to wake you."

"You didn't," he answered. "I can't sleep if you're not home."

"I'm home." She crawled into bed between them.

Mom rolled over and ran her fingers through Ria's hair. Murmured, "It's so soft."

"You missed a documentary on blood-borne parasites tonight," said Dad.

"Don't remind me," Mom groaned.

She felt too big for the space but couldn't make herself get up.

"What do you think happened to Esther Talley?"

"Oh, sweetie. What happened?"

"She'd be in high school now. Cotton still misses her. He thinks she's going to come home. He doesn't want to go to college because he wants to be here when she comes back."

"That was an awful thing, Ria. I didn't know it still bothered you." Mom sat up.

"I didn't either. But I think it should. We can't completely forget about her." Her voice was ragged and thick with tears she hadn't known were there. "Cotton would do anything to find her. He's always looking, wondering. He misses her all the time." The idea of carrying all that heavy missing forever pressed on her chest, making it hard to breathe. "Do you think she's alive?"

Mom wrapped an arm around Ria's waist.

"I hope so," said Dad.

"I don't. If she's alive, out there somewhere, it's too awful to think what she's doing. She can't be the same anymore. Not after all this time."

Dad rolled over to face her. "People can get through things. Our brains and our hearts, they help us. We have to hold out hope that she's all right. And maybe, by some miracle, she's going to show up again."

A nod was as much motion as she could muster. Her body had turned impossibly heavy.

"She has a family who loves her and misses her. That goes a long way," Dad continued.

She'd never minded being an only child, but now, seeing how her entire family fit on the bed . . . if anything ever happened to her . . . or either of them . . .

"Benny doesn't have anyone."

Neither of her parents answered. She could feel them waiting, biting back the questions and worry. It was true. He had no family, no girlfriend, not even a pet. They used to have him over for holidays, partly so he'd remember not to schedule practice. He had no one to say goodbye to.

"Ria, babe, I watched the video the other day. Of your fall in LA."

She groaned. They'd watched it so many times that day to see if the other coach had done anything even slightly wrong. There was nothing to see.

"You looked so scared. I didn't notice before." Mom's voice sounded thick and teary. Like maybe she could forgive Ria for getting it wrong.

"Do you remember how Benny got me pink boots for my tenth birthday? You said they were too expensive. . . ."

"And impractical! They had those ridiculous heels."

"Damn, I loved them. I wore them every day to practice."

"Yep. You clomped all the way from the car to the pool."

Tears streamed down her face. She had no idea what to do with all this mess. "We used to have so much fun. The whole team did. We worked hard, but we played games, too. Like Suicide Squad. And Romeo and Juliet. He even let us play hide-and-seek in the gym."

"The slumber party fund-raiser was the most exhausting night of my life," Dad said.

Ria laughed. "You did a backflip! You were the coolest dad."

"And I paid for it the next day."

"I miss my pink boots." Ria let out a loud, shuddering sigh. Wiped her eyes on the sheet, knowing she was smearing makeup on it. It wasn't the boots as much as the *her* who had worn them. She'd been so sure of herself back then, so confident. She missed not knowing that the thing she loved most could sour and stain.

She missed little Esther going out to play, too.

She was being ridiculous. Her missing was nothing compared to the hole in Cotton's family, and yet she couldn't seem to hold herself together. Everything that had always been her—Ria—was leaking out the hole that diving had left.

If Cotton had the chance to end his missing, he'd take it. Even if it meant facing something new and awful. He'd be brave and charge in.

"Sean and I broke up."

"I'm sorry. . . ." Mom stroked her hair.

"Don't. I'm fine. It was my idea."

"Was it because of . . . something with Esther? Did something happen?"

"No. I wasn't even thinking about her until I was lying here like I did when she first disappeared."

"What about Cotton?"

"I told you. He misses her all the time."

"I meant you and Sean," said Dad. "Did you break up because of Cotton?"

"I don't know." Of course they believed her. Her not-knowing was typical. Something understood.

TWENTY-EIGHT

Seeing as Sean had been Ria's first boyfriend, he was also her first breakup. She doubted he wanted to see her any more than she wanted to see him, but she was still grateful for her shortened class schedule. It would involve less deliberate avoidance time. The weirdest thing was how everyone seemed to be talking about what had happened.

She kept getting looks of sympathy. Or maybe some of those looks were more satisfaction. Delight. She hadn't known anyone would even care. She never expected to be the focus of this kind of conversation. Whether they had it right was more than she could figure out. She hadn't tracked Maggie down to translate.

Ria was used to being watched at meets. Judged. Envied and scorned in equal measure. She'd practiced the high-chin, shoulder-back, not-gonna-look-you-in-the-eye saunter. She knew how to look like she was calm, cool, and collected, no matter what was going on inside her mind. Most of her school days were filled with pretending anyway. It had always been a matter of going through the motions.

One of her special-ed teachers in middle school had a poster on her wall. A cartoon student sat in a desk, looking eager. Along his spine was the word *SLANT*. Otherwise known as the secret for success: Sit up. Lean forward. Act interested. Nod your head. Take notes. There was no need to "fake it till you make it." That may never happen. Just fake it.

Instead of taking the trail that evening, Ria ran through the neighborhood, following the rough asphalt and broken sidewalks, past the houses that all looked the same, or at least related. Her legs felt strong, her body in line with itself. All her muscles and tendons and bones and organs united, keeping her going. Even though she was straining, pushing, her breath rough and ragged, the sweat streaming along her skin, she wished she could go faster, still faster.

In the past, she never would have run along the streets to Maggie's house. Benny hated his divers exercising in public. He only wanted them getting attention for certain things—his right things. Winning first place, qualifying for bigger meets, being a standout diver in some way. He took pride in their hard work, but only in the gym or at the pool, not for everyone else to see. Maybe he wanted it to seem like their talent was some kind of magical experience. They needed to be the best, but no one should know how they got there.

She knocked on the front door, then paced back and forth

along the walkway, cooling down and catching her breath. Her face felt hot and swollen, but her arms and legs felt almost weightless. She'd crossed an endorphin line.

"Ria?" said Maggie, peeking through the screen door. "What are you doing here?"

When she'd been in motion, all the words she'd been keeping inside felt loose and ready to be released, but now, standing still, she wasn't sure where to start.

"Do you still have swings?"

"I'll meet you out back."

In the scruffy backyard, Ria headed straight to the crooked metal swing set. She stood on the black rubber seat with one foot, then squished her other foot in too. She held the rusty chains and pushed herself forward, then back, building momentum. The trick was to keep her body straight and tight. It was a good alternative exercise—she was surprised Benny hadn't thought of it. If he had, he would have brought swings into the gym.

Maggie took the swing next to her, sitting and swaying.

Still on her feet, Ria swung high enough that the drop made her queasy. Not in a bad way, simply in a reminder-of-gravity kind of way. She knew it wasn't physically feasible to do an actual 360 around the top bar, but she pushed anyway, trying to defy all the invisible forces keeping her within a safe border.

"School was awful. I don't know why everyone cares that Sean and I broke up."

"He was really upset." Maggie undid her bun, let her hair fall around her shoulders. She checked the ends, played with the frizzy parts.

"I know." Ria didn't expand. She'd never liked talking about her fails.

"He tried to do something nice for you and you . . . well, I guess it doesn't matter since you're leaving anyway."

"I didn't tell you about the NDT because . . ."

"Because you thought I'd be jealous. You didn't trust me to be happy for you."

Ria caught the ground with her foot, stopping her swing. "I might not go."

"Right. You might not take the exact opportunity you've always wanted. As if you'd actually say 'Gee, no thanks, I'd rather not follow my hopes and dreams.'"

There was no room to explain, not with the way Maggie was so certain.

"I'm thrilled for you, Ria. Honest. I know more than anyone how hard you've worked. I know what you've done to get this. I've been there even when you've forgotten about me." Maggie crossed her arms. "It was always all about you, the chosen one. We all knew you were the reason Benny showed up. We were all there for you. But I still can't believe you didn't tell me."

It was true that Maggie had been with her, more than anyone. They'd pushed each other, on and off the board. They'd massaged each other's cramps, cleaned scrapes, iced bruises. They'd coaxed and coddled and cheered. But still, even through all those hours shared, there had been things they didn't talk about. Some pains lay too deep to be uncovered, exposed to the sun.

"I didn't know Benny would come too. He can make calls for you. You can still get a scholarship. You'll see. You should call Coach Ling at Dayton Hill University."

"I want Uden."

"You could be in the big leagues, Mags. With your new dive, and more on the way."

"I don't want the big leagues. I want to win."

"Obviously. Why else compete?"

"I won't win if I'm at a school like Dayton Hill. I'll always be behind someone like you. If I'm at Uden, I have a chance."

She knew Maggie was right. But she also knew, for her, those wins would feel hollow. Being the best had to be real, not a convenient illusion. Moving up through the ranks, toward the Olympics, narrowed the field to only the top competitors.

"I kissed Sean." Maggie stood up.

The words didn't mean anything. Not at first. They were too unexpected. Out of context. Surreal. But then, they hit. "Sean? Like Sean . . . Sean?" She'd almost said *my Sean,* even though that obviously wasn't true.

Maggie's eyes looked full, ready to overflow. If Ria didn't know what to do with the *words,* the *tears* were completely inexplicable.

"It just happened. He was upset and wanted to talk. We were drinking . . ."

"The wine."

"And, well . . ." She scrunched up her face. "One thing led to another."

Ria could imagine it. Each and every detail. As if she'd been there. She knew them both, implicitly. Maggie, curvy and confident, and Sean with his roaming hands and shiny metallic hair. His skin the color of Maggie's freckles. A perfect match. Now that she could see them together, she couldn't look away.

"How many things?"

"What?"

"How many things were led to?"

"Just kissing. Maybe a little bit more than kissing. We were pretty buzzed."

Ria pushed off the ground, started swinging again.

"I'm sorry. We both are. You have every right to be pissed. We're going to make this up to you somehow."

"How?" she asked, genuinely curious. "What does that even mean?"

Maggie's lip trembled. The crease between her eyebrows deepened. She looked the way she did whenever she got sidelined at practice.

"It's okay, Mags. It doesn't matter."

Sometimes Ria said things she wasn't sure were right or true. And held back plenty more that she knew were true, but couldn't say the right way. She wasn't sure where these words fit. She didn't know if she believed herself.

TWENTY-NINE

Ria jumped on her trampoline. No flips, no twists. Just jumps. Hundreds into thousands of jumps. She was buzzing from her exchange with Maggie. Anger and hurt and confusion mixed into a toxic concoction flowing through her bloodstream.

The truth was she and Maggie didn't have anything to bind them together anymore. They weren't teammates. They had no future together. They never would have been friends in the first place if they hadn't spent all those hours together in the alternate universe ruled by Benny. All that lack of normal.

And now, Maggie and Sean. Together. Kissing. More than kissing.

She wondered who made the first move. Who crossed that line first? Not that it mattered. It was clear the result had been mutual.

And why did she care? Things had been off with Sean for a while now. If they'd ever been aligned in the first place. Benny had been the reason they got together and she hadn't even realized. She'd always thought Benny understood her. That the reason he never needed to ask her why, or how, was because he already knew what she was thinking. He hadn't been thinking of her at all. She didn't belong to herself. He'd given her away and Sean had played along even though he'd wanted Maggie. Everything was finally how it should have been.

But Maggie and Sean felt guilty. That's what left this sour taste in the back of her throat. *They* felt like what they'd done was wrong. It was a big deal to *them*. But they'd done it anyway.

And what was the deal with kissing? How did *that* get started? And when? Did cave people grunt and slurp and press their faces together? Not that she blamed them. When she was doing it, kissing made sense. It was only when she sat back and thought about it that she felt bewildered. Yet another way her body and her mind moved in different directions. She'd spent an entire math class evaluating each of the boys, imagining and wondering how they might kiss.

And then there was Cotton.

Except he was completely different.

Worse than hearing the news about Maggie and Sean was the way her parents were being horribly, awfully, unbearably nice to her. Mom made lasagna, an old, indulgent favorite. She even included garlic bread. All of it loaded with calories and fat. An overload of carbs. A victory meal. She brought it out to the trampoline and insisted that Ria stop jumping. That's where they ate, standing along the edge, as if it was an enormous flexible table.

She forced herself to eat a few bites, then rearranged the rest on her plate. It sat, heavy and weighty in her gut.

Dad tried his best to make witty conversation. He invited her to watch bad reality shows. Her parents both looked so sad, so worried. They were making her feel worse for herself.

"Maybe this is a good thing," Mom said. "You don't need the distraction of a boyfriend when you leave."

"If I leave."

"But now that you won't have him to miss, it will make your decision easier."

Could Mom actually think Sean was a reason not to go to the NDT? Mom had never even liked him much. Or maybe that's why she'd never liked him. Because he was a *distraction*.

After Mom took the dishes inside, Dad turned to her. "I know you're upset," he said. "But maybe it would make you feel better to move forward. This feels like a good time to finalize details with the NDT."

"But I'm still not ready."

"They aren't going to wait forever, Ria. This is a special opportunity. They want you, but it's not an open invitation. They need to know you're serious."

Later, in her bed, her thoughts and wonderings came too fast, too random, too changing to be useful or productive. Her whole body carried her confusion. She forced herself to do her breathing exercises, the ones Benny had taught her. Sometimes, if she focused on her body, on telling it what to do—lungs: take deep, slow breaths; fingers: stop tapping; legs: stop shaking, sweat glands: stop overreacting—she could slow the frantic urge to move. But tonight her body stayed on high alert. Fight-or-flight mode. The night stretched out in front of her, hours to kill and fill.

She finally texted Cotton around two. Nothing more than a hello, simply a check to see if he was sleeping. He answered immediately. Sometimes he was plagued with the same insomnia she faced every night.

She texted: **I can't sleep. I wish we could go caving.**

He didn't answer. Not right away. It was long enough that she assumed he'd drifted off to sleep. But then he answered: **Let's go.**

In the dark?

It's always dark in the cave.

She laughed to herself. Of course it was.

She waited on the trail, not far from her house. The night air was cool enough to see her breath. The sky was dark and heavy. She could see faint lines of thick, puffy clouds. Not even the stars shone through. She wore an extra layer of clothes beneath her mud-stained sweats, hoped it was enough. The zing of anticipation warmed her insides, but her fingers felt cold and her face stung in the windy air.

When Cotton's light appeared along the trail, bouncing toward her, she moved to meet him. "Thanks for coming."

"You're welcome," he said, not pausing in his steps.

Only the soft thumps of their feet on the dirt trail and the swoosh of his coveralls filled the quiet night. When an owl hooted, low and mournful, it raised Ria's heartbeat, made her feel a wave of anxiety and thrill.

The entrance of the cave smelled stronger in the night. Damper. More alive. But once they'd stepped inside, it felt the same. By the time they reached the narrow entrance tunnel, she was sweating. She hadn't needed the extra clothes—the cave was the same temperature at night as it was in the day. Time didn't matter here.

It felt good to maneuver her way around the rocks, to climb and crawl and feel her way along the slick walls. It took enough concentration that her mind settled. Her body felt strong and agile making its way through the dark.

They paused at the end of the tunnel, readjusting after the crawl and scoot. "I've never taken you to the right. Right?"

"Right."

"Right," Cotton echoed. "It's small and dead-ends. There wasn't much to map. But it's still interesting."

"Right on," said Ria. "Let's go."

It wasn't a long walk to the spot where he paused. "You go first. I want you to see it pure, without me in the way."

The space was small, but there was room to step inside and

turn around. The walls looked like thick ribbons. Or snakes. Twisted and folded into each other. And then, appearing in various spots, were holes. At least a hundred openings from floor to ceiling. Like storage cubbies, or mini shelves.

"It's a brain. I think the holes are pockets for memories."

"I knew it looked like something," said Cotton. "But I couldn't remember what."

"How much time do we have?"

"More than usual. I had to wake up my parents, so they didn't ask a lot of questions. I was vague about the specifics."

"Sneaky. I like it."

"The night is long," he said. "When you can't sleep."

Each of them chose a rock to settle on, leaving a few feet of dim light between them. The soft shifts of shadows and dark surrounded them.

"Sean and I broke up."

"Oh."

She waited, but that was all he had to say to the news that felt so big and momentous.

"You were right about Leo and Flutie. They're dating."

"What about you, Cotton? Have you dated anyone?"

"I don't know."

"You don't know?"

"Candace Bonner and I made out after several robotics competitions last spring. But we never went on a date."

"Oh."

It was weird to feel a twinge of jealousy. She felt embarrassed that she'd assumed he'd never been kissed. She thought his sensory issues would have interfered. But apparently making out was no big deal. And neither was her breakup with Sean.

"Are you sad?" he asked.

"About the breakup?" She paused, wanting to get this right. "Is sad the same as disappointed?"

"No. I used to have a feeling chart with different faces . . ."

She knew what he meant. Ms. Q had one in her resource room.

"Sad and disappointed are on the same line, but they're different. I think disappointed is still hoping, but sad has given up."

"That helps, Cotton. Then, I am sad. It's definitely over. He and Maggie kissed already. So, I also feel inadequate."

"Lacking."

"Lacking," she agreed.

"Inadequacy is an emotion derived from external relativity."

"Translate, please."

"It's a matter of perspective. It's based on comparison."

"Isn't everything?"

"No." Cotton leaned back, his helmet scraping against the rock wall. "And comparison to others is an inaccurate way to measure one's value."

Benny used to say something like that to the team. *The only person to beat is you*. He meant that everyone should only worry about their own scores, their own improvement each meet.

She'd never fully believed he meant it. Not for her. That was for someone who wasn't going to win.

"Squid," she said.

"Squid?"

Squid on Benny who always hijacked her brain.

"Squid on Sean," she said. "Squid on Candace Bonner, too. I don't want to talk about them anymore."

"Yes," said Cotton.

They sat together in the dark, breathing, being, existing. It was enough.

Finally, Ria stretched and stood up. "Let's go. I'm finally getting tired."

They made their way back along the path. Some of the rocks and formations looked familiar. She might have a chance of finding her way out on her own. She gestured toward the tunnel. "You go first."

Even though she'd gotten used to the feeling of the walls close and narrow all around her, she still preferred to follow him. To remember she would fit too.

They'd made it through the tunnel and almost reached the exit, when Cotton stopped. She bumped into him, knocking her helmet sideways so it slipped down over her ear.

"Listen."

A swish, or a swoosh, filled the air. It didn't sound like wind, but almost. It was the wind's cousin. The space filled with a flutter of fly. Ria leaned forward, felt a brush of something near her cheek. She gasped, grabbed Cotton's arm. All around her, the air grew thick with movement and rush. The flickering shadows made her stomach lurch.

"Bats," Cotton whispered. "They're coming home."

Knowing what it was helped. Even so, a primal urge to run pulsed deep within. She leaned against the solid warmth of his side, ready to tuck her face into him, but at the same time unable to stop watching the bats swoop in and around the rocks, ducking into their cranny of a home. She swallowed, blinking back inexplicable tears.

It might have been a minute. Or two. Or maybe it was closer to all night, but by the time the bats had settled and the dark was quiet once again, her fingers felt stiff and cramped from clutching Cotton's sleeve.

"Oh," she sighed.

"Yes."

"I've never . . ."

"Never," he agreed. "This feeling isn't on the chart."

THIRTY

The next day Ria pulled a map from the glove compartment of her car. Dad had insisted she keep one in case her phone died or the GPS ever malfunctioned. It was crisp and clean, never unfolded. She opened it carefully and spread it across her bed.

Their cave wasn't marked. There was an expanse of tan that signified undeveloped land, but its creator hadn't cared about what was beneath the surface. The actual look of it—the rocks and the plants, the ups and the downs, none of that was included. Not even the secret hole to slip inside. Which meant no other caves were included, either.

She loved that different maps showed different things. Cotton's map of the cave showed whatever they'd discovered. There was a power in being able to name and label what mattered while keeping other places secret and hidden.

A new palette shaded and framed the rolling images she saw when she closed her eyes. A map started forming in her head.

Not a mathematically scientific one. Not like this one, or the ones Cotton made. Her map was more color and shapes.

She'd set up paper and colored pencils on her desk when her phone rang.

"Ria?" Cotton said before she finished saying, "Hello."

She could hear his labored breathing. "What's wrong?"

She hated herself for dreading what he'd tell her. For a second, there'd been that lift in her middle, knowing he was calling. But now, if he told her something about Esther . . .

She had to know the answer, no matter how it made her heart hurt.

"Do you remember that award ceremony?"

"Yes. Did you figure out what your award is for?"

"The ceremony is tonight."

"Are you all dressed up? Did you have to write a speech?" She smiled and leaned against her desk chair.

"Can you give me a ride?" His voice sounded shaky and rough.

"Where are you?" She stood up so quickly her head felt light and floaty.

"I'm home."

She was missing a vital piece to the puzzle, but she'd find it later.

"I'll be right there." Her heart thrummed against her rib cage as she ran down the stairs, feeling a touch of dread, even if she wasn't sure why.

Fifteen minutes later, after a quick explanation to her parents, she pulled up in front of his house. Cotton, wearing dark slacks, a light blue button-down shirt, and a tie, stood at the end of his driveway. The slump of his shoulders made her middle ache.

He opened the door, leaned in, and said, "I don't want to go."

"Get in, Cotton."

The way he obeyed so easily let her know that was the right answer. She turned around in his driveway, then headed out to the main road.

"Is your ceremony at school?"

"It's at the Alexis Center. In Travis."

Ria raised her eyebrows. That was thirty minutes away.

"Never mind. I don't want to go."

"You have to."

"But I'm already late. It's too far for you to drive."

"I don't mind. Now I'll finally know what your award is for. But I don't understand. Where's your family?"

"At my award ceremony." His voice sounded crooked. Off-key.

"Without you?"

"Yes."

She'd gotten used to his limited answers, but right now she needed more. She didn't think there was time for discovering the exact right questions. "Did you tell them I'm bringing you?"

"They don't know I'm not there."

"How did that happen, Cotton? It's *your* award."

"My mom thinks I came with my dad. And he thinks I came

with her. I was feeling anxious. I couldn't decide which car to go in, so I kept changing back and forth. I went in the garage to think." He shrugged. "They left."

Not choosing was a way of choosing.

"You better text them. They're going to be worried when they realize you aren't there."

"It's too complicated for texting."

"Then call them. Put it on speakerphone and I'll explain."

He sighed but did as she'd asked.

"Hello, Cotton?" His father's voice came through the speaker while Cotton stared out the window, not answering.

"Hi, Mr. Talley. This is Ria Williams. Cotton is fine. He's here with me. We'll be at the ceremony soon."

"You will?" Maybe his father was used to Cotton's surprises because he said, "Um, okay. Right. We'll see you there."

Cotton had been right. They hadn't yet realized he wasn't there. Now they wouldn't have to.

"I don't care about the award. I would have done the work anyway. I don't need a certificate."

"I like winning," she said. "When I first started diving, having those medals hanging around my neck was the best feeling. I'd wear them all day. I loved the sound when they clanged against each other. I was so obnoxious."

"That's different," said Cotton.

"Exactly. Your award matters. My medals were stupid. How is diving going to make the world better?"

The Travis Center was enormous. White marble steps led to a front wall made of glass and steel. Beside her, Cotton walked slowly, his shiny black dress shoes clicking against the tile floor. Ria wished she'd thought to change her clothes. Her leggings and T-shirt seemed rude next to him. Except, he also looked wilted.

"When you go on stage to get your award, you need to stand up straight," she said. "Push your chest out and throw your shoulders back."

"Like this?"

"Yes. It makes you look confident." She smiled.

From across the enormous lobby, Mrs. Talley called out, "Cotton! There you are! You need to be sitting with the other winners." Then, barely pausing, she smiled at Ria. "I didn't know you were coming."

"Me neither."

"You should have told us you made other plans," his mother said, hustling them down the hallway.

"I didn't," said Cotton.

"I know you didn't. But you should have." Her voice was calm but firm. "Take your seat, Cotton. We'll find you afterward."

As he headed toward the front row, Mrs. Talley said, "Sit with us, Ria. We'll squish in."

Once they reached the row of Talleys, bodies shifted. Jelly moved to sit on her father's lap and Ria sat between Bo and Flutie. The lights dimmed as she leaned back in her seat.

It was clear this was a ceremony for the smartest teens in Virginia. Over and over again, names were called, accomplishments were explained and reveled in. Ria's hands stung from all the clapping. A thin, serious-looking boy had attended a world peace summit in France. One girl sold a novel to a major publisher. A group of teens created a daycare for homeless children. Other awards were for things she didn't know existed. Experiments with something rhyming with ooze. Articles on mono-something-or-others. She wondered how much actual at-the-desk-time was spent working on the math equation that took three months to complete—it's not like the girl skipped every other bit of life, was it? Ria could probably drag out any of her assignments that long too, but she wasn't going to be rewarded for it.

Finally, when Cotton's name was called, she willed him to throw his shoulders back. It must have worked because on the stage, he stood straight, towering over the man at the microphone.

"We are pleased to award the Rotary scholarship for achievement in the area of cartography to Connor Talley."

All around her, his family exploded into applause and cheers. Relief flowed through her that Cotton was here. She was grateful there wouldn't be a wave of sadness wrapped up in this moment.

After the ceremony, the families and guests milled around the lobby, sharing congratulations while eating cookies and drinking punch. Ria stood to the side as the Talleys surrounded Cotton. More people gathered to celebrate his brilliance.

She felt out of place now. She wasn't meant to be part of this moment.

He looked at her suddenly, from a few feet away. She smiled, gave him a double thumbs-up, then felt goofy. She held up her keys and pointed at the door. He started to head toward her, but his mother grabbed his arm, leading him toward a group of grown-ups.

The air was cool outside, the moon high above in the stunning sky. So beautiful in its enormity and never-endingness. She either felt exhausted or invigorated. She climbed into her car, started it up. Waited for the defroster to do its job. A knock on her window startled her.

"Diving *does* matter," Cotton said through the rolled-down window. "It's brave. And beautiful. It lets everyone know that the unexpected is possible."

Damn, she liked him.

"Why aren't you celebrating?"

"I am."

Feeling him looking at her, seeing her, wanting to be with her, filled Ria with a zip of something an awful lot like adrenaline. Except warmer, and deeper. Like hope, even if she wasn't sure what she wanted.

"I wish I could see you dive," he said as he buckled into the seat beside her.

Ria bit her lip, thinking. "I could do that. If you're serious."

"Isn't it too cold? And dark?"

"Not everywhere."

THIRTY-ONE

Ria parked on the street, amid the dark, hulking buildings. As they approached the dry gym, she took deep breaths, scolding her thumping heart into behaving. This used to be one of her favorite places. She hated the way her nerves now felt jagged, and adrenaline waves sizzled and popped throughout her bloodstream.

The key was still hidden in the fake rock beneath the bush. She'd been the one to put it there. She was probably the only one who'd ever used it. The team spent enough grueling hours inside, no one else wanted to go to the dry gym more than Benny required. It had never been enough for her. She'd always wanted more. Here she was again, feeling eager and impatient.

She jiggled the key as she turned it, pressing her shoulder against the metal frame. Then the door opened and the smell of the gym—the dust of chalk, and the metal of the equipment, mixed with a hint of sweat and Bengay and something else, unidentifiable yet always there—stopped Ria in the shadowed opening.

"Is anyone here?" Cotton whispered behind her, warm and close.

"No." She could feel the emptiness. The wide expanse of the place. No rustles or movements. No music. No creaking of the trampoline springs or *ka-thump-bump-bump* of the dry board. They were alone. The space was dim—the only light came from the front glass doors and the vents along the back wall where Benny had knocked out the metal grates.

It was cold, too. Eventually he would turn on heating fans and lamps, but that would be later, in full-blown winter. Until then, he'd make them work for warmth. They'd practice in mittens and head wraps, leggings and scarves; anything to keep the chill away.

Unless he was with her and the NDT. Then this place would be an empty warehouse.

She kicked her shoes off by the door and Cotton did the same. The words *~~GOOD*BETTER*~~BEST* were still scrawled across the walls in black paint, but the first two words were slashed with red, making them irrelevant. There was only room for the *BEST* here.

"This is interesting."

"Yeah?" She tried to see it through Cotton's eyes. The three trampolines, the row of weight machines, the mats on the floors, the walls, everywhere.

"Is this legal?"

"Us being here?"

"This place. All this stuff. It looks so dangerous."

"It's safe."

And yet, it wasn't the same gym she saw in her mind. Maybe it was the cold and the dim. Or the oppressive silence, broken only by the sound of their socks slipping along the mats. It seemed smaller than it used to be. Or emptier. Dingier and dustier. It's not like she'd ever thought it was pristine, or even civilized, but now it looked more off-color, one step closer to condemned than she remembered.

Cotton picked up a competition manual. He'd found the one thing to read in here.

She slipped past the row of cubbies, and into Benny's office. This was the place where he plotted and planned for each meet, compulsively checking scores and rankings.

"Which of your dives has the highest degree of difficulty?" Cotton called to her.

"Springboard or platform?" She opened the top drawer of Benny's desk, but there were only pens and scrap paper. Ria pulled out a plastic bag holding at least fifty Sharpies.

"Springboard."

Distracted, trying to sort through the papers in the second drawer, she said, "Probably one of my twisters." The degree of difficulty was a way to measure a dive's challenge. The higher the points, the harder to be perfect.

"What's its dive number?"

She couldn't find the NDT paperwork. Benny had given her the packet of information, but she didn't have the paper she'd signed. She wasn't sure where he fit into the words and lines of promises.

"If it's a twister, I'm assuming it starts with a five."

"You already know more than most people." It was funny that he found the order and math of diving so interesting.

"Can you do a four hundred one dive?" He stepped inside the office, holding the open book.

"It's a four-oh-one. Basic inward. You could do that dive."

"No. I don't think I could."

Ria wanted a copy of that agreement, free of her parents' eyes. Even if it was too complicated to read. Cotton could have helped her. But Benny hadn't left it here. She looked around the office, quickly making sure it looked the same, then joined Cotton at the door. She took the diving manual from him and set it back on the empty bookshelf by the cubbies. "Let's see what you *can* do."

Needing something to hang on to, she took Cotton's hand. He pulled back at first, but then squeezed her fingers. She led him across the spongy floor mats to the far side of the gym.

"Is that a diving board?" He dropped her hand.

"It's a real board, the same one that's on any pool. Except for the water."

She climbed the ladder, walked across the board, peered over the edge into the pit of foam blocks. She bounced, gently at first, then, higher, pushing harder, launching herself as high as she dared, then a little higher, to the point where her insides were out of sync with the rest of her. Adrenaline still felt like a healing potion. Necessary doses required.

As she slowed again, Cotton clapped from his spot along the side of the pit.

"You can't clap yet. I haven't done anything." She raced down the board and threw herself off with a flip and a twist. She heard the clang of the board before she hit the pit, sinking into the soft pieces of foam.

"I don't think we're the same species. That was amazing."

"You're too easily amazed. That wasn't even a real dive." She waded through the armpit-high mess of foam and stood on the soft and uneven floor at the edge of the pit.

"Show me something real."

"I can, but I have to land them feet-first since there's no water."

This was why she'd brought him here. It's what she was craving.

Her body remembered the moves. She barely had to think. She was on automatic, going through her collection of dives, in every direction. Front. Back. Reverse. Inward. And twisters, her favorite because they could be everything combined.

Finally, she met him where he leaned against a stack of mats pushed against the wall. "Come on. It's your turn. You should take off your tie."

He loosened, then slipped it off his head, tossing it to the side. He unbuttoned his shirt and removed that too, leaving on a white T-shirt with his dress slacks.

"While you're at it, pants could be a problem too. They might get messed up."

"No, thank you." Cotton moved slowly across the rough and springy surface and stood at the end of the board, looking down.

"It's like a trampoline," she said.

"Yes. Except for all the ways it's not."

She laughed. "That's true about everything. Just jump. You don't have to do anything fancy."

"My jumping will be fancy." He hurled himself off the board, letting out a yell as his arms and legs waved for the brief second he was in the air. He sank deep into the blocks, then came up wide-eyed, with teeny bits of foam in his hair.

"Let's play copycat. Whatever you do, I have to do too."

Most of Cotton's tricks consisted of flailing limbs and making lots of noise, so after a few very similar versions, they made their way to the edge, laughing.

"I had no idea falling was so exhausting." He sounded out of breath.

The soft and stretchy ground of the pit sank below them each, but proportionally. The result was an illusion of being the same height. Eye to eye. Nose to nose. Mouth to mouth. Species to species.

A flash of light from across the gym startled her out of the moment. Instinct made her tense up. Freeze. She heard the door click shut before she turned to see who she knew was there.

Damn. Damn. Damn.

"Victorious?"

"Benny," she whispered, but it was clear Cotton already knew. She hated the panicked look on his face. She shouldn't have brought him into Benny's territory.

"I know you're here."

"Go away. I don't want to see you." She hoisted herself out of the pit.

"This is my gym." He sounded amused. "No one tells *me* to leave."

With her stomach doing flips, Ria scrambled across the mats to join him. Her mouth felt dry and sticky. His face looked weird and shadowed under his hat. She willed Fear to stay quiet and hidden. It couldn't help her right now.

"What were you working on? Dives or conditioning? The NDT facility is going to blow your mind. It's going to make this place look like a kids' playhouse."

"That's not it."

"I knew you couldn't stay away. I figured you were up to something. I sent the NDT your video of the other day. They're happy. But impatient for you to pick your starting date." He crossed his arms over his chest. "How many other times have you come to work out?"

"None. I'm not."

"Right." He wasn't listening. Or not comprehending. Definitely not believing.

"I didn't come to work out. That's not why I'm here."

"Is that right? You came for the view?"

As he stepped toward her, she kept her eyes on his hands.

"No, Benny. Please. Don't." She deserved to punished, but she couldn't bear for Cotton to see it. "I'm with someone."

He stared at her, jaw clenched and pulsing, looking confused.

"I'm 'experiencing.' Being a teenager. Like you told me to."

He scanned the gym. His eyes stopped on Cotton's shirt and tie, then found Cotton. A look of queasy disbelief rolled across his face. "Here? You brought him here?" Benny's face turned steely and cold. He worked his mouth like he'd tasted something gross.

She bit back the apology, swallowed the urge to tell him they weren't doing what he thought. Instead, she ignored the heat in her face and the stickiness on her skin.

"We'll leave."

"You better get the hell out of here, Romeo," he yelled in Cotton's direction. "You're trespassing on someone else's property." Then he leaned in close, his breath hot and stale on her face. "We're not done."

He turned and left her standing alone on the foam mat. He went to his office and slammed the door.

Cotton heaved himself up and out of the pit. He rushed to the spot where he'd left his shirt and tie. Without talking, she led him out the door, into the dark of the night.

THIRTY-TWO

Ria woke up with her mind racing, and her body restless. Her parents' voices hummed and buzzed through the wall.

She wondered if Benny would tell them about her visit to the gym. He hadn't been mad. Not at first. It was more like he'd expected her. He'd assumed she'd been there before, and it was dumb luck that he'd finally caught her.

And when she'd begged him not to explode, he'd listened. Sure, Cotton had been there, but also, she'd never said no to Benny before. Maybe that's all it took. Maybe things could be different if she worked harder to stop him. But, he'd made her the best she could be. What would she have lost by saying no?

She'd surprised him, bringing Cotton to the gym. And poor Cotton looked shell-shocked on the way home. They'd both been quiet, holding tight to their own thoughts.

She had to see him.

The Talleys' house looked dark. She sent him a text, then sat on the curb at the end of their driveway waiting for his response.

She rested her arms on her knees and tucked her head into the crook of her elbow.

"My parents want to know why you're sitting out here." She must have dozed off, because his greeting startled her.

"It was too early to knock on your door." She blinked, still waking up.

He turned and walked away. When he got to the porch he looked back. "Come in. It's not too early anymore."

Their home smelled of vanilla and maple, mixed in with the savory scent of sausage. Ria's mouth watered and her stomach rumbled a ridiculous deep and gnawing, begging sound.

Breakfast at their home was like a dance with too many steps to count. Everyone in the warm yellow kitchen, each of them moving in their own direction, but perfectly aligned, as if choreographed to avoid collisions. Flutie walked out with a piece of toast as they walked in, but she greeted Ria with a smile before she headed upstairs. At the table, Mr. Talley and Bo watched something on a tablet while Jelly announced, "I'm being a self-cannibal. I'm having jelly on my grits."

The table was covered with more food than Ria's family served in a month of breakfasts.

"Cotton, feed your guest." His mother waved her spatula like it was a magic wand.

"No, thank you. I'm fine."

"But you're also hungry," said Cotton.

"Did you hear about the restaurant on the moon?" Mr. Talley asked as they sat down.

"I don't think so."

"Out-of-this-world food, no atmosphere."

"I bet it's a great place to rock out."

He looked surprised, then burst out laughing. "I like this girl, Cotton."

"Me too," Cotton said, scooping applesauce.

Once they'd finished and rinsed their dishes, with Ria feeling like her thank-you wasn't nearly sufficient, Cotton led her out to the garage.

As soon as they stepped into the quiet, dim space, he stuffed his hands into his pockets. "Your coach was angry last night."

He was, but she'd seen worse.

"I thought he was going to hurt you."

"We shouldn't have been there. Not without permission." She sighed at the frown on his face. She had to try to explain. "I know it's wrong when Benny hits me."

"Yes."

"But he only does it because he wants me to be the best. It never lasts long. Diving hurts too if you do it wrong."

"That's different. Hitting the water is not the same as being hit."

But they *were* the same, too.

"The first time he hurt me, I thought it was an accident. I didn't even know he was mad."

She'd been goofing around, showing off. She had her teammates cracking up. She'd slipped off the board sideways. It had surprised her, almost scared her, but not enough to slow her down or make her stop laughing. Then, as she'd lifted herself out of the pool, Benny had grabbed her arm, at the elbow. She'd thought he was helping her out—not that he ever did. But that's where her head was, in a place where he always took care of her.

"I was too young and dumb to know he could do that."

He'd wrenched her arm back, then down. She'd hit the cement, hard, hips skidding and scraping, but the look on his face had shocked her into biting back any protest. His words made a cloud around her, she hadn't heard what he'd said, not with the way her heart raced and eyes stung. But she'd understood what he meant: She was stupid and foolish. And her whole team knew it. Embarrassed, she'd shaken it off, acted like nothing had changed. The way no one else protested or even said a word told her the truth: She deserved it.

"After it happened he was so sorry. I thought he was going to cry. He even bought me a candy bar after practice. He was so proud of me for forgiving him. But of course I did. I had to. We were partners. We needed each other. He gets angry because he cares."

"There are better ways to show caring."

She didn't argue, but it wasn't as simple as he thought. Like with all the different ways to go in the cave—the easiest trail wasn't always the one he'd choose. The destination, the getting farther into the cave was the reason he'd squeeze through a too-tight tunnel and slip down muddy and treacherous hills. He'd risked climbing in the dark with ropes, and the reward was finding that pool. It had been worth it. The part that sucked was also the part that made the magic happen. Benny had led her to the top.

"I've been thinking, Cotton. You should go to college. You got that scholarship last night. You could do anything, go anywhere."

"No. I can't."

"There are different kinds of schools. Big and small. Not so far away. You could . . ."

"Squid," he said, loud and harsh.

"Sorry." She blinked, blushed hot.

"You don't need to apologize. You can say what you think. That's what friends do. But then I can say squid. I'm not angry. That's why we have the word 'squid.'"

The sting in her eyes started to calm. She'd forgotten the easy rules of being with Cotton.

"I have to be here when Esther comes back."

There was no way to argue, even if she thought she should. *Squid, squid, squid.*

"I want to show you something." He gestured for her to take his chair at the desk. "I've been thinking about your suggestion." He knelt on the floor and clicked something on the computer. Damn, he smelled good. "The idea of overlapping maps is interesting. It took some adjusting and manipulation, but I got them both to scale.

"This whole area is Pierre. Judging by our mileage and direction, I think we must be heading . . ." He paused, intently focused on the map. She watched as he made sense of what he was looking at, saw that moment when it clicked. The way his eyes lit up made her grin.

"Here! I think the underground pond must be right around here." He let the mouse hover over a spot on the map, not far from her house.

She laughed at the magic of it. To think the cave was another layer, below the streets.

"It's not exact. That mileage is including elevation and side-tracks. It's not direct, not like a bat flies."

"What about the other caves? Where are they?"

"It's hard to know. Not all caves are identified publicly."

"Best guess."

"If I overlap them, it seems as though there must be one here." Using an icon tool, he marked a spot on the map, then two more. "And these are reasonable possibilities. It's all theoretical. No guarantee."

"But this one"—she tapped the screen with her finger—"seems like it could be the other end of our cave. If—and I know it's only an if—this could be the other side of the same cave. So, we need to find it. To know where we might end up."

"Huh," he said, but she couldn't read the look on his face. Until he broke into a wide grin. "It's worth a try. I'm going to get my log book."

Waiting, she wandered through the garage. Everything surrounding his desk was a jumble of a mess, but his drawing surface was clear. He'd tucked all his papers into stacks and slots along the side. His other maps were stored neatly on the shelf.

She pulled out the papers. Studied the maps he'd made. She recognized their neighborhood, each street carefully labeled. Another was all lines and squiggles. A topographical map. But not of anywhere she knew. Not the cave. Or at least not any part she recognized. There were curved areas. A big room at the bottom of the page. Or maybe it was the top. She rotated the page to look at it from a different angle. Her name was printed in neat letters in the bottom corner: *RIA*. She must be missing something. She'd have to ask him. She set it on the table and moved to survey the collection of toys. She pulled out a purple plastic ring. She'd always loved the Hula-Hoop.

He came through the door carrying his notebook, a few moments after she'd gotten the Hula-Hoop in motion. The key was all in the hips. A gentle rocking, a shimmy from side to side. Too much motion would make the ring go off-kilter and lose its rhythm.

"You don't mind me using this, do you? I couldn't resist."

"It's not mine," he said. "In sixth grade you and Maggie did a Hula-Hoop routine to music in the talent show."

"You remember that?" Her laugh messed up the flow of the hoop. She shifted, got it back.

"You swung them around your necks! I thought . . ." He stopped. Now he looked panicked. A little pale. Maybe even queasy. Still rocking, she followed his gaze to the table. Where she'd set down the map. That from here looked like . . .

She let the Hula-Hoop fall to the cement floor with a clatter.

It wasn't a cave system. It was a body. The room at the top

was the head. Arms to the sides. The waist curving into hips, the elevation of breasts. Cotton had made a topographical map. Of her. She saw it now. It was her body he'd drawn.

She joined him at the table, studying what he'd mapped. It was strange.

But wonderful, too. He'd studied her. Thought about her. All the many lines. The time and care it took.

"Is this how you see me?"

He stood, frozen in place, looking pained.

"Because it looks to me like this," she said, pointing to the shoulder spot, "is right here." Facing him, she took his left hand and matched it with her right shoulder. "And this is the curve here." She followed the line of the map down with her finger, and then moved his right hand down to the spot above her left hip bone. She could feel the heat of his chest through his shirt. She was sure his heart was racing as fast as hers. He must have been holding his breath because he suddenly let out a kind of sigh. It made her insides turn loose and warm.

She started the kiss. But then he kissed her, too. It was both of them. Together. Ria kissing Cotton and Cotton kissing Ria. Not one thing, still two. Each of them moving and shifting and breathing, exploring the other.

She wasn't sure how he could knock her over and hold her up at the same time, but he did. In his hands, she felt like something amazing.

So what if he was easily amazed. She was too.

THIRTY-THREE

Ria still wasn't ready to see Maggie. Or Sean. She'd been purposefully late to school, then dawdled everywhere, hoping to stay invisible. It wasn't hard to avoid them. They had so little in common now. And yet, she couldn't relax, wondering if they'd come face-to-face. It wasn't until she was in the parking lot with Cotton that she finally melted with the relief of being seen. She felt a warm flutter, thinking about all their many kisses. It was probably good that Jelly had burst into the garage, searching for her roller skates, otherwise they might never have come up for air.

Now, inside her car, she waited, but he didn't try to kiss her.

"I made you a map," she said.

"A map? You made me a map?"

"It's simple. Not like yours. But yeah." She grabbed it from the backseat and handed it to him.

She loved the careful way he unrolled it, bit by bit, inch by inch. He spread it across his lap, gently curling the ends back so the paper would stay open. His finger traced the lines and shapes and colors she'd made for him.

"We've been so many places together."

She nodded, even though he had his eyes on the map, not her. She watched his face, serious and thoughtful, shift and react.

"What's this?" He pointed to a swirl she'd marked beyond the dry gym, outside of town, past the industrial area, but not so far as the Travis Center.

That was her biggest surprise. If she was right.

"I think that's the cave that might connect with ours."

When he turned to her, his gaze felt like he was peeking into her mind. And liked what he saw.

"Let's go find it." He buckled his seat belt.

She drove, with Cotton giving directions, using a combination of her map and his GPS to guide her to the spot she'd marked on the map.

When they got there, it looked like someone's yard, surrounding a small white house, with rose bushes growing by the door. Nice. Ordinary. Except for the barbed-wire fence surrounding it. Metal signs had been nailed into the large wooden posts between the lengths of wire: *KEEP OUT. NO TRESPASSING.*

"Too bad. It's on private property."

"Let's get out and look around." She buzzed with the maybe of a new cave.

"We are not allowed here. There is barbed wire."

"We'll park in that parking lot we passed," she said, turning the car around. "We can go for a walk—*outside* the barbed wire—and see what we see. They'll never know we're here."

Even though he looked reluctant, she pulled into an empty parking lot. She drove behind a large cement building and parked. He had his head down, and his fingers fidgeted with the seam of his jeans.

"We can simply go for a walk."

"We can simply go for a walk," he echoed her words.

Ria tried to read his quiet as he walked beside her along the road. She wasn't sure if it was worry or concentration as he scanned both sides of the road. Maybe he was working out the map of it in his head. She imagined his brain taking in each rise and fall of the ground, absorbing the spot where the trees faded into shrubs. At least his shoulders were back now, his head up, eyes wide and bright. It was good to be moving.

When the fence drifted away from the asphalt, he followed her through the thick and overgrown grass. It felt isolated. It was hard to remember—or even believe—that the road was a short fifteen-minute walk away.

The barbed-wire fence jutted up against a wall built of stones and mortar. She ran her hands along the rough of it. It was old and crumbling, but she loved the way it felt somewhere between natural and made.

She turned to ask Cotton about it and found him staring at her. Damn. He hadn't even touched her, but still her body quivered and tingled. She felt melted and buzzed and tired and wired, all at the same time. Logic not required. She licked her lips with anticipation, waiting for his kiss.

He looked away. Walked along the line of the wall.

Ria swallowed. Forced her inner core to return to normal temperature. Misread. She looked up, eyeing the rocks.

She scrambled up with the rocks and mortar serving as a precarious ladder. At the top, she sat on the damp mossy ledge with her legs dangling.

"Come down. It's still their fence. Even if it's not barbed wire."

"Why would they mind us being here? What are they hiding?" She kicked her feet against the rocks.

"Fences are for protection. They want to keep their family safe."

"We won't hurt anything. Besides, once we're in the cave, that's a new place. That's not what they own."

"They would disagree. If a cave entrance is on your property, then it's yours."

"But how far in? At some point it's not their land anymore." She wasn't sure why she was arguing the point. It's not like she had any reason to doubt he was right. Except it didn't seem like a cave should be owned. "What if the cave goes on for miles and miles? Where do you draw the line?"

"There are rules. Property lines."

"Come on, Cotton. Let's take a quick peek."

"Squid."

Ria stopped, mid-argument. She needed to change the focus. "You know what would be amazing?" She leaned forward, enjoying the dizzying feel of looking down. "Building a house around the cave. So it's like a room. You could even put a door on it."

"It might keep the house cool as well. It would add another level of playing Dungeons and Dragons. I could be the ultimate geek."

She laughed, happy he was playing along.

"Perhaps the rocks mark the end of private property," said Cotton. "We could check the county development maps for property lines."

"Or we could climb over and have a quick look to see if we find a cave. Maybe this isn't even the right place."

"No. This is right. We're within the correct coordinates."

Even though he was firm in refusing to cross the line, he seemed sure she'd gotten it right. That was almost as good as seeing it with her own eyes. She turned at the waist, maneuvered herself down. Now she could feel the moist earth ground into the front of her shirt and the seat of her pants.

"You should have worn your caving clothes," said Cotton. "You're muddened."

They were quiet on their walk back. She wanted to take his hand, too much to try, in case he pulled away. She didn't think hand-holding was something he liked. Especially since he hadn't even kissed her once all day. If she'd come here with Sean, her lips would be raw from making out by now. They might not have ever gotten out of the car. She didn't want to be with Sean, but she wouldn't have minded Cotton pressing her up against that stone wall, either.

She was relieved to see the large cement building in the distance as they made their way back to where they'd started.

Except, maybe not. Her car wasn't where she'd parked it.

She double-checked the parking lot. Same gray wall, same green dumpsters. And a sign—one that she must have missed—stating *CUSTOMER PARKING ONLY. VIOLATORS WILL BE TOWED.*

THIRTY-FOUR

The parking lot was two cars and one pickup truck away from completely empty. Her car was definitely gone.

"Where is it? Where is your car? You parked it right here. I don't understand."

It wasn't fair how utterly bewildered Cotton looked. He was the smart one. She couldn't help but think he should have noticed the No Parking sign in the first place.

He paced back and forth along the fence line. His hand flapped and fluttered against his thigh. He was upset. More than upset. Flustered. Agitated. Approaching wiggy.

Ria felt pretty close to wiggy herself. No matter what this place was, it seemed completely unreasonable that they'd towed her car. The longer they stood in the spot where it should be, the more pissed she felt. It would take a while, but she could run home from here. Except Cotton couldn't.

They needed to call someone, but they'd left their phones in the car. Along with her money, ID, first-aid kit, maps—all the things her parents wanted her to have, just in case. They hadn't anticipated the just-in-case being losing her entire car.

She moved around the corner of the building to the front. Its dark windows were dressed up with iron bars. Above the door, gigantic curly pink and purple letters named it *Big Top*. Female silhouettes posed in acrobatic moves. Their bodies were wrapped in silver ribbon squiggles that continued along the building. It was circus-like. Sort of.

"Let's go inside. They have to let us use their phone." She looked to Cotton for some kind of confirmation of—or warning against—her plan. When he didn't reply, she headed to the darkened door and peered through the tinted glass. She couldn't see anyone, but when she pulled, the door opened.

Inside, the Big Top glowed with an eerie purple light. As her eyes adjusted, she took in a large carpeted room with silver poles positioned throughout. Some poles had animals—with mouths wide open—at the base. It was like they'd run away from a merry-go-round, only they hadn't traveled far. Around each pole was a patch of wooden flooring. Some areas were elevated like mini stages.

"What kind of circus is this?"

Cotton looked dazed. Frozen, like the animals trapped on their poles.

"You kids lost?"

"Did you tow my car?" She dragged Cotton to the man behind the counter.

"No."

"Are you sure? It was parked around the corner, behind the building. Now it's gone."

"I didn't tow it. But our service did. The lot is only for customers."

She looked around the empty space. "I can see why you're worried about filling up the lot. Sorry if I took someone's spot."

"Company policy."

What a jerk. "How do I get it back?"

"Call this number. You'll have to pick it up at the yard." He reached under the counter and pulled out a card.

"Can't you tell them to bring it back? Please? My parents are going to kill me."

"Sorry, sweetheart. Once it's gone, it's gone." He stared at Cotton. "Is he drunk? You gotta get him out of here."

"No, he's not drunk. He's . . ." Ria turned to Cotton, trying to see him through the bartender's eyes. Sitting on a purple stool, he had his head folded over his lap and was muttering something to himself. His hair still managed to look unruly even after the haircut. "Can we get some water?"

The man frowned but filled two glasses and slid them across the counter. He watched as she forced one into Cotton's hand.

"Tell you what," the man said. "I'll give 'em a call and see if we can save you the impound fees. You'll still have to pay for the tow, but maybe they won't put it in the lot."

As he moved down the bar, with the phone against his ear, she turned to Cotton. "How are we with time? How much longer until your mother starts to worry?"

"Seventy-two minutes."

She sighed with relief. That should be enough time to figure something out.

"She doesn't watch the time like I do." Cotton took a gulp of water. "I worry more. I want someone to notice if I'm gone."

"They'll definitely notice. I'll notice, too."

"You know what someone said after Esther disappeared?"

"What?" She tried to adjust to this new place he was taking her.

"'Well, at least you have all these other children.'"

Damn.

"They were wrong. People are wrong all the time." She leaned into him, letting her weight speak for her. He leaned on her in reply.

"When someone goes missing, they always suspect the family. That's the first guess. That someone in the family hurt her."

"But that's so awful. And unfair."

"It's based on factual data. Proven situations. Kidnappings, abuse. We are most likely to be hurt by someone we trust."

He wasn't meeting her eyes, but she couldn't look away from his hard to read, expressionless face.

"All right," the bartender said, interrupting. "As long as you get there today, you won't have to pay the extra fees."

She had no idea how she was going to make that happen, but one step at a time. "Can I use your phone?"

"That's it? No thank you?"

"Seriously? You want me to thank you for towing my car? Even if you did it for free, it's not a great deal."

He laughed. "Sweetheart, when you get a little older, let me know if you want a job. I think you'd hold your own around here." He handed the phone to her, the long curly cord easily reaching from the wall behind the bar. "What's the number?"

Neither of her parents answered. There was no point leaving a message since they couldn't call her back. She couldn't call Cotton's parents. He didn't like talking on the phone and she wouldn't be able to explain. She wasn't talking to Maggie, and no way would she call Sean for a ride.

There was only one other number she knew by heart.

THIRTY-FIVE

Outside, the sun seemed unbearably bright. As she held her hand to shield her eyes, she had a panicky moment of feeling lost. But then Cotton was beside her. They sat on the curb to wait.

The red SUV pulled into the parking lot, driving too fast and taking the corner too short. Benny had always been a terrible driver. He was eternally reckless, completely impatient. He hopped out of the car and ran his eyes up, down, and around the situation.

"Thanks for coming," Ria said, getting up. "My parents didn't answer. I didn't know who else to call."

Cotton stood too, then moved between her and Benny.

"Nice to meet you," said Benny, holding out his hand.

"We've met before." Cotton scowled and tucked his hand behind him.

Benny stared at Cotton for a minute before he gave up and

put away his hand. He opened the back door and gestured for Cotton to get in. Ria headed toward the passenger door.

"You're not getting in my car wearing those filthy clothes."

She eyed Benny, waiting for the punch line. He'd always been fussy and fastidious. He insisted the team wear matching uniforms from suits to warm-ups at meets. Their bags at the pool had to be neatly lined up against the fence. He liked everything orderly and clean. But.

"I mean it. You're not getting whatever is all over you in this car. You can either take them off or walk back to town."

Benny had seen her body in her tight, practically skin, swimsuits an infinite number of times. Minutes multiplied by hours by days, weeks, months, years. He'd watched her grow from skinny little kid to awkward preteen, on to where she filled out a bikini in all the right spots. The shape of her body had always been irrelevant. It was the thing that took her from the board into the air and water. But that was before. Her body wasn't only a tool for diving anymore.

And it was hers.

She headed inside the bar again, straight for the bathroom. She took off her shirt and pants, turning them inside out. The mud, some of it dried and some still damp, rubbed against her skin as she returned to the parking lot.

Without acknowledging the smirk on his face, she went around to the passenger door and got in. She looked back at Cotton, whose cheeks had turned pink. She wondered what they'd talked about.

"Funny place to start getting modest." Benny eyed her, looking amused, then turned the key and pulled out of the parking lot, thumping over the curb.

"He means because we were in a strip club," said Cotton.

"A what?" She looked back and forth between them. Benny busted up laughing.

She frowned, mostly to hide the fact she'd missed his laugh and wanted to hear it again.

"It looks like a merry-go-round in there, with all these animals. You mean those poles are for . . ." She trailed off, trying to imagine it. "That guy said I could work there."

She'd called Benny because she knew his phone number. And she knew, even after everything else, she could count on him to show up. She hadn't thought about the ride home, what that might look like. She never would have guessed she'd feel like the odd man out.

At the Talley home, Cotton opened the door and got out without saying goodbye. She stepped outside, keeping one hand on the door. "Sorry about this hassle. I'll talk to you later."

"You're staying with him?" His hand tapped his leg and he looked like he'd eaten something sour.

"I need to get home. I have to figure out how to get my car."

He stared at her, not smiling, not heading toward his house.

"You knew it was a strip club, Cotton? And you didn't tell me?"

"Benny told me. It felt inappropriate to discuss further."

"Yeah," she agreed. Then, because she knew he was still

unhappy, she added, "I'll be fine," then got back inside before he could change her mind.

Benny pulled onto the road. "Good to see you finally ditched the pretty-boy lifeguard. I guess I had your type wrong. I didn't know you'd go for . . ."

"Don't." She'd never forgive him for saying anything bad about Cotton.

"I was about to say your taste has improved. That boy is not a pushover. He has spirit. Like you."

She stared out the window so he wouldn't see her smile.

"I owe you an apology, Ria. I didn't know you could do it."

"Do what?" she asked, feeling wary, knowing she was caught in a balancing act where she wasn't sure which way was down.

"Quit. I never thought you could actually do it."

There was nothing to say. Not when he was still talking.

"I didn't think you were the type to choose mud wrestling and strip clubs over traveling the world doing something most people don't even know how to dream about.

"I've been thinking it was such a waste," he said, taking a turn too fast. "A waste of talent, of your parents' money. Of my time. But I guess you were doing us all a favor, cutting it off when you did. Because the truth of the matter is, if you *can* quit, you should."

She scooted against the door, wondered what she'd hurt if she jumped out.

It used to be: she screwed up, he got angry, she apologized, they got back to work. And for a while, there would be a respite.

The storm of his frustration would lead to a truce. She wasn't sure which stage they were at.

"You already blew the biggest meet of your life! Now you have an unbelievable opportunity and you're blowing it again."

He stopped his car at the corner, out of sight of her house.

"You're meant for greatness, Ria. You've never been ordinary. You're not like everyone else. It kills me to think you might miss the chance to do what you were born for."

"There are other teams. The NDT isn't the only one."

"We belong with the NDT."

He turned toward her and she flinched. His shoulders slumped. He took off his hat, played with it in his hands.

"They're the best. And so are you."

That's all that mattered to him. It's why he'd claimed her. She suddenly wished she'd been average. Normal.

The NDT was what she'd wanted. What her parents wanted. What everyone wanted. She'd been stupid to hesitate. She never should have let her head get in the way. Fact was, she didn't belong to herself. She'd already given Benny everything. Her time, her body, her head, her future.

She'd been so wrong to think she had a choice.

"I'll go," she said.

"Good."

Relief at his approval flowed through her. Finally, she could breathe again. This was the prize for a job well done. Success. Acceptance. Things that didn't exist outside his atmosphere.

THIRTY-SIX

Friday morning, Ria found Maggie waiting for her in the school parking lot. Ria hadn't lost her car privileges like she'd expected. Her parents hadn't been nearly as mad about the car-tow as she'd expected. Apparently misreading a parking sign was a minor offense. They hadn't even asked many questions about the how or why or who she'd been with. Leaving out the messiest parts of her life was remarkably effortless.

All that mattered was she'd said yes to the NDT. They'd immediately sent the first payment and were planning her move. Once she was cleared by her doctor, they'd buy the plane tickets.

She'd made them—along with Benny—happy, at last. They were thrilled she'd finally gotten the right answer, the one they'd known all along. She was still waiting for her own happy to kick in.

"It's a beautiful day," Maggie said as soon as Ria opened her door.

It was true. The sun was shining. The reds, yellows, and

oranges of the trees looked vivid against the blue of the sky. There was a hint of crisp cool in the air, but only barely. The sun was making a late-fall rally. The only thing wrong was that Maggie—who used to know her best, her worst, her in-between—had slipped away to a place where she was talking about the *weather.*

Inside a cave, weather didn't matter.

Ria cleaned her glasses with her shirt. Now that she was going to be diving 24-7 she could give up her contacts.

"Scale of one to ten, how mad are you?" asked Maggie.

"Off the charts." She paused for a moment, then added, "Because it's not worth rating. I'm not mad."

"Bullshit."

"It's true. I'm not. Sean and I were broken up—"

"Barely."

"Both of you were drinking. I get it. Things happened." She wanted to get out of the car, to put some space between them, but Maggie blocked her exit.

"If you're not mad at me, then where have you been?"

Caving. Making maps. Kissing Cotton. Nowhere Maggie would recognize. Places and things she had to leave behind.

Maybe if she and Maggie were busy diving, she could find the words to explain where she'd been. There was something about having her body occupied—and her head, too—that allowed truths to flow more freely. Here, with each of them measuring the other, looking for hints, there were too many hazards in the way.

"Did you know there's a strip club over past Industrial? It has a circus theme." She eyed Maggie, waiting for a hint that Benny had told her they were leaving. Officially.

"You're still Random Ria."

She didn't feel random.

"Do you want to go to the quarry today?" Maggie asked.

"Why?"

"To go," she said with a shrug. "There's some lame college fair all day. We thought the quarry might be a better way to spend the day."

Ria had been wanting to go back there. The quarry tugged at her mind. Even though it had been such a brief visit the night of that party, it was a place she settled on when she was running, stuck in class, or falling asleep. She wanted to see if her memory was right. She didn't have much time before she had to leave.

"I don't need to talk to any colleges. I committed to Uden."

"Good. That's what you wanted." She had to tell Maggie her decision. "I'm going. I'm joining the NDT."

"With Benny."

It wasn't a question, but Ria nodded anyway.

"All the more reason to come with us today. While you still can."

Ria hesitated. She wanted to tell Cotton she was leaving school, but Maggie wouldn't understand. Besides, he needed to stay and go to that college fair. "Let's go."

Maggie moved around the front of the car. She opened the

passenger door and plopped into the seat where she hadn't ridden in weeks.

"How's Sean?" Ria asked, keeping her eyes on the road.

"Fine."

Like the weather.

They joined the line of cars parked outside the chain-link fence. Peeking through the metal weave, Ria saw only boulders and enormous piles of gravel. The hole and the cliffs weren't visible from here.

At the bend in the fence, she grabbed the edge and pulled it up.

Maggie scooted under, getting stuck briefly on one of the wire bends because she tried to get up too early.

"Now hold it for me," said Ria.

She could hear the crowd—laughter, shouting, and music—before they made their way along the path and around the corner.

The quarry didn't look the way she'd remembered. Today, the water at the bottom of the hole was the deepest blue she'd ever seen. The light was different, too. It was earlier in the day, but later in the month. The sun felt farther away, or weaker. The way its rays hit the rock walls set off even more variations of color. They revealed the creases and cracks. The walls might be what the inside of a cave would look like in the sunlight. Cotton would know if that was right.

A scattering of blankets and towels and chairs and coolers

claimed the one nearby grassy patch, but most people had gathered closer to the edge.

"There's Sean," said Maggie. Then, as if to make up for the enthusiasm in her voice, she added, "And Charlie and Tony. Everyone is here."

Not everyone. There was no Cotton. But he wouldn't fit in here. Maybe she didn't either. Even after all of Sean's lessons on how to be normal, she'd fail the final test.

Ria took a cup of something red when it was offered to her. It was spiked, the heat of alcohol warm and thick in the back of her throat. No wonder Sean looked so happy. Maggie, too.

The two of them didn't act like they were together. They didn't hold hands. Or slip their arms around each other or into each other's pockets or belt loops. Nothing obvious. It was worse. A constant series of bumping into each other. A collision of arms, hips, legs. Over and over, like bumper cars. Or magnets. Two people desperate to touch each other.

Now that she was watching, Ria spotted the sideways looks between them. Sean typed something into his phone and seconds later, Maggie read hers. Whatever he'd sent made her smile and play with her hair.

Charlie stumbled, his feet slipping and scrambling in the gravel, precariously stopping inches from the edge. "Shit! I thought I was going over!"

Hysterical giggles broke out, but Ria's heart raced as if she had been the one sliding.

"Someone should jump in!"

"Ria said she could do it," said Tony. "Right, Sean? Didn't you think Ria was gonna do it?"

"Shut it," Sean muttered, still not meeting her eyes.

"I bet Maggie will do it," Ria said.

"Somebody do it!" yelled Charlie.

Cheers and laughter erupted around them. People chanted, "Do it! Do it!"

She turned and faced Maggie. "It's not much higher than platform."

"Wait." Sean grabbed Maggie's hand. "Are you sure? You don't have to."

"I've got this." Maggie shook off his concern. She'd always worked harder for an audience.

Ria and Maggie didn't talk during the walk to the other side. Once they reached the spot directly across from the crowd, Maggie waved. Then she turned to Ria. "Are we really going in?"

"We have to. No balking allowed." She didn't have to say Benny's name for them both to know he was here, in their heads. He'd never forgive them for being this close, at the edge, then not following through. There was no running away, not anymore.

"Besides," Ria continued, "this spot is safe. Some places have old equipment or rock shelves to worry about, but here it's open and plenty deep." She eyed Maggie to see if Fear was nuzzling up to her.

"Have you done this before?"

"No." She'd only imagined it. Over and over again. This place had haunted her, the idea of falling off the edge jerked her awake when it popped in her head at bedtime. But she'd worked it through in her mind. She'd picked this spot based on the map Cotton gave her. Now it felt inevitable.

"Are you with me or not?" Ria asked.

"You're not even wearing a suit."

"True. You didn't tell me to bring one."

"I didn't think you'd come. I thought you might be going somewhere with Cotton." Maggie raised her eyebrows. "I've seen you leave school with him every day for a month."

Ria shrugged, ignoring the heat in her cheeks.

"I thought we were best friends. But you don't tell me anything. You don't trust me."

She wanted to argue. Wanted to prove that wasn't the way it worked in her head. There wasn't always a "why" to the things she did and didn't do. But maybe Maggie had it right.

"Let's get this over with." She tucked her glasses into her pocket. Then pulled off her shirt and slipped down her shorts. She ignored the sudden burst of cheers as she stood in her bra and underwear. "On the count of three. Keep your body tight. All the way down. It'll take longer than platform."

"I know what to do." Maggie's fear sounded like irritation.

"One," counted Ria.

And then Maggie was gone. Pencil-straight, toes pointed. She hadn't waited for three, or even two. She'd simply jumped into space. Cheers erupted from across the quarry.

Ria waited for the splash, then set herself. Erased everything. No more crowd. No breeze blowing across her skin. No sand beneath her feet. She was alone. Just her, the air, and below, ready to catch her, the water.

She paced four steps back. Lifted her arms, twisted her torso. Then, hurdled off the edge.

There was the leap, and then the fall. The oh-so-familiar rush of thrill. Controlled recklessness in her illogical attempt to be free of the world. She gripped her legs, kept every muscle tense for her desperate race against gravity. She fought to keep her head up, straining her neck and shoulders, every bit of her tight and strong. She made the first flip, then circled around again, and even again, all the while plummeting downward, with no true sense of time and space, then again, once more, taking her dangerously close to the edge of impossible. Then, easy, like taking a breath, she recognized the moment to kick and open up, to reach for the water. Wild abandon met exact precision.

It took forever. It took no time at all.

The impact stung her skin, the water rushed around her, a wall of noise and froth. She rolled into her save and headed for the surface. She gulped air, then burst out laughing. From above she heard the hoots and hollers. They echoed off the sheer walls of the quarry.

"We did it! Benny'll never believe it." Euphoria rushed through her.

"You dove? You bitch. You said jump."

"And you said on three. It doesn't matter. Everyone knows we're awesome."

"Yeah, but they think you're better, don't they? You always have to show me up."

Ria's body racked with shivers now. Her teeth clattered together as she treaded water.

"You always have to be tougher. Stronger. Better." Maggie hit the water with her hand. "Did you see how Sean doubted me? He didn't think I could do it."

"Because he cares about you."

"You didn't even care that I fooled around with him."

"Is that why you kissed him? To beat me? To win something?"

With a burst of splash, Maggie swam for the edge, to the place where they could pull themselves out.

Ria wished she could stay where she was, wanting to melt and disappear. But instinct kicked in. Self-preservation propelled her to the rocks. By the time she reached the shore, her arms and legs felt heavy. Dead weight. Half asleep from the cold.

Maggie stood dripping and shivering on the rocks.

"You don't need to be jealous. He liked you first, Maggie. Sean wanted to ask you out."

Until Benny got in the way.

"I know. Believe it or not, I'm not jealous of you, Ria. I used to be. I cried because Benny didn't care about me the same way. Can you even see how screwed up that is?"

She couldn't see much of anything. It was too cold, too wet, too true.

"You need to hope there's no one better than you when you get to the NDT. Otherwise he might forget all about you, too."

Then she was gone, up the trail. Ria was sitting in her underwear, alone and shivering in the bottom of a big hole.

Hope doesn't win. Winning beats hope. That Bennyism didn't sound quite right, but she was too numb to try to rearrange it in her head.

She stumbled her way up the path, following Maggie's damp footprints. At the top, she ignored the crowd, bolted for the spot where she'd left her clothes. She stumbled back to the fence, pulling them on along the way.

In her rush to escape, Ria slid under the fence too fast. The pain of metal slicing into her leg didn't register until she was on the other side, panting. Blood, thick and red, poured from the gash downward, pooling in the dirt where she stood. It looked like a mangled heart.

THIRTY-SEVEN

By the time Ria made it home, her entire leg, hip to toes, ached. The cut itself burned and throbbed. As she stepped out of the car and stood up, her head felt light and her vision moved in and out of blurry. She took a deep breath and concentrated on walking from the car to her front door. She couldn't decide if she was relieved or irritated that her parents weren't home.

Inside, she headed to the bathroom to investigate. She'd wrapped her shirt around her leg and now it was stuck tight to the gash. Her blood had dried, brown and stiff, marking a pool in the fabric. When she tried to lift it, the cut gushed again, bright and red, with a metallic smell that made her eyes water. She clamped the shirt back down and sat on the edge of the tub.

She'd never been badly hurt before. It was one of her assets. The fact she'd avoided injuries was remarkable for an athlete of her caliber. Most everyone broke or tore something eventually. After chipping her tooth, this was her second diving-related injury of significance. Both times she'd gotten hurt while running away.

Damn. It hurt.

She pulled out her phone, expecting a series of missed texts and calls. It felt like she'd been gone for way too long. But her phone was blank and empty. No one was looking for her.

Cotton answered his phone immediately.

"It's Ria."

"Yes."

"How are you with blood?"

"Mine or yours?"

"Are you bleeding, Cotton? Are you hurt?"

"No. I thought this was theoretical."

"Not theoretical. Actual. I cut my leg."

Twenty minutes later he called her from her backyard and through the phone she directed him step by step into her house. "The glass door should be open."

She heard it slide along its track and echoed through the phone. "It is."

"Come in. Through the family room and up the stairs."

"There are a lot of pictures of little Ria. Most of them are of her wearing medals at the pool."

"Ignore them. My parents are short on imagination when it comes to household decor." She could hear him down the hall. "Keep walking. Second door on the right."

"I'm here." He knocked.

"Come in." She was still holding her phone.

The door opened slowly, and Cotton peeked in, looking wary.

"Can you help me?" she asked, not entirely sure what she wanted him to do.

"Yes." He placed both their phones on the counter.

"I don't want to go to the hospital." She needed this taken care of before she had her physical for the NDT.

"We need to remove the covering and clean the area."

"It won't stop bleeding." She stuck her leg, T-shirt and all, under the faucet the way Cotton guided. The water stung, and her blood flowed down the drain all the while she soaped and rinsed the gash.

He took a clean towel from the shelf and sat beside her on the edge of the tub. He'd never be able to lie down for a bath; he was way too long. He pressed the towel firmly along the cut. "Where can I find sturdy tape?"

She waited for him in the bathroom while he followed her directions, returning with a roll of duct tape and scissors. After she applied antibiotic ointment, he held her leg across his lap. "Butterfly bandages can work as well as stitches. It's a longer cut than usually recommended, but I think we can take care of it."

Once he showed her what he had in mind, they worked together to fold and cut the tape into the rough butterfly shape. The buggy part—the middle—was folded over so as not to stick to her wound, and then he used the wings to pull the two sides of her skin together.

Slowly, methodically, crisscrossing each one over the other, they worked together, bit by smidge by part by piece, closing the two sections of skin back together. Somewhere midway along her thigh she realized she wasn't thinking about the pain anymore. Instead she focused on the feel of Cotton's capable fingers. It was very distracting that he smelled like fresh bread and that indescribable him-scent.

"Will I have a scar?"

"Probably." He took the bit of tape she offered and put it into place. Only room for one more piece.

"You could be a doctor. You're smart enough. And calm. You have a reassuring bathtub-side manner." She tried out his name: "Doctor Talley."

"No." He tilted his head, eyeing her leg. He ran his finger along the edge of tape, as if measuring it by touch. "I wouldn't want to give anyone bad news."

Damn. She reached out and placed her hand firmly against his cheek.

He leaned into her touch, then pressed the last butterfly into place.

"I look like a mixed-up treasure map." She eyed the row of bandages. "X marks the spot."

"You're going to need to leave them in place for about a week. Don't get them wet."

"But I can still cave. Right?"

Cotton was quiet. For long enough that she worried he was avoiding telling her bad news. Then he said, "Do you want to spend the night in the cave tomorrow? In order to have more time for mapping? My parents approved our plan."

"Seriously?"

"Yes, seriously." He paused, with a funny look on his face. "Flutie is coming too. Leo has been taking her caving. He assures me she will not be a liability."

"Is it weird that your best friend and your sister like each other?"

"I don't think I have clear parameters on 'weird.'"

She laughed. "I think it's nice. And an overnight cave slumber party sounds incredible."

"Is your answer yes? You will come with us?"

"Yes, Cotton. My answer is definitely yes."

He gently moved her leg off his lap and stood up to wash his hands. Looking at her through the mirror he asked, "How did you cut yourself?"

"I went to the quarry with Maggie. She didn't want to go to the college fair."

"I didn't want to go either. You know I can't go to college. I looked for you."

"I wish you'd been with me."

"You didn't ask me to come."

"I'm sorry. I didn't think. I mean, I was thinking about you.

But I didn't think you'd want to be there. Or I didn't think to invite you. It wasn't really your group."

"I don't have a group."

"Me neither. Even Maggie hates me."

He didn't argue or question. She stood up. Her leg still hurt, but it was easier to ignore now, especially if she leaned to the other side. The bathroom was a tight space, Cotton was close. She focused on his reflection.

"We could be a group," she said to him in the mirror. "You and me. A small and exclusive group. There could be . . . kissing in our group."

He tilted his head. "You liked that?"

"Yes, Cotton. I liked that." She laughed. "Very much. Couldn't you tell?"

"It's not like I ever thought someone like you would like someone like me."

She wasn't sure how to answer that. She was missing something. She pressed her hands against her temples. Smoothed her hair away from her face. Lifted her chin. Maybe she could hide the way she felt shaky now. A bundle of jangled nerves. This was Cotton. They could figure this out together.

"What does that mean? 'Someone like you' or 'someone like me'? Do you think someone like me wouldn't like someone who's kind?"

"I have trouble with flexibility. I worry about time and rules. And everything."

"So, someone like me wouldn't like someone who actually cares about things?"

"I'm geeky."

"You mean smart. And I'm not."

"You're smart. But you're also beautiful."

"I'm a mess."

"Yes. You're kind of filthy and your hair is doing a strange twisty thing. And you still have blood on your shirt. But, you *are* beautiful. You're strong and fit. And I'm . . ." He hunched over, his cheeks pink and flushed. "I'm not."

"But you are. And you're more. You're . . ."

He'd never be able to see himself the way she saw him. He could never have her exact perspective. She reached out and took his hand. She needed to touch him even if he pulled away. But he didn't.

"Humdiddle?" she asked.

He looked as surprised as she felt. Then his eyes crinkled into that Cotton-smile.

"You make me happy, Cotton. Even when I'm not."

Words weren't good enough.

She moved closer. Guided him to the toilet seat. She straddled him, flinching because her leg still hurt like hell. But then she nestled in. She tangled her fingers in his hair, and he pulled her closer. She traced his eyebrows, his nose, his lips. She kissed his neck, his cheek, and finally, his mouth. He tasted like something sweet and rich, but mostly, best of all, him.

THIRTY-EIGHT

Later, after Cotton had left, and her parents came home, Ria took the evidence of his surgery work outside to the garbage can.

The night air felt cool and damp. It smelled like a campfire. She looked up at the stars and was hit with a faint wave of vertigo, but too quickly her body adjusted to the new point of view. She was stuck firmly on the ground.

Damn, that dive in the quarry had given her an adrenaline rush. It had been wild and reckless. And fun, too. It made her miss the raw part of diving. The thrill of not knowing balanced with faith in her body.

A video clip had already been posted online and liked repeatedly. Maggie's jump was there too, but separate. As if they hadn't been together. In the video, Ria stood at the edge of the quarry, clearly in her bra and underwear. No doubt it was her. Then, suddenly, she was in motion. The lift had been as good as it felt. Her pike form was tight, her legs straight, toes pointed the whole ride down. It was a beautiful dive, made more stunning by the backdrop of the rocky walls. She felt a flicker of pride. Before she could wonder or doubt, she sent Benny the link.

She walked down the sidewalk to the neighbor's driveway, and onto the street corner, evaluating the pain in her leg. It had ached and throbbed all through dinner, but her parents hadn't noticed. They had no idea she was hurt. They never did. She was too good at hiding her bruises. Even when she'd wished they'd notice her skinned knees, battered shoulder blades, she'd worked to keep the pain out of view.

They didn't even know she'd been to the quarry today. Or that she and Maggie had fought. They still didn't know about caving or kissing Cotton. She could feel her secrets adding up, building to some kind of crash.

Sometimes it was better to fall apart in a million ways all at once, rather than one small way on its own. One missed homework and her teachers would be angry. Two or three, they moved on to concerned. Skip it every single day and everyone quit caring. They'd give up. Diving had been like that too. The smaller an offense, the greater Benny's wrath.

If a dive's mediocrity could be traced to one small slip, one minor glitch, one teeny tweak, the more likely he would rant and rage. The closer to perfect a dive went, the more likely his assigned correction would feel like a punishment. If she had a strong approach, great lift in her hurdle, tight form, fast flip, but then botched the entry, he'd rage about that one last piece of the dive. She'd be in entry purgatory, standing on the side of the pool doing lineup after lineup, concentrating only on the moment of breaking the surface, the rip of the water, the act of sliding in, willing her body to act paper thin. But, if everything went wrong, he'd shake it off as if it didn't happen. She'd simply have to do the whole dive again.

Back at her house, she paused and watched the neighbor's smoke twirl up from their chimney, melting into the sky.

Then Benny was there, standing in the spot where her driveway met the street. She'd known he'd come.

"I saw your video."

She stood straighter, shoulders back, chin lifted.

"The higher you go, the prettier you fall." His voice sounded husky, thick with the night. He stepped closer, moving up the driveway. "There's no one like you, Ria. Strong. Brave. Graceful. You're the real deal." He tilted his head and stared at her, into her. "I bet that dive felt incredible, didn't it? Out in the wild, with a crowd watching. Even if they don't understand what they're seeing. They know it's amazing. They know *you* are amazing."

Exactly.

"What the hell were you thinking?"

She frowned. The dive had looked good. Great, even.

"I said, *what the hell were you thinking?*"

She'd thought she had to do it. That he'd never forgive her for being in a moment of possible and not going for it. She'd done it for him. Everything. It always came back to him.

He grabbed her shoulders, squeezed tight, then, in a flash, shoved her hard. She stumbled backward, bumping her shoulders and head against the retaining wall. An involuntary yelp escaped at the way her leg flashed a white-hot dagger of pain. She sucked it back in, denying her body's reaction.

"You could have killed yourself."

She softened. He'd been worried about her. "It was easy. I have no idea how that boy lost his head. The one you told us about. I would have had to try to hit the wall."

"Damn you, Ria!"

"No, Benny. Stop!"

She ducked her head away from his rage. His elbow connected with her ribs. Her reflexes had gotten slow.

"The NDT is not going to see it that way. If they see this video, we are screwed." He stepped closer again, fists at his sides, his eyes narrow slits. Ria backed up, shifted sideways to protect her cut leg. She was pressed against the cold metal of the garage door, could feel the faint vibration of it behind her, an echo of her own adrenaline-fueled heart racing.

When the slap came, she was ready. Now she remembered how to hold her breath and tears. She was one step out of her body by the time the second one connected.

He grabbed both her arms, squeezing tight, shaking her, rattling her.

"You're in violation of your contract, Miss Victoria Marie

Williams. You can't take unnecessary risks. You can't do whatever the hell you want. You belong to the NDT."

As he let go, she blinked to refocus. His fist was inches from her face, his teeth clenched. She braced herself. Her old friend Fear whispered sweet nothings in her ear.

Finally, he stepped back. He was done. His hands opened, and he flexed his fingers. The way he always did when the rage had dimmed. Her own fingers stretched and then folded inward. Her chipped tooth felt rough under her tongue.

THIRTY-NINE

Everything hurt more in the morning. Her jaw was tender, and the back of her head, too. Most unfamiliar was the cut on her leg. Ria had been aware of it all night, in the background of her sleep. Every time she moved, she felt the burning sting of the skin flaps tugging against each other under the mish-mash of crisscrossed bandages; but if she stayed in one position too long, it throbbed with a dull ache. She'd ripped open up the largest organ of her body. It had to hurt. Besides, hurting was easier than thinking.

She pushed the thought of Benny's visit into the darkest part of her brain. She couldn't think about going to the NDT. With him. It was too confusing, too many unknowns. It was like she was back trying to learn algebra—mixing numbers and letters had never worked for her. Each one on their own was tricky enough.

Instead, she concentrated on getting ready for caving. She wasn't going to miss the overnight trip. Not for pain, not for anything. She might never have another chance. Besides, it was the only way to skip the constant replay of last night. She'd convinced herself she and Benny could start over, fresh, with new rules, but last night felt too familiar. It was an echo of too many other times she'd screwed up.

She showed up at the Talley's house with her backpack, but it held only her toothbrush and shammy towel. She'd told her parents she was spending the night with Maggie. They didn't know enough to doubt her.

Other gear was lined up in the garage. It was clear she'd missed a lot of planning.

"You need to carry your sleeping bag. Here's your share of water to carry." Cotton handed her a gallon jug.

He divvied up the other items between them. A first aid kit, extra batteries, ropes and straps, food bags. More than reasonable precautions.

"I think I'll drink all the water now so I won't have to carry it," she said, placing her heavy backpack on her shoulders. Then, to the horrified look on Cotton's face, "I'm joking."

"Where can I put my makeup?" asked Flutie. "I have my hair dryer packed already. But I was hoping whoever brought the microwave could . . ."

"You are not amusing," said Cotton.

"He stole hours of my life last night telling me what I could and could not bring."

At the gate, Mr. Talley made them pose for a picture, all weighed down, and shiny clean.

"I can't wait to see the before-and-after. You might not recognize us," said Ria.

"It's still good to have documentation of clothing and appearances before taking a risky journey. In case we go missing," said Cotton.

A pained look crossed Mr. Talley's face. But then he forced a smile. "Stick together. We'll see you this time tomorrow, walking through this gate."

It seemed that each of them felt the same tremor of expectation urging them along the trail. Flutie was a chirper, singsong talking the whole way. Besides their height and a general kind of unruliness to their curls, it was hard to see where she and Cotton were related.

As far as talking, and pace, Ria and Cotton matched up more evenly. "How's your leg?"

"Okay." She wished he could know about Benny's visit without her telling him.

"Okay," he answered. She wasn't sure if it was simply an echo. Then he added, "I know yesterday made you feel."

It was a funny, Cotton-esque way to put it, but it sounded right. Damn if she knew what to call this feeling either.

By the time they reached the entrance, her back felt damp and sweaty beneath the extra weight of her backpack. The heaviness of her helmet felt reassuring, instead of annoying.

It had been decided that Leo would lead the first part with Flutie, then Ria and Cotton at the back. The extra gear and people made the cave sound more muffled, and felt tighter, more crowded. When they reached the tunnel—still her least favorite part—they stopped to rearrange the extra gear.

"Move your backpack to the front," said Cotton.

"So my backpack is now a frontpack?"

"Yes. Backpack, frontpack. Backpack, frontpack."

"Just do it," said Flutie.

Ria waited at the tunnel's entrance, letting Flutie make progress ahead of her. She wanted to be sure she had some extra space before she started through. She reached her hand behind her, found Cotton's. She squeezed, then let go.

Caving had filled her empty days. And along the way, she'd fallen for him. Or maybe it had been more of a climb. Either way, she liked the view. "How are you feeling, Cotton? Where are you on the chart?"

"I'm excited. Anticipating. Curious. Oh, and happy."

"About making more maps?"

"Yes. I think this is going to be a very satisfying challenge to incorporate all the new data."

"I love it when you talk maps."

"Which part? The creation or the interpretation?" He paused. "Are you teasing me?"

"A little bit. But not completely."

"Where are you guys?" Leo's voice came through the dark.

It was an odd feeling to crawl with her backpack strapped to her chest, drooping down toward the floor, but better than having the extra weight on her back where she wouldn't be able to control it. Her leg hurt more in this position, but the sharp ache was a distraction. She waited as long as she possibly could before she started counting. That trick still worked.

By the time they made the long trek and climb down into the pool room, they were all ready for a break. She needed to pace her water intake, but the mix of being thirsty and knowing it was the heaviest part of her load made it hard to sip slowly.

Flutie sat by the edge of the pond and peered in. "You seriously went swimming in here?"

"Yeah, I couldn't resist. Not an entirely great idea." But it hadn't been awful, either. It was the kind of risky impulse she could be proud of now. Like the quarry. Even if she'd been wrong to do it, she was glad she did.

"I didn't bring a swimsuit," said Flutie. "But we could skinny-dip."

"No," said Cotton. "We can't."

Ria nodded in agreement. She loved the way her helmet light added emphasis. It wasn't only that she had to keep her bandages dry. The idea of swimming naked with Cotton was one thing, but with his best friend and sister, well, that was entirely something else.

"It would be physically impossible for me to skinny-dip," said Cotton. "I would have to chunky-dunk."

Their laughter echoed around them. A few minutes later, when Leo and Flutie had moved to the other side, she squeezed his hand. She liked his dunkability.

"This is where we head into uncharted territory," said Leo.

"Good," said Cotton. "I thought you and Flutie might have gone past this point."

"You're so annoying," Flutie groaned.

"This is a great place to camp," said Leo. "We could leave our extra gear here and plan to come back for the night."

"No," said Ria. "We want to go as far as we can. There will be another good place. We'll keep going until we find it."

"I'm not sure that's smart," said Leo.

"That's what we're doing," Cotton said loudly. "The whole reason we planned this trip was to make progress. You're losing sight of the goal, Leo."

"And you're being bossy. As usual," said Flutie.

"You don't get to make decisions. This was one of the guidelines we agreed on. You're here as a guest. You don't have the knowledge or the experience to make choices. You are to do as you are told."

"But you don't get to be a know-it-all."

Ria stepped into the dark channel, away from their harsh words. As she moved along the slick trail, acquainting herself with these particular walls, another light's glow came behind her. Leo had followed her.

"You're smart to stay out of it," he said.

"They sound so upset."

"This argument is nothing. This is pleasant conversation. They'll quit soon."

She used to wish she'd had a brother or sister. Now she wasn't so sure. But Leo's prediction proved right, and soon Cotton and Flutie were with them again.

If it wasn't for Leo's alarm set to go off every half hour, Ria wouldn't have had any idea how long they'd been inside the cave.

With no sun and no outside world interruptions, there weren't any of the usual ways to mark time passing. Reading the numbers on her mostly useless phone stopped meaning anything. They'd done some climbing after the pool room, enough that she wondered how close they were to the surface, but then the path flattened out so they could walk.

And walk. And walk.

Every so often, Cotton took a picture of a formation or variance in the rock. "To keep a record, so we know we're on the right path."

It didn't seem entirely reliable, but it was something. Even the most distinct rocky shapes had started to look way too similar. She couldn't swear they weren't walking in one big circle. At one point she built a rock cairn, hoping they wouldn't pass it again.

"I need a break," Flutie said finally.

Ria was exhausted too. It didn't matter in time how long they'd been going. It was the walking and climbing, but it was also the strain of the dim light. Of having to be aware of her head. Always thinking about where to put her feet, and hands, all of her.

"We need a place to break for real food and sleep," said Leo. "We could probably make it back to the pool room."

"Or we could see what's ahead," said Ria, unsure if she was being unreasonable. Going backward seemed like they'd be ending the trip. They'd be giving up before getting anywhere worth the difficulty of the work. She was still waiting for amazing.

"If we get too tired, someone is going to get hurt."

The compromise was Cotton and Leo going on ahead, leaving Ria and Flutie waiting and sipping hot cocoa from Leo's thermos.

"I want to see something," said Flutie. "Like, really see it. Not with all the shadows and darkness."

Ria knew what she meant, but it wasn't an option at this point. No point wishing. Instead she said, "Hot cocoa was an excellent choice."

"Mmm. Are you Cotton's girlfriend?"

"Yeah." She'd thought that was obvious. Maybe a vague sort of cluelessness ran in the family.

"Leo swears you've even kissed him. But wow. It's so weird to think of him that way. He's not exactly easy to please."

"Me neither," said Ria, realizing it was true.

"You're so different from each other."

In some ways, maybe. Ria leaned back against the rock wall. "Sameness is not the same thing as being in love."

"Oh my God. You sound like Cotton. And you said 'in love.' My mind has been officially blown." Flutie paused, then added, "In a good way."

A clatter and stomping of boots on rock announced the return of the boys as they burst around the corner. There was a loud *thunk* and Cotton's helmet flew off.

"Cotton!" Ria jumped up and grabbed it. "You knocked your light out."

"I hit my head."

"Duh," said Flutie. Then, more gently, "Are you okay?"

"I think so." He took the helmet from Ria. Jiggled the light, but it stayed dark. "Good thing I have another bulb."

"And, we found a place. There's a cool grotto ahead. Ria, you were right."

"She usually is," said Cotton.

She was certain that no one in the history of Ria had ever said that about her. He had such a different way of seeing things.

Once they'd fixed his helmet, they moved along the next passageway. Excitement and renewed energy radiated off all of them. The walls in this part of the cave were slick and even. Too smooth to take note of. Every inch was the same shade of brown.

And then, it wasn't.

The cave opened up. The space wasn't wide or long. It was bigger than her trampoline, but not by much. All around them were a dizzying collection of rocky shelves—they could almost be called stairs—embedded within the rock walls, leading upward and downward, sometimes both, at the same time. Each variation dripped with brilliant stalactite crystals. The whole room glowed with a hint of blue, or yellow. Green and almost orange. Except the subtle colors seemed to shift and change when she tried to study them.

She moved to the wall, shining her light. Up close, the crystal looked grayish-white, but as she stepped back, the faint hue of color returned. "It's us! The colors are us. We're in the reflection." She laughed at the surprise of it. "It's a kaleidoscope room."

There was a buzz among them as they set up a simple camp,

all the while playing with their reflections. They spread a tarp on the ground so they wouldn't be resting in damp earth and mud. Cotton set up his camp stove on one of the lower steps. The flame of it set red and orange dancing on the wall. The smell of the stew he'd brought felt like it was thick and rich enough to earn a reflection too.

"I think this is the best thing I've ever eaten. In fact, there's no point in eating again. Nothing will ever be this delicious."

"Sounds like a challenge," said Leo.

"Yes," said Cotton. "I look forward to passing your expectations."

The room was big enough for their four sleeping bags, but small enough that there wasn't any arguing about the arrangement. The girls were in the middle and the boys were on either end. They were all too close and cozy for any kind of kissing. Especially knowing the way every rustle of the sleeping bag sounded louder in the dark.

Ria didn't feel tired enough to sleep, but she closed her eyes against the nothing to see. A lullaby of scents and sounds and knowing she wasn't alone mellowed her mind, sending her onward.

FORTY

Ria woke with a sudden shock. She wasn't sure what had startled her awake. She blinked wildly, felt close to panic when her eyes didn't work. There was nothing to see in this darkest of dark. Her heart thumped too hard; she felt sweaty on the back of her neck. Her jaw ached. She'd been gritting her teeth so tight they didn't feel like hers. Especially when she couldn't find the chipped one. But it was still there.

Fear was here, too.

She rolled over, her knees bumping against Cotton. He sat up. She sensed him reaching out, then a small light appeared, forcing her to squint against its surprise. She grabbed his hand and tugged.

Wordlessly, they left their sleeping bags and headed out of the crystal room. The sweat under her clothes left her feeling shivery. She had no idea how long they'd been asleep. Or what time it was. They made their way along the trail, as if they knew where they were going.

A few minutes later, after turning twice, Cotton stopped walking. She could smell her own sweat mixed with his. It wasn't unpleasant. Closer to reassuring. Their bodies were working. Her cut still hurt. She was tender in the spots Benny had hit. Also, her hips felt sore and her shoulders were tight. But it was the low-grade burn of fear she'd woken with that had left her unsteady.

"What's wrong?"

"What would you miss most?" she asked. "If we got lost down here. If we never made it back, what would you miss?"

"We aren't lost," said Cotton. "I know exactly where we are."

She felt relief to hear him say what she'd trusted and assumed. Hoped.

"I'm scared," she said. But it wasn't the cave that had her feeling shaky. It was Benny. He didn't belong here, but he'd slipped in, crawled along beside her, nestled into the spot that made her breathing feel tight.

"How do you carry your missing every day?" She barely recognized her own voice, all strangled and twisted. "I know you miss Esther all the time, so what do you do with the missing? Where does it go so you can do other things?"

"It doesn't go anywhere. It's still here. I miss her now. Right here. But you're here too. And that's good. It's both."

She reached up and he bent over, and in the middle space, they kissed. It was an awkward reach. Her arms felt too aware of themselves and helmets made kissing difficult. Left on the ground with the light on, was much better.

Cotton was right. This was good. The cave wall behind her felt cold and damp, but it was such a trivial discomfort, irrelevant compared to the heat of him, warm and solid, pressed tight against her. Even with the ache and swirl in her head, kissing him felt right and real and now. In the dark, tightly wrapped together, missing took on a different color. But Fear was here too.

"I'm scared of Benny."

"He's not here."

"He's always in my head. All the time. I'm scared he's going to find out I'm here. He won't like it. He'll say it's dangerous or reckless or a waste of time. I've kept this place a secret from everyone I know because of him. Someone else would have told him, not because they want to hurt me, but because he always finds things out. This cave is the one thing he doesn't know." Her voice was thick in her aching throat.

"It was Benny who scared me at that meet. The other coach yelled, but in my head it was *him*. I thought I was being chased, so I ran. I know it doesn't make sense, but I was running from Benny."

"He won't find you here. You're safe."

But she couldn't stay here forever. And when they left the dark, Benny would be there, waiting for her. They'd be headed to Colorado and the NDT where she'd have to keep her balance—and Benny's, too—in a whole new place with all-new pressures and coaches and comparisons. The unknown was too enormous and dark, filled with shadows and worries.

Cotton wrapped his arm around her. For now he was someone to lean on. Now was her new favorite time.

"If he's so awful, why do I miss it so much? Why do I miss diving?"

"Diving is not the same as Benny."

But for her, it was. Diving had always been wrapped up in his orders and approval, and control.

"I don't know how to dive." Cotton's voice was deep and warm. "I understand the different parts: approach, hurdle, lift, flip, entry. And I know logically that you control your muscles and move your body in a particular way for the desired motion, but I don't understand how you put it all together. It seems impossible."

"It takes practice. Hard work."

"Yes. But I still don't fully understand it. I couldn't do it. Most people can't. Not like you. So maybe I have this wrong, but I keep going back to Ms. Q's rules."

"What do you mean?"

"It's not acceptable to hit. We use our words, not our hands."

She didn't know whether to laugh or cry. Benny didn't follow Ms. Q's rules. Or anyone's but his own.

"Cotton? Ria?" Flutie sounded worried, from somewhere along the rocks.

Ria pulled herself away from him and called out, "We'll be right there." She handed him his helmet and said, "We're being summoned," the way she knew he was about to say.

After a quick breakfast, they were all eager to get moving.

It was a tight fit now. Four times two was a lot of feet too close together. She needed to move, to leave this cramped space and to shake off her haunting worry.

"The dark is seriously getting on my nerves," said Flutie.

They all laughed, but Ria agreed that something about this part of the cave felt different. The echoes here were a lower pitch. It was like the walls had a different composition. Or maybe it was a thickness of the air.

When Cotton suddenly stopped, she crashed into him. She heard Flutie slip seconds before her boots collided with the back of Ria's heels. Then the bump of Leo at the back.

"Cotton! Warn us if you're going to stop," fussed Flutie.

He didn't answer. He took off his helmet and turned it over in his hands. Ria shone her light so he could see. He fiddled with the inner lining, then ran his hand over his head. "I think I have a knot. From last night."

Ria reached out, ran her fingers through his hair, roaming his scalp. "Whoa, Cotton! Yes, you have a knot. That must hurt."

"Please stop pressing it."

"Sorry."

"Are you good to keep going?" asked Leo.

"Yes." Except he still didn't move.

"What's wrong?" Ria asked.

"Listen."

At first, all she heard was breathing. All four of them were slightly winded. There was a creak from someone's gear. Then, she realized she heard a roar of white noise in the background.

Faster and steadier than the sound of bats. "What is it?" she asked, bracing herself for the answer.

"Water," said Cotton.

She laughed—they all did—as fear and hesitation morphed into thrill. "Let's find it."

A few minutes later, they turned a corner, and the roar intensified. Ria could feel moisture in the air. Little bits of cool spray hit her face, her hands, the only parts of her exposed. Tiny droplets on Cotton's eyelashes glowed in her helmet light.

"It must be close. The ground is slippery."

As if to prove his point, he slid, crashing sideways against the rock. His helmet illuminated the wall and the black spray-painted words: *Jerry loves Joey.*

"I hate that," said Leo. "It's so Neanderthal."

"Someone else was here." Disappointed, she looked around, as if she expected Jerry and Joey to appear. She turned to Cotton. "Did you hit your head again?"

"I don't know." He stood up straighter, throwing his shoulders back. "I think I'm fine."

Flutie said, "Well, except for the big dose of awkward to go with your bruises."

"Let's keep going." Leo maneuvered his way in front. Ria stayed in back, behind Cotton and Flutie.

Around one more twist of the trail, they—all of them at once—finally and suddenly saw what made the thunderous roar. A waterfall. A real, honest-to-goodness, water-gushing, spray-streaming, water-falling waterfall.

It started up high, above Cotton's head, at least twice his height. The water looked like it was being poured from the rock. The tremendous force of it formed a white and frothy wall pulsing and throbbing, surging and retreating. And loud. So loud. Each and every splish, splash, and whoosh echoed, making a roar of noise with no particular shape and border. Ria wished she could pause the sound a minute, just to catch her breath and take in the waterfall without feeling quite so overwhelmed. But maybe she was supposed to be overwhelmed.

"Where does the water go?"

"There's a pocket in the rocks. I can hear the water under us. There's a river below. There must be a whole other layer of cave down there." Cotton was in observation mode. He'd already started taking measurements, making notes.

Leo and Flutie moved to the left side of the waterfall, holding out their hands, letting the water pour into them. Ria slipped off her shoes for a better feel for the terrain, then clambered over the rocks, trying to get another view, and to see if the sound wasn't quite so intense on the other side.

There was an opening behind the waterfall, possibly leading to more cave. She couldn't see much from where she stood. She saw a way to get there through a narrow, horizontal slit between the rocks. She called to Cotton, but her words were lost in the roar. He was busy studying something. The others might not fit this way, but she could take a quick peek and see if it was worth exploring. Flat, with her stomach against the rock, she moved feet-first backward, into the chasm. At the last second she realized her helmet wouldn't fit while it was on her head. She took it off, pulled it through, and turned to see where she'd ended up.

Her foot slipped and the rest of her followed, down, down, sliding downward along the slick rocky wall, with a rush into a cold pool of froth.

The water gurgled and roiled, over her shoulders, into her mouth. A current, strong and whirling, pulled her still downward. It wasn't enough that she'd slipped down this chimney-like space; the water pulled her even lower, under the surface. Panic hit, hard. She couldn't breathe, couldn't yell for help, couldn't think at all. She squeezed her eyes shut. She couldn't bear to lose her contacts, too. Her legs kicked reflexively, her arms reached for something, anything, but only found slick rock.

She was going to drown. The pull was too strong, too everywhere to think she could win this fight. There was no point struggling. Everything was over. Fear whispered, "Let go."

Eyes still closed, she leaned back into the pillow of bubbles.

She didn't sink.

The churning waves still raged against her arms and legs and spine, but floating near the surface, she bobbed instead of dragged. She'd lost her helmet in the fall, but when she squinted, peeking with one eye, the space glowed faintly, eerily—wherever it was, its bulb was still lit. As long as she stayed prone, she floated, slowly spinning and dipping, but able to breathe.

Her feet bumped against the wall. The surface felt nobby and craggy—climbable. She sat up in the water and immediately was thrust downward. Being vertical made for dangerous suction. She returned to her back-float position and braced her fingers against the slick walls behind her head. Carefully, slowly, desperately, she spun her body clockwise, reaching for the rougher place she'd felt with her toes.

Once her fingers found the rocky handles, she paused to catch her breath and bearings. To be sure she knew which way was up. Now she could see her helmet sitting on a ledge, only a few feet above. Close enough to look possible.

Keeping her head back, she bent her legs, then, ignoring the dread of returning upright, braced her feet against the rock and used all her strength to lift her torso up, above the water's surface, scrabbling for the rock, and grabbing on, precariously hanging in the middle.

"Cotton?" She could barely hear her own voice over the sounds of the waterfall and the whirlpool below. She couldn't yell again; she had to focus on her grip.

There were only inches above her fingers to the ledge where her helmet sat or inches below her feet where the water swirled and roared.

Inches in either direction.

The direction mattered more than the distance. She needed to go up. But the pull of gravity urged her down.

The water swirled below her. Circling, twirling, calling to her. It looked beautiful in the dim and eerie light. It would be so easy to let go.

FORTY-ONE

Leo's face appeared above her, looking curious, then annoyed. "What are you doing? That's so dangerous. Do you have a death wish?"

She couldn't hold on much longer. But at least now someone knew where to look for her body if she got sucked under. Her parents wouldn't have to wonder where she'd gone.

Then Leo reappeared through a different, wider opening and sprawled facedown on the ledge.

"Grab my hand. I'll help you climb." His hand was only inches away, but she couldn't make herself let go. Everyone knew Fear brought about a fight-or-flight response. But too often, in between those two choices was paralysis. The instinct to freeze. Even though her fingers ached and felt ready to slip, to move them would require something she didn't have. Something called trust.

Leo must have understood, or he was tired of waiting,

because he reached down and grabbed her wrist. Only then was she able to let the rock go and grab his wrist in return—and then they did it again with her second hand. Her feet pressed against the notches in the rock, her legs lifting the rest of her along with Leo's tug.

Finally up, she scooted herself into sitting position, pulling her helmet back on her head. Her panting echoed loud and rough. The cold hadn't fully kicked in yet.

"Figures you went swimming. You can't see a pool and not dive in." Leo sounded amused, only slightly annoyed. Definitely not like a hero who'd saved her life.

Too out of breath to speak, she shrugged. He had no idea she'd almost died. Vanished. Gone forever.

She followed Leo out of the whirlpool chasm, back to a space near the waterfall. He climbed down to the path where Cotton and Flutie were looking at something carved into the rocks. She'd almost died and everyone else was exactly the same.

"There's a chimney pool behind the waterfall. Ria went swimming, of course," said Leo.

Flutie laughed but Cotton frowned.

"Did you get your bandage wet?"

She nodded.

"Your clothes are wet too."

"Can you bring me my pack so I can change?"

It was bizarrely easy to act like nothing bad had happened. There was no point in crying now but her eyes filled anyway.

She was so tired of this heavy, annoying dark.

Cotton brought her the pack along with her shoes. He focused on examining the walls while she awkwardly replaced her wet clothes with drier ones. She slipped on her shoes and tied them. She completed her transformation as though she'd never fallen into that whirlpool. It felt crucial that they not know. It would only upset them. And her. She had to pretend she was the same. She was okay.

"Is this yours, Cotton?" She picked up a pocketknife a few feet away.

"No. Where did you find that?"

"Look. There's also a water bottle. Hey, do you think this is Australia? Is this where everything falls?"

"No. That's not right. Those are not our things."

Now she saw that deeper back on the shelf where they sat, in a crevice—a cave within a cave—a blanket lay spread across the rock. It looked inviting. She reached out to touch it, then pulled her hand back. The blanket was wet. Cold and clammy.

Cotton's smile was gone. His face looked crumpled. Melted. Then it turned hard and full of lines. The shadows intensified his glare.

"Get down, Ria. Don't touch anything." His voice sounded raspy, afraid.

A sickly panic rushed through her.

"What? Why?" She slid down, following him, hurrying, blood rushing in her ears, instinct making her scramble. "What's wrong? What did you see?"

"What's going on?" asked Leo.

Ria could feel Cotton trembling. The shaking rumbled through his chest, down to his hands now gripped tightly around her biceps.

"Stay away from there," yelled Cotton.

"You're hurting me." She twisted out of his clutch. Gasping, feeling like the air was too thin and pale, "What did you see?"

"That thing. It's wrong."

"The *blanket*? Probably some couple fooling around left it here." She looked back at the shelf, still unable to find what had hit him so hard.

"Don't you see the stuffed animal?"

Now she saw something brown. A bunny, judging by the ears.

"Do you recognize it?"

He stood, staring. She wondered if she needed to remind him to breathe. Flutie was silent, visibly pulling back, stepping behind Leo.

"Is that bunny Esther's?" Ria whispered, leaning into his arm.

"No." His voice was impossibly small. Fragile.

"Hey, Cotton. It's okay," said Leo.

"We have to tell someone." His voice sounded urgent now, desperate.

"Tell who? And what do you want them to know? I don't get it." She bit her lip, trying desperately to understand.

"Someone's been using this cave."

"People hang out in caves. People like us." She pointed in the direction of the graffiti. "People like Jerry and Joey."

"There are so many sickos in this world, Ria. People do bad things. All the time."

Flutie started crying.

"That's enough, Cotton," said Leo.

"We have to tell the police."

"What will you tell them?"

"They need to do DNA testing on that blanket. Someone must have brought a kid down here. They need to look for a body."

"That's . . ." Ria bit back the word "crazy," because it seemed too true. Cotton looked wild. Unhinged. Out of his mind with misery. His hands smacked against his legs. "We don't know who brought the blanket and stuffed animal there. Or why. There are plenty of reasons behind things. That's an awful lot of filling in the blanks."

"It's a stuffed animal!" His voice was a mix of rage and tears. "What if we could save some kid?"

"Stop it, Cotton!" Flutie sounded harsh. "You're spiraling. Get a grip."

"No! No, no, no!"

"Don't yell!" Leo sounded awfully close to yelling. Beside him, Flutie slipped and knocked against the wall.

"We can't help anyone until we get out of here." Ria swallowed the deep lump of sad in the back of her throat.

"Yes," Cotton said in a rush of motion, heading back the way they'd come.

"Wait." With Cotton so close to hysterical, adrenaline and confusion made it even harder to transform her thoughts into words. She said, slowly, trying to figure out if she was as right as she thought, "I think we should keep going the other way."

He didn't argue. But he didn't agree, either. He hummed softly, fidgeting with his coveralls. Flutie moved in next to him, wrapped her arm around his waist.

"I think this must lead us to another entrance," said Ria. "That's what we've been looking for. I think we found it. That's why there's this stuff here. They didn't come the way we did. There has to be another way in that's closer." The logic of it sharpened in her mind. If she was right, Cotton would see there was another explanation for what they'd found. "We need to go this way."

Now that she'd said it, she believed it even more strongly. Every inch of her sensed there was another way to reach air and light.

"We need to get Cotton out of here, now," said Flutie.

Leo wasn't as easily convinced. "You don't know where we're headed. Even if you're right and there's another entrance, we have no idea where we'll end up."

"We have some idea. We haven't gone that far. It's not like we've left the planet."

"Think how long it took us to get here."

"Exactly. This has to be shorter and faster."

"No, it doesn't. It could be as far, or even farther. Or not at all." Leo had his arms crossed over his chest.

Anger bubbled up inside her. Leo looked so damn stubborn. Like he knew everything. She felt like shoving him into the rock. Slapping him. He'd thought she was messing around back there, like she was dumb, impulsive Ria, leaping in with her clothes on.

But he couldn't know what she didn't tell him.

"I didn't go swimming behind the waterfall. I fell. There was a current or something swirling all around me. I kept getting pulled under. Leo saved me, but he didn't even notice. Thank you, by the way." She took a deep breath.

"You could have drowned," said Cotton. "You could have died. You could have . . ."

"I'm fine. None of that happened. But yeah, it could have. And right now I need to get out of here. We all do. And our best chance is to find a different exit."

"Seriously?" Leo sounded confused. Then he added, "It's up to you, Cotton. Which way do you want to go?"

She'd understand if they wanted the sure thing. Even if they didn't follow her, she was going on her own.

"Let's go." Cotton started to walk the direction she'd hoped he would. It was more of a shuffle than a step, but he was moving forward.

Their progress was slow. Especially with the beat of *hurry hurry hurry* matching her heartbeat, urging her to move, to get out of the dark. Each step felt too long, the rocks too rough, everything too, too much.

A whoosh of wind swirled around her face, startling her, setting goosebumps along her skin. She wanted to hurry away from it, but Cotton grabbed her arm. "Wait."

In a steady monotone he said, "It's a pit cave. We can get out that way." He pointed up.

They circled around him to see. A slit of light shone down, hitting the walls of the rocky chimney that reached up, way over their heads.

Leo went first, scrambling up the rocky wall. "I see the opening. The tunnel flattens out. We're almost there."

Wherever *there* was, they'd find it soon.

Cotton lifted Flutie, and Ria coached her climb, pointing out the knobs to reach for, the crannies where she could tuck her foot. And then it was Ria's turn.

She didn't want to leave him down in the cave alone, but Cotton had to boost her to the spot where she could get her foot on a ledge. She scrambled up, the bulk of her backpack scraping and bumping against the last bit of cave. She paused for a second and was relieved to hear him following.

Finally, they reached fresh air and sunlight. Ria hoisted herself out of the hole, then Cotton came too. Both of them stood in the sunshine, blinking back tears against the light.

FORTY-TWO

The world was wide and bright. Blinding.

Ria looked down the hole to see what it looked like from this angle. It was as deep a fall as she'd felt climbing out, but the dank, dark of it smelled sour and wrong. Or maybe that was them. Their sweat and extended time in the cave had caught up with them in the fresh air.

"Do you recognize this place?" Leo pulled out his GPS unit.

"Yes. Ria climbed that wall, from the other side." Cotton's voice sounded clipped and monotone. He started walking in that direction. "We're on someone's property. We need to leave."

That's what she wanted to do. Escape. Bolt. Vamoose.

The climb over the wall wasn't hard, but they moved slowly, getting reacquainted with the sun and the sky and the living growing things. The others were talking and making a plan. They made calls and arrangements, but she wasn't listening. The buzz in her ears, the hum in her torso, the ants-in-her-pants squirm of *gotta go* made everything else fade away.

If Cotton was right about the blanket and the stuffed animal, she couldn't bear it. She didn't want to know the how or the who or the what. She knew it was weak and cowardly, but her heart couldn't take knowing something bad mixed in with the cave. Their cave.

Even if he was wrong, and the blanket was only a blanket, that was awful too. Because that horrible idea was in him, close to the surface, ready to bubble up. He carried that with him, always. It wasn't fair that he knew things that made him see the world that way. She couldn't look at him now. She didn't want to see that hurt in his eyes. She wasn't strong enough.

Losing Esther had changed him. He had scars, thick and twisted. Most of the time he kept them buried but now they were out in the open, raw and tender.

Hers, too.

She'd buried her hurts for years. Ashamed of pushing Benny to the point of exploding, she'd hidden the truth. She'd worn all his disappointments, his frustrations, his anger, and covered them, keeping them tucked away, out of sight. But the tender spots had reshaped her, made her heart beat to a different rhythm. His anger had twisted and rewired her mind, making it hard to trust her own senses.

As they reached the road that would lead them back to the strip club, she dropped her backpack and helmet on the ground.

And then, without looking back, she ran.

The wind felt sharp and cold on her face. Her eyes watered. Or maybe those were tears. She concentrated on running. Her battered body could take her away from thinking.

The sharp pain in her leg, along the bandage line and stretching out beyond, past the tug and pull of her skin, became her focal point. A way to count her steps and regulate her pace. It reminded her that she was, in fact, moving.

At some point, it stopped hurting. She was too busy concentrating on breathing. Her lungs felt tight and hot. It was like being stuck in the moment of resurfacing after a dive. Desperate for air, but wary of the water all around. Her body, untrusting and unsure.

She'd known somewhere, in the back of her mind, where she was headed. Seeing the Aquaplex building in the distance gave her a burst of adrenaline.

Her rubbery legs carried her up the sidewalk. She staggered past the outdoor pool, closed now for fall and winter. She headed around the building, to the back, where she knew Benny had entered. He refused to use the entrance at the front. Not slowing her momentum, she crashed against the door, hard.

Her fingers wouldn't cooperate to work the handle. It was slippery and overly complicated, and she couldn't see through the mess of sweat and mud dripping in her eyes. But then, suddenly and wonderfully, with a rush of light, like the moment the sun pops up over the horizon, the door opened and she fell forward, with a crash onto the cement floor of the storage room.

She crawled, lifted into a crouch, grabbed one of the shelves to steady herself, then stood upright. She made her way through the crowded room, out to the pool deck. She moved across the tiles, slowly, smoothly, careful not to slip.

Voices echoed around her as she headed for the three-meter board. She knew, in one small, distant part of her brain, that she looked deranged and lost. Mud on her ragged clothes, streaked with sweat on her skin, her hair mussed and plastered.

A whistle from the lifeguard pierced the air as she made her way up the ladder, leaving a trail of mud along the rail. The minerals within the muck shone in the artificial light. They looked so pretty, sparkly and brilliant, against the shiny chrome. She headed up and up, back to where she belonged.

On the board, she wished she'd taken off her shoes. But it didn't matter. She'd dealt with far worse inconveniences before. She looked out over the pool area where her team had stopped diving, stopped talking, stopped everything. With her contacts in, she could see everyone. Clearly, finally. All eyes were focused on her.

Benny's, too. But he couldn't touch her here. The board was her refuge.

"Hey!" Sean frantically waved his arms from the lifeguard chair, then blew his whistle as a bonus. "Ria! What are you doing? You have to get down."

She moved to the edge of the board.

"No! Use the ladder! Ria! Don't go in the pool like that!" Sean sounded hysterical. "Benny! Do something! Get her down!"

"Turn around and climb down that ladder." Benny stood up from his chair, moved to the edge of the pool. She knew what he might do. What he was capable of. What he'd already done to her. Because she'd let him.

"I can't," she said. "That's against the rules. *Your* rules. Once I'm on the board, there's only one way down. No balking allowed."

She peered over the edge. The blue of the water rippled and shimmered. It was fake, that blue. It wasn't the water. It was only paint. An illusion. Water didn't have any color at all.

"This used to be the scariest part of diving for me," she said. "Standing here, knowing I had to do something hard, something I wasn't sure I could. Fear would keep me company up here. It reminded me to slow down and be careful. It wanted to help. Fear helped me be a better diver. But you messed that up, Benny." She bounced once, feeling the spring of the board.

"I almost died today. I was in a dark place, all alone. Scared of being lost, forever. Fear showed up, but it couldn't save me. It didn't even want to." She bounced slowly, rhythmically. "Because the thing is, if I disappeared, then *you* wouldn't find me. I wouldn't have to be scared anymore."

"You're obviously upset." His voice was calm, reasonable. "Get down so we can talk."

She hesitated. Wondered if talking could work.

"I trusted you." She bounced harder. "I believed everything

you said." Each bounce lifted her a little higher. Each *thunk* bolstered her more. "I did anything you wanted. I gave you everything." She launched herself several feet into the air. There was the illusion of being out of control, but then she landed on the narrow plank, caught her balance. "I never complained, I never told anyone the truth about all those times you hurt me."

"Come on, Ria. Get down." He was begging now. If she didn't know better, she'd think he sounded worried. Maybe even scared. "If you turn around and climb down that ladder, we can figure things out. Together. You'll see how things really are."

"But I see everything from here." She opened her arms wide.

"Don't do something you'll regret."

Someone, somewhere, splashed in the pool. Voices were building in the silence, or maybe they'd never stopped. Time went on, always. There was no pause button, no way to stop and move in reverse. It was too late for regret. She had to go on.

"I chipped my tooth that day in Los Angeles. When I fell, I hit it on a rail. I never told anyone. I've been too used to keeping your secrets."

"That fall was your own damn fault. Your head got screwed up. Like it is right now."

He was right, but wrong, too. They'd both gotten so many things wrong.

"You're the reason I ran at that meet. You, Benny. I was scared of you." Tears streamed down her face, taking with them the embarrassment of that day when she saw the shock, the confusion of everyone who couldn't understand why she ran.

"I didn't touch you." His voice had turned hard.

"You didn't have to. You'd trained me to be scared. Every hit, kick, slap. All the times you screamed and pushed. All that training." She ignored the tremble in her voice and kept going. "You know what the hardest, scariest part of the dive is for me now? It's when I come up for air and see you, Benny. I never know when you're going to hurt me. Or why. But I always know you can."

"That's enough!" He turned and kicked the deck chair. The way he'd kicked her, too many times to count. "Get down here or . . ."

He charged toward the ladder. For a terrible moment Fear was there, taking all her air. But there was another blur of movement, all across the deck as her teammates moved, rushing to beat him there. Her team stood at the base of the ladder, blocking him.

Sean's whistle blew, loud and sharp. Warning. Reassuring.

Maggie slipped through the crowd and headed up to join Ria on the board. She moved beside her, their shoulders touching.

Benny crossed his arms, glaring. "You're blowing your future all over again."

"You mean *yours*. I can still dive without you. *You* need us—all of us—we're the ones on the board. Without us, you're nothing. I'm going to tell the NDT about you. I'm going to tell everyone."

"You really think the NDT will want you knowing what a head case you are?" He laughed, cold and steely. "You've lost it worse than I thought."

She faltered, then felt Maggie squeeze her hand.

"You're right. I have lost something. I've lost part of myself. The fierce fighter part. The part of me who would have saved herself today. The part of me who would never hesitate at a second chance with the NDT. But that's because you stole it from me. And now I'm taking it back. You don't get to take anything more. Not from me, or anyone else."

"We're done. It's over!" He turned and headed for the exit, awfully close to running.

Ria had never felt so sure she had the right answer. But being right didn't mean being safe.

"What happened to you?" Maggie stared into her eyes, looking worried, like she cared.

"It's a long story. A long way from there to here. I have so much to tell you."

"Then let's get out of here. I think we'd better hurry. Security is coming."

She was still wearing her muddy clothes, but she couldn't take them off, couldn't let go.

"How?"

"More up than out." Maggie grinned.

"Come with me," she begged.

Maggie knew what she meant. They'd done this before. It

was a way to show off, but also a way to share the trip down. Ria flipped into a handstand at the edge of the board. Maggie moved in, grabbing Ria's muddy ankles. Maggie oscillated gently, then more surely. Ria let her do the work of it.

"One, two . . ." Maggie counted.

On three, they lifted off the board, bodies pressed tight together. Ria's face mushed against Maggie's shins as they moved into a layout flip. Bodies straight, aligned, and holding on tight, spinning as one, feeling as if there couldn't possibly be time or space to rotate . . . until they did.

She remembered now, there was a joy in falling.

FORTY-THREE

When Ria finally got home, there were hours of talking to her parents. Even though the Talleys had called and done the heaviest explaining, Mom and Dad had questions on top of questions. She'd had a few answers, and then she'd had questions, too.

Her parents sat with her while she told them everything. She almost stopped talking when Mom started to cry, but she was stronger than that. She wasn't a quitter. And so, she went on, giving examples and details. The police weren't sure what charges could be filed, but they wanted her to make a formal report.

The International Diving Association assured her they'd complete their own investigation. Benny's coaching privileges were on hold, frozen until they could gather more information.

Her parents were going to call the NDT and all the other elite teams too. They'd help her figure out her options. They'd take her to meet the new coaches. And to talk to the other divers. It was up to her to figure out what she wanted.

Without Benny.

Finally, nestled between them in bed, she collapsed into a dark, dreamless sleep.

The next morning, they still treated her as if she was fragile. Ready to splinter. Once they finally, thankfully, left for work, she was hit with a wave of exhaustion and went back to her own bed.

When she woke again, she felt disoriented. She still wasn't used to the new arrangement of her bedroom. She reached for the wall, expecting it to be an arm's length away, forgetting it was now on the other side of the bed. She heard a noise from outside. She knew it, and yet couldn't think what it was. It felt misplaced.

She wandered downstairs to investigate.

Through the glass patio door, she spied Cotton on her trampoline. Standing—or no—that stiff-legged motion was what he called jumping.

She slid the door open. "Bend your legs."

He turned to look at her. "Will you teach me to flip?"

She hesitated, then stepped outside. He was still doing his almost-kinda-sorta jumping as she lifted herself up to join him.

"Why are you here, Cotton?"

"I wanted to see you." He tilted his head, looking at her intently, as if to prove his point. "I'm sorry I hurt you. When I grabbed you in the cave."

"Thank you. But I'm sorry I ran away. I left you alone when you were upset."

"I wasn't alone. I was with Leo and Flutie. I've been worried about you."

"No, Cotton. I was worried about you."

"We can worry about each other."

She liked the balance in that. "What did the police say about the cave?"

"They will investigate. My parents say the best thing to hope for is we never hear anything more."

"It's hard to hope for nothing."

"Yes." He slowed his pseudo-jumping. "But I don't want to expect the worst, either."

Sometimes the worst sneaks up on you anyway. Other times you cling to it, keep it close.

She slid across the springy surface until he was within reach. "Are you ready to flip?"

"Yes."

She moved to the center of the trampoline and said, "Start with your legs bent." She showed him, patting the spot beside her.

Cotton scrunched his long legs beneath him. "Like this?" he asked, toppling to the side.

"Except hold it." She waited for him to get it, then said, "Look at the edge of the trampoline. Good. Now push off with your feet and throw yourself backward."

"Backward is too scary."

"It's easier to go that direction." Seeing the look on his face, she laughed. "All right. Then throw yourself forward."

The blank look on his face told her he wasn't going anywhere, yet.

"Let's try a somersault first. Squat with me. Now, tuck your head. Try to land on the spot below your neck." She ran her hand from the place where his hair ended down between his shoulder blades. When she felt him shiver beneath her hand, she pressed more firmly, so as not to tickle. "Make this spot touch the trampoline."

Cotton moved forward, tucking and folding, then landing like a crooked lump.

"I think I forgot to straighten my legs."

He'd also missed several other steps, but what he lacked in skill, he bolstered with effort. Again and again, he threw himself forward, his body in varying degrees of curled, stretching at the last second like he might land on his feet. At one point she was sure he was going to launch himself off the trampoline, but somehow, miraculously, he landed in a crumpled heap inches from the edge.

Eventually, he lay still on his back and let out a huge sigh.

"You're a good coach."

"That's what I thought I would do. I wanted to be a coach. Like Benny."

"Not like Benny. Like Ria."

She rolled onto her back, looking up into the branches.

"I want to dive. I want to see how good I can get. I want to qualify for the Olympics and I want to win a big kick-ass gold medal. I want to be the best." She sighed. "But if diving doesn't work out, I guess I could be a stripper at the Big Top."

"Yes. You could."

It didn't make sense to be insulted. It was her idea, and he was simply confirming something she already knew was true. She was athletic and graceful. Showing her skin was a matter of anatomy. She could keep her head and feelings to herself. And yet, she didn't like Cotton agreeing so quickly.

Little bits of cloud floated behind the tree branches. They looked closer than usual. "Is it true that the sky isn't really blue?" she asked. "Is it only an illusion?"

"What does 'blue' mean?"

"I don't know. It means . . . blue." She could feel it, sense it, maybe even taste it. But there wasn't any better word to explain it. "I think the sky is blue. But it's a different kind than the blue of water. Each blue is all its own."

She rolled onto her side, facing him. She placed her hand palm-side down and stretched her fingers apart, wide and star-like. He did the same, placing his fingers carefully between hers. She could feel the heat of his skin near hers. It made her wish.

Her toes found his. Their feet pressed against each other, as if she was standing on his feet, and he was lifting her. She shifted again, bringing her hip into alignment with his. Not touching, but near. Their sizes didn't seem so unevenly matched from this view.

She thought about kissing him, but he seemed too far away. It would take too much effort to get there. She might get lost.

It was all so confusing to want something that felt so terrifyingly, ridiculously inevitable and also completely impossible. She wished wildly that being with Cotton could be easier. Easy might be nice right now.

"I think you're geeky, Ria."

"That might be the nicest thing anyone has ever said to me."

"It's true. You ask good questions and think hard thoughts. And you see things I miss. Plus . . ." He broke into that smile she loved. "You must be geeky, to be with me."

"Yeah. I must be a supergeek. Maybe I could get a cape."

"You could wear your cape to work at the Big Top." He sounded a little too matter-of-fact to be joking. "But there are lots of other things you could do instead. You could be a hairstylist. Or a reporter. You could teach kids like me to do flips. You might want to be a cartographer and make maps. There's not one right answer."

Ria's heart felt a little bit lighter. It would be nice to think she had choices. Choosing meant something. It was like winning, but better.

"I'm hungry," she said. "Let's choose something to eat."

Inside, Cotton cooked, while she cleaned, step by step, behind him. It was amazing what he could put together using the contents of her refrigerator and pantry. He hadn't smuggled in any contraband ingredients, but his brown rice with vegetables mixed in, topped with something cool yet spicy that he called "volcanic fruit salad," all tasted better than anything her parents ever made. Maybe she could learn to cook. He hadn't followed a recipe, so there wasn't a worry of muddling the instructions.

"I'm not the reason Esther will find her way home."

She set her fork down.

He pushed his plate away, even though there was still a pile of rice on it. "I'm considering going to college next year. I've arranged to take a tour of Tustin University. It's only ninety-seven miles away."

"That's great."

"I'd like you to help me see it. You'll notice things I'll miss." He looked into her eyes, searching. "Will you come with me?"

"Yes." Not a lot of words fit around the ache in her throat.

"Good." He frowned. "I can't tell how you're feeling. Your face looks wrong."

"I'm happy you might go to college. But I'll miss you."

They both knew missing too well to pretend it wasn't real. But missing meant you'd had something once. And maybe you'd have something again someday.

They moved into the family room. Without food to distract them, her house sounded overwhelmingly quiet. It was contagious, hard to interrupt. She faced him, not talking, not touching, not knowing what to do with her hands and arms and legs and the way she kept focusing in on his mouth.

"Do you want to watch something?" she asked.

"No."

"Do you want to listen to music?"

"No."

He lifted his chin, looking left, as if the ceiling corner was the most interesting spot in the room.

"What's wrong, Cotton? You look worried."

The crease between his eyebrows deepened. "I like kissing you, Ria."

She waited for him to explain the *but* she heard in the space around his words.

"When we kiss, my body gets in a hurry."

"Mine too, Cotton."

"I don't want to squid you."

"Do we need rules?"

"Yes."

"Kissing. Sitting up. All clothes on. For ten minutes."

They didn't set a timer—although she had a feeling Cotton wanted to—but it was pretty close to exact by the time they came up for air.

"I like that."

"Me too." Her body was warm and trembly with proof.

She never used to think her head would be helpful in matters of kissing. But setting the rules, the step-by-step procedure of hands and hips and here-right-here, was incredibly freeing.

Hands roamed over, then under, and between. All of it negotiated and tried and savored. There wasn't worry and nerves and whoa, oh no. It was only yesyesyes, and thisthisthis in the moment.

Her mind was a swirl of senses, a melting of colors alternated with the awareness of four hands roaming, two mouths breathing short and fast. Both of them kissing, holding, thrumming. Their bodies had taken over. Her inner density had changed. They were both wonderfully rumpled and hot and wrinkled and messy, wrapped up in a tangle of two.

It was like following a map. Or being the map. Longitudes and latitudes. North, east, south, west, and everywhere in between. One place leading to another. Being both lost and found. It was the thrill and the fear wrapped around an unknown adventure, searching and exploring, only to find they'd been here all along. This was the place they knew best.

EPILOGUE

A year later, Ria had been to seven different countries, and within those, even more cities and towns. She'd managed to officially graduate from high school and had even made a quick trip home for prom, which was not at all a horror-movie bloodbath, though she'd ruined her dress when they'd gone caving after the dance. And then she'd had to board a plane in the morning. Cotton had given her a logbook, and in it she'd recorded the coordinates of each place, as well as sketches and notes to go with the maps and photographs she collected along the way. She sent menus to Cotton, highlighting the dishes she wanted him to try to make.

Following her therapist's advice, she kept track of her feelings too, using colored markers and symbols when words weren't clear enough. There was no right or wrong way to feel. Old memories turned into maps, where there was room to mark missteps and victories, the good with the bad. In the same logbook, she kept records of her scores for each of her many meets. Her placing within the ranks of contenders. Any bits of advice she'd gathered from her coaches or other divers. All of it combined would help her to remember where she'd been. There's never only one way to see something.

Wherever she went, and whatever language greeted her, the pools welcomed her. The smell of chlorine and sunscreen, the rippled reflections across the water, the sound of splashing and talking and whistles and, most of all, the rhythmic *ka-thunks* of the diving boards made her feel at home.

This meet mattered more than the others. Added to what she'd already achieved, her scores would decide the next part of her journey. At the end of the day, she'd be pointed in a certain direction. Her future would take on a new shape. But she knew any journey has its ups and downs. There's never only one way from here to there and back again.

Before reaching the board, she paused and waved her shammy toward the stands, where she knew a crowd was cheering her on, even if she couldn't see their faces.

She stopped by her coaches for a last-minute instruction. They looked at each other, then back at her. "You know what to do."

And she did. Everything she'd learned and endured was with her now. It was all up to her.

At the base of the ladder, Ria dried herself with her shammy. She checked the side of her leg, like she always did before a big dive. The cut from the quarry had left a purplish-blue scar. It looked like a river on a map.

She climbed, up, up, counting each step.

At the top she waited for the ref's signal. There was no reason for Fear to be here.

She was ready.

Set. Breathe.

Four steps to her hurdle. Lift, and go.

She was in the air. Spinning. Too fast to breathe or see. Feeling lighter than she'd ever been. Gravity had been tricked. It hadn't caught up yet. In this flash of a moment, anything could be imagined. Hope and faith and maybe kept her aloft between the board and water.

This was the easy part of impossible.

ACKNOWLEDGMENTS

My father instilled in me a deep love and appreciation for the natural world, stories, and family. He taught me how to explore the outdoors, including underground caves. This story wouldn't exist without him. Unfortunately, he is also the reason I learned early about unexpected loss. I was lucky that my brothers, Eddie and Andy, let me tag along as they pursued their own passion for caving, rock climbing, and more—even though I had a much closer relationship with Fear than they ever will. I'm also grateful for my mother, who allowed us to take risks and learn from our mistakes, and for my sister, Suzanne, who is the braver, smarter, and sweeter half of the Singing Sisters.

As for the actual book in your hands, many people helped bring it to light!

I feel lucky to be working with the fabulous team at HarperCollins; most especially my consistently amazing editor, Alyssa Miele. This story is stronger due to her thoughtful guidance and her ability to see what's on the page as well as what's buried beneath. Many thanks also to Alexandra Cooper and Rosemary Brosnan for their early and ongoing support. Sensitivity readers and copy editors provided additional and much appreciated help. The beautiful cover is due to the talents of the design team, including David DeWitt and the work of artist Samantha French.

This story greatly benefitted from the attention and encouragement of my agent, Catherine Drayton, and also Claire Friedman of Inkwell Management. Thank you both for your brilliant insights and for keeping the light on while I was lost and wandering.

Readers everywhere, I adore you. Readers who have sent me messages, reminding me that words have the power to connect—you have buoyed me far more than you know.

The community of Vermont College of Fine Arts continues to provide sparks of inspiration and motivation, most personally including my graduation class of Unreliable Narrators and the SoCal-VCFA retreat group. Jen White, you know which scene is all thanks to you!

Retreat gatherings made all the difference in writing this story. Sharry Wright, Cindy Faughnan, and Tamara Ellis Smith provided collective brain (and heart) power during our Plum Crazy Island time. They were with me at the start and during two of the times I "finished" this novel. My Wylld women, Kelly Bennett, Andrea Zimmerman, and Marty Graham fed my head, body, and soul in crucial ways.

My ongoing readers Andrea, Suzanne Santillan, Carolyn Marsden, Denise Harbison, and Janice Yuwiler have put up with me and my scribbles from dark places for a long time. Thank you for your wonderful (and oh so annoying) ability to see what I miss. Group-think at its finest!

Elizabeth Stranahan provided an unexpected beacon of light at a critical point of the journey.

Writer friends have provided encouragement like concert-style lighters in the dark. In particular, Darcy Woods offered cheers and peels of support for me and this story, even when that meant reading one random line at a time. I am blessed with way too many other friends to list them all, but special appreciation is owed to the fabulous and enthusiastic San Diego SCBWI community, as well as my colleagues and students at UCSD-Extension. Here's where I slip in a sincere and loving pat of acknowledgment to Luna: dreamer, listener, loyal friend. As a dog she was never much of a reader, but she kept me company the many hours and miles it took to figure out this story. She is missed.

Sometimes it feels as though my day job working in public schools competes with my writing time, but kids like Ria and Cotton continually enlighten and inspire. The students and staff make me want to be a better human. I feel lucky and hopeful to see our future leaders as they learn and grow.

This story is a tribute to student athletes everywhere, but especially divers, who sacrifice comfort and safety for something far more stunning and impressive. You amaze me.

My own children have taken me on adventures far better than any I could have imagined—thank you for giving me so many reasons to cheer for you. And to my husband, Tom, thank you for making the impossible goal of happily ever after feel like it's going to be easy.